A Knave By Any Other Name

Ladies Who Dare
Book Three

Tanya Wilde

ARE YOU SIGNED UP FOR DRAGONBLADE'S BLOG?

You'll get the latest news and information on exclusive giveaways, exclusive excerpts, coming releases, sales, free books, cover reveals and more.

Check out our complete list of authors, too!

No spam, no junk. That's a promise!

Sign Up Here

www.dragonbladepublishing.com

Dearest Reader;

Thank you for your support of a small press. At Dragonblade Publishing, we strive to bring you the highest quality Historical Romance from some of the best authors in the business. Without your support, there is no 'us', so we sincerely hope you adore these stories and find some new favorite authors along the way.

Happy Reading!

CEO, Dragonblade Publishing

Additional Dragonblade books by
Author Tanya Wilde

Ladies Who Dare Series
Almost a Scoundrel (Book 1)
By No Means a Gentleman (Book 2)
A Knave By Any Other Name (Book 3)

Chapter One

"WHO AM I . . .?"

"Selena Savage, heiress, and sister to the Earl of Saville." Theodosia King cast her a sidelong look. "This is known."

"But what does that *mean?*" Selena asked her good friend as she stared, with a mixture of emotions, down at the betting book of White's and a pair of Turkish trousers that were nestled in the center of her bed. The book had been stolen from White's weeks ago but had been handed over to her by Harriet Hillstow, the Marchioness of Leeds, only a few days ago. The trousers . . . well, those had been delivered to her front door by an anonymous source.

"It means you are rich, titled, and have the world at your fingertips."

"But it's not at *my* fingertips, is it? It's at my brother's. I'm merely an extension of him." Selena glanced at her friend, her eyes widening as a thought—horrible, yet ridiculous—occurred to her. "Oh, Lord, does that mean I am a fingertip?"

"Don't be silly." Theodosia pointed at the book. "Just because a few men decided your best and worst attribute is your brother, doesn't mean that they are right."

Her friend made a good point. Selena had all but accepted that most men were lechers. Not that she'd ever been treated as anything but a lady, but she had grown up watching her brother and his friends break the hearts of many a woman without a second thought to what the women themselves might be feeling.

Tales of their debauchery had filled the halls of her home. Of course, they never caught on that she had, at times, blatantly eavesdropped entire conversations. Other times, she'd overheard snippets of their excursions she rather wished she hadn't. Yet those tales had given her a certain, rather unwelcome understanding of men.

Any romantic ideals she might have fostered as a little girl were questioned, shattered, and crushed one tale at a time.

She no longer trusted charming smiles. Charm and sincerity seldom went hand in hand. Nor did she believe pretty words to be anything but empty flattery. What a man whispered to a woman in a sweet moment was rarely ever what he meant. From what she understood, charming smiles and empty flattery not only formed part of a gentleman's duty to the fragile opposite sex but also served as a means to attract a temporary mate, like a peacock displaying its feathers to enthrall a female.

Nothing romantic about that.

Which was why Selena's view on romance had dimmed. She didn't need the fuss, and she didn't want the trouble. What she wanted, no man could offer.

In some ways, she was grateful to her brother and his friends for removing the scales from her eyes. In other ways, she wanted to throttle them.

But for now, she'd settle for escaping.

Her brother had all but imprisoned her in their home. No callers of the male variety were accepted either. This new protective attitude supposedly stemmed from the part he had played in the chaos that seized London. Chaos she had also had a hand in creating. But it was chaos he had helped set in motion.

"This is all his fault . . ."

"What are you muttering about?"

"My brother." She clenched her hands. "At first, I saw it as my duty to take the men of society down a notch to remind them that we women are a force to be reckoned with."

"We did. We are."

"Then why do they go about their days as if the trouble we caused them is nothing but a fly buzzing about their dinner plate, easily swatted away? Why am I still being ordered about?"

Theodosia laughed.

"It's not funny, Theo. It's infuriating." What she hated most was being told what to do. Had she been born a man, she'd have boxed her brother's ears and left him in the dust. Not only was he the cause of all her recent misfortune, but he had also assigned a guard dog to fend off the very rogues he was responsible for setting on her path! And unfortunately, it was one guard dog that was proving difficult to shake . . .

"One act of defiance won't change centuries of belief and partiality," Selena continued. "That's why we are wearing these trousers."

"*Are* you going to wear them or not?" Theodosia asked, fumbling with the waistband of her trousers. She'd already shrugged into hers while Selena's mind had run wild with their purpose. "They are strangely comfortable. And," she grinned at Selena, "it's one step closer to proving you have the world at your fingertips."

"They are also quite colorful, aren't they?" Selena eyed her pair, still untouched on the bed.

"I believe that is the point."

"Do you think it's *them* who distributed these trousers to the lovely women in Mayfair?"

"You mean the women who started a secret club?"

Selena nodded. "I still cannot believe we have not been invited to this club. Shouldn't we be invited? After all, we did do all the work when it came to stealing the betting book and distributing copies of the wagers all over London. We exposed their husbands' silly hobbies. We are the ones on that heiress list."

"Why do you want to join the club so badly?"

"It's a club. Secret. Only women. Who would not want to join?"

"Me."

"I still can't understand why not."

Theodosia shrugged. "I don't know anything about the motive of the club."

"To annoy the men of London. Same as us."

"How optimistic you are. If this club is so 'secret,' why do we know about them at all?"

"They want us to know about them."

"Exactly. But why? Also, they couldn't have been recently formed."

Selena turned to her friend. "How can you tell?"

"Wouldn't we heiresses have been invited if they had been formed because of the book?" She pointed at the culprit, still sitting serenely on the bed. "There is something about them that I can't place my finger on. Like you said, we, the heiresses, weren't invited. So why not?"

"A question worth asking them when I find them. Regardless, there can't be a secret women's club that I'm not part of."

"Then I suggest you change into these trousers and join the parade outside. If the club did send them, showing your cooperation is the first step to lure an invitation."

"Fine. But why are you joining the parade if you don't wish to join the superbly all-female, super-secret club?"

"To try out these trousers, of course."

"And annoy my brother."

"Naturally." Theodosia gave an exaggerated sigh. "Why couldn't Warrick be the one chasing *my* every move? Why does it have to be your brother?"

"Neither of them should be following us around."

"True."

"In any event, I did take a pair of scissors to his favorite waistcoats."

"Also true," Theodosia said. "Are they even aware of how

bad they are at keeping watch over us? They obviously mean to keep it secret, yet they are remarkably obvious."

"I believe that is simply a failing of the male brain." Selena tapped the side of her head. "The male brain has a particularly interesting function, one which allows the male in question to pretend something to be true and then believe that truth beyond a shadow of a doubt, even when hard, solid proof to the contrary is provided."

"That is disturbingly accurate."

"I, on the other hand, cannot pretend I don't see Warrick skulking behind lampposts and darting behind carriages when I make a simple round through Bond Street." Of all her brothers' friends, his brawny figure had always been the one to catch and hold her gaze. Unfortunately, she preferred a man with brain and brawn, not just brawn.

"Weren't you besotted with him?"

"That was ages ago." Selena lifted the pair of trousers into the air to study them. "Besides, I've been smitten with all my brother's friends at one time or another."

"Deerhurst?"

"Lasted one whole month."

"Avondale?"

"Just short of a day."

Theodosia whistled. "You are astonishing. Then how long did the Warrick fascination last? A minute?"

Strangely enough, her infatuation with him had lasted the longest. However, that wasn't the point. The fact of the matter was that the spell did not last forever. As with all her previous infatuations, it faded until nothing was left but a vague memory of a slight doting.

She avoided Theodosia's question with one of her own. "Have you ever been smitten with a man?"

"I can't say that I have."

"How dreary."

"Speaking of dreary, your brother and your watchdog are

downstairs. How are we going to slip out without them notic-ing?"

"Oh, I have no intention of sneaking out. Their reaction is what I'm going to enjoy most. That and finding a clue about my future club." She brought the trousers up to her face, pressing the fabric against her cheek. "Soft."

"Your determination is inspiring."

"Why thank you. I live to be an inspiration to all women. However, with Warrick following me about town and my brother on alert, I have to be more careful in my search for clues."

"Good luck with that, my friend."

"What I need," Selena said, "is a bit of subterfuge. A way for them to believe I'm doing one thing while doing another." Easier spoken than accomplished. But she either needed that or more ears to the ground to help ferret out these women.

Selena inspected the garment from top to bottom, drawing a raised brow from her friend.

"What are you doing?" Theodosia asked.

"Looking for clues."

"You truly believe they were delivered by your little club? If so, surely, they won't—"

"Aha!"

"What?" Theodosia brought her face closer. "What did you find?"

"Look at this."

Theodosia traced a finger over the small patch of needlework adorning the ankle. "A symbol?"

Selena sent her friend a wide grin. "A signature." Her gaze returned to the black sword entwined with crimson thorned roses, and giddiness spread through her. A magnificent clue.

I have you now.

"When you find this club, please don't join them willy-nilly," Theodosia cautioned. "First determine what they are about."

"Rest assured. I am not so careless."

"Are you certain? Why do I get the feeling that the moment you receive an invitation you will grasp it with your hands and feet regardless of the consequences?"

"Don't be such a delight dasher. I will not join them willy-nilly."

"Good." Theodosia tossed a pillow over the book while Selena shrugged into the trousers. "Aren't you afraid your brother will discover their club's prized book so out in the open?" So far, the book had been handed from heiress to heiress exactly to *avoid* the men from getting their grubby hands on it again.

"He already had servants search my chambers."

"Are you certain he won't do so again?"

"The male brain."

Theodosia rolled her eyes heavenward. "Of course. I heard the Duke of Mortimer is also searching for the book."

Selena pulled a face. "Good luck to him."

"My sentiment as well. Have you combed through all the wagers to find anything useful about your brother and watchdog?"

"I tried but didn't get far."

"A difficult read?"

"Do not jest. Some wagers are as clear as fresh water while others seem to be written in code. Also, the names are abbreviated. I gave up after my fourth attempt." As delightful as it would be to blackmail those two scoundrels, the process of deciphering the wagers had proved more painstaking than learning French. Whatever blackmail material she could unearth was not worth the harm being done to her brain cells, which seemed to wither whenever she laid eyes on the bold scrawls across the pages.

"What a pity."

Yes.

Ever since she learned, according to the list in the book, that both her most praiseworthy attribute and her most regrettable flaw was her brother, a burning anger tightened her heart in a grip that refused to let go. Did she not have an identity of her own? Was her brother truly the sum of her?

Her *brother*?

He'd cared for her from the time she was still young, ever since their mother had remarried and moved to Scotland with her new husband. Saville had done his best with the hand he was dealt—they both were dealt—she knew this well. But was she even recognized as a person at all?

Finding the women of the secret club was not just about unravelling a mystery, it was about finding herself, too.

An identity.

Worthiness.

Meaning.

Because at the moment, Selena felt rather meaningless. More than that, she felt *alone* in her meaningless. And it was a pitiful feeling that didn't sit well with her.

"Why don't *you* read through the book?" Selena suggested.

"Lord no, I value my time too much."

Selena shook her head with a small smile.

"Besides, without the book, those wagers are all but hollow. On the other hand," Theodosia stuck out a leg at a jaunty angle, "we look positively scandalous!"

That's right.

Scandal and rebellion.

Selena could find meaning in that. After all, did rebelling not mean she stood for something? Even if that rebellion mostly just meant annoying her brother and his watchdog while she searched for those elusive club members.

"Shall we go shock my brother into heart palpitations?"

Theodosia chuckled. "Weeds don't wither so easily."

"Hah! Did you just call my brother a weed?"

"Some titles are deserved."

True.

Selena grinned. Like the one she would soon be claiming for herself.

⇛⇚

"I'M DONE PLAYING nursemaid to your sister."

Phineas North, Earl of Warrick swallowed a sip of strong, black coffee. No sugar. He swirled the remaining quarter. Two cups were usually enough to get him through each tormented day. Unfortunately, torment seemed to be the latest theme of his life.

He was already on his third cup. He needed another.

"What did she do now?" the Earl of Saville, a longtime friend, asked in an impartial tone.

"Nothing. However, I still don't understand why I must be the one who chaperones your sister in secret. She is your sister."

"You saw what she did to my wardrobe. Selena and I have never been able to keep our tempers when we disagree with each other. For our relationship's sake, it's better if you keep her out of trouble."

For their relationship's sake? Warrick almost snorted. When had those two ever not been a volatile, bickering duo? No, Saville's reason . . .

On second thought, better not to take a jab at a bear. Even so, he needed out.

"Commission more waistcoats. I'm done."

"I'll pay you."

Warrick's brow shot up. "Are you that desperate?"

"Yes. Name your price."

"It would be less expensive to purchase more waistcoats."

"I assure you, it won't." Saville cast a scowl in the direction of the window, where the sound of chatter grew louder with each passing second. "What the devil is that ruckus? Has a swarm of bees descended upon London?"

"Perhaps it has." Like a curse . . .

I do not believe in curses.

Yet, the day after he had turned thirty years of age, the tide had turned on his luck. From losing Avondale's list of heiresses to witnessing firsthand the fireworks that followed and being charged as a "guardian" to Saville's sister. Even more appalling, he'd been chased down the street by a woman brandishing a deuced candelabra. His arse had been pinched more times than he cared to count, and he was pretty sure he was shedding hair like a Pomeranian. At this rate, he would be bald in six months. Would he even be able to find a wife then?

There are no such things as family curses.

But the evidence . . .

What madness was this so-called family curse anyway? If he didn't wed by the age of thirty, calamity would befall him? Such an absurd superstition must have been concocted by his forefathers to ensure the obedience of their sons and to carry on the family line.

If he was going to dwell on curses, it would be best to approach it one curse at a time—starting with a certain friend's sister and relieving himself of the responsibility of being a deuced guard dog.

"Brother!" An excited chirp came from the door. "Warrick! Good morning!"

Warrick's gaze jumped to the current bane of his existence as she flounced into the room, and he nearly splashed coffee over himself as his whole body jerked in reaction to the sight of her.

Mother of Christ. What insanity was this?

Saville shot up from his chair and half growled, half croaked the question that had flared in his own mind. "What the devil are you wearing?"

Lady Selena twirled, shamelessly displaying the scandalous fit of a pair of trousers that should be—if it were not already—outlawed in Britain. "What do you think? They are pretty, are they not?"

"Pretty, my arse!" Saville snapped.

Warrick wrenched his gaze from the odd-looking yet terrifyingly seductive trousers to the fair, and thoroughly smug, complexion of Selena Savage. Waves of sandy hair cascaded down to her hips, further enhancing this unholy picture. She was not looking at him, but he knew those vivid blue eyes held a sparkle of trouble.

His gaze dropped to the thin material of the trousers again, clinging to her legs, not quite revealing their shape, but serving as a promise of what lay beneath. With the already scandalous trousers, she wore an equally improper, yet perfectly fitted shirt. He instantly recognized this as part of the men's attire the women wore at the Stewart ball when they distributed the copies of White's betting book.

Warrick stifled another groan. So much provocation in one outfit.

He may not be truly cursed, but he surely felt that way.

"Tsk, tsk, such foul language."

Only then did Warrick notice Lady Theodosia. He stifled another groan. Double the trouble.

He would not be able to escape his duty as a guard dog today. Damn it. Though he was not without fault in this. While he'd been tasked by Saville to protect Selena from fortune-hunters, he could have declined. At the time, guilt had driven him to agree. Guilt aside, Warrick had never been a man to walk away from the consequences of his actions.

Selena's grin widened. Never a good sign. "By your tone, brother, am I to assume you do not approve of this fresh style of fashion? Theo and I are quite enjoying this craze."

"What fashion craze? This is a mutiny."

Agreed.

Lady Theodosia directed a sidelong glance at Saville. "Are you certain you are using the word mutiny correctly?"

Saville's eyes took on a glint of steel. An equally foreboding sign. "I see both of you are determined to get a rise out of me this morning."

Warrick rubbed his temples. *Here we go.*

"As we should," Selena said.

I should add a dash of brandy to the brew.

Saville pointed a finger at the trousers the women were boasting about. "What is the meaning of dressing like this? If it's to annoy me, congratulations, you succeeded."

"This might come as a shock to you, brother, but not everything is about annoying you. It just so happens that we are joining the parade."

Warrick's ears twitched.

"Parade? What parade?" Saville demanded. "I have no knowledge of any parade."

Ah. So that's what the buzz is about.

"The one outside your house." Theodosia tilted her head to the side. "Care to join us?"

"No, I do not." Saville shook his head in emphasis, then suddenly stopped to clear his throat. "I mean, you are not setting foot outside this house."

"I should like to see you stop us, brother." Selena's smile took on a different sharpness, and Warrick instantly recognized the honed devilry within that slight arch of lips. "If you dare."

"Do not test me, Selena."

"Test you? Brother, have you not been testing me ever since your betting book got stolen?"

Warrick emptied his cup of coffee and began sweeping the cabinets for alcohol.

"I've been protecting you ever since you and your friends released copies of that damn book and caused scandal after scandal."

"Well, I shall not point out who is to blame for that, since you already know."

"What do you imagine this rebellion of yours will prove?"

"Good question, brother. I shall let you know once I have the answer to that as well."

Damn it. No alcohol.

"If not to aimlessly annoy me, then your true purpose must be to drive me to Bedlam."

"You give me too much credit, brother. However, since the wagers became public, the world of women has changed. This is a journey of self-discovery."

"The world of women?"

"It has a pleasant ring to it, does it not?"

Warrick sighed, pouring himself more coffee. At this rate, one pot would not be enough. He glanced at the women, his mind spinning on how to prevent the explosion that was about to follow this bout of bickering. "What is the parade you are joining about?"

"No one is joining any parade," Saville bit out.

Lady Selena extended a long, shapely, unwelcomely tempting leg. "Why, showcasing these Turkish trousers."

The trousers? Surely there must be a deeper plot here. "Is that all there is to this parade?" Warrick asked.

"Is that not enough?"

More than enough. They alone were a shock to any man's heart. A statement? A war cry? At this point, he couldn't tell anymore. The women had all misplaced their wits. The men not far behind. But one thing was clear beyond the shadow of a doubt—the challenge in both women's gazes.

But why had they boldly declared their intention? *Were the two women testing or teasing them?*

"You might as well just come along," Lady Theodosia said, her smile matching Lady Selena's. "You are going to follow us anyway."

Christ, both, then.

Saville's hands slammed on the table. "You are not leaving the house dressed like that in those . . . in those . . ."

"Turkish trousers," Theodosia supplied before she narrowed her eyes. "And why are you looking daggers at me? I'm a guest. I can leave whenever I want."

"Guest or not, neither of you are leaving this house dressed in those godawful things."

A chill slithered down Warrick's spine as Selena's gaze turned to him. "Why, brother? Can't the watchdog you've put on my tail just follow us? He's been doing such a smashing job of it so far."

The chill turned to frost.

They knew.

Warrick caught Saville's glare. "What?" he defended. "I've been careful."

"Not careful enough."

"In all fairness . . ." Lady Selena's tone dripped syrup. "A behemoth with no sense of awareness makes for a terrible spy."

Warrick drew his brows together. "What do you mean no sense of awareness? I am very aware." Of *every* situation that includes you.

"Really? Then have you noticed the way people whisper and stare at you when skulking behind lampposts in Bond Street?"

He hadn't.

His attention had always been firmly on her. Which was the entire bloody point, wasn't it? This was all Saville's fault. And if Selena knew he'd been following her, then looking back, he had a suspicion he'd been led around by the nose on more than one occasion.

Very well. He supposed she had a point. His awareness of his environment had become dismal.

"Not to even mention when Harriet was kidnapped in broad daylight a fortnight ago. You missed that entirely."

"I was concentrating on you," Warrick said, once again defending himself. Another theme of his life lately.

"Then I should applaud your focus. That at least, is truly remarkable."

"Do not change the subject," Saville spoke up. "Join this parade if you must, but you are not leaving this house unless you change to proper attire. That is my final say on the matter."

"You are the worst." Selena grabbed hold of Lady Theodosia's arm. "Come, let's leave before I strangle my brother."

The women sauntered from the room without so much as a backward glance.

Finally, Warrick could breathe again. He pushed his coffee away. The brew had failed him today.

Saville lowered back into his seat. "Damn females."

Warrick shifted in his chair, tugging at his cravat. Had the temperature risen a degree or two? "Are you sure they will listen? Perhaps we should not have let them quit the room like this."

"Don't concern yourself with their antics. It's an act of rebellion and nothing else. What can they do?"

Was Saville not paying attention, or was he in denial? "They can do a whole lot."

Saville scoffed. "Then should we escort them back to my sister's chamber to oversee their compliance? Those two won't disobey me."

A door slammed shut, the bang so close it rang in Warrick's ears. That was no bedroom door.

Warrick arched a brow at his friend.

Not disobey you? Was that not their entire purpose?

Chapter Two

"I NEVER IMAGINED I would live to witness such a spectacle."

Scores of women gathered in Mayfair dressed in Turkish trousers. Some were wearing masks. Others—like Selena and Theodosia—were boldly claiming their identity. Everyone already knew they were *the* heiresses. The ladies who arrived at the Stewart Ball clothed in breeches and top hats, scattering copies of pages from the betting book of White's from atop the staircase.

But most importantly, in this crowd, *those* women—the members of the secret club—must be present.

But would they be wearing masks or not?

"I'm obsessed with these trousers," Theodosia said for the tenth time. "I shall wear them every chance I get from this day forward."

"Your brothers would object."

"My brothers aren't in London."

"Yet."

"Which is why I must seize every opportunity until they return."

"Enjoy your freedom while you have it, my friend." Selene surveyed the crowd. "What's next do you suppose?"

"We parade around. Consort with our fellow rabblerousers."

"Perhaps this morning is more of a display, a chance to see

who claimed the rebellion and who did not." Selena's gaze flicked over the women who gathered in the street, admiring each other's fit. "*They* should be here. Watching us."

"You sound like a wife trying to catch her husband in an affair. Are you that dogged in your attempt to find them? Does it not bother you that they are using us to fan the flames of discord?"

"They are seizing an opportunity, just like you."

"Well, I can't argue that."

"All these trousers . . ." Selena still couldn't believe the ladies of Mayfair had embraced these foreign garments to such a degree. It was a spectacular sight. "How colorful." A thought occurred to her. "The trousers must have been manufactured in London. If not, the crest must have been added here. If I can find the company . . . or whoever delivered them to our doorstep . . ."

"A secret club will leave such a gaping hole in their plan?"

"Perhaps not. But even so, I am determined to find a member of the club here today. I shall not be thwarted."

"Then go ask around. I shall help you look out for suspicious behavior."

"That would be too conspicuous." Her gaze flicked over all the women with masks. "I should probably whisper my request into some ears and see if it does the rounds. Who reacts, who does not."

Theodosia gave her A Look.

"What?"

"I'm marveling at your dedication to enter this club. Truly riveting."

"Do not tell me you aren't even a bit curious? You don't have one tiny speck of curiosity?"

"They are too suspicious for my taste."

"I have wondered at their aim, as well. But as an heiress on *the* list, a lady of society, what is the ending for us, Theo? Marriage? A life as a pariah? Are those our only options?"

"Spinsterhood is another."

"As a pariah! Why must we be labeled when men who remain unattached are not?"

"Pariah, spinster, wife . . . they are mere terms."

"And rain is *mere* water, but it can still cause a flood and wash your house away. If our fate is already decided, we might as well discover who we are beyond the riches, the titles, and this biased world you claim is at our fingertips."

"You decide your future."

"If you say so." Selena cast her friend a sidelong glance, recalling a particular detail. "Has your mother not been hosting morning callers which she's disturbingly named 'blind matchups' to find you a husband and remove you from the chaos?"

Theodosia's hand shot out to cover Selena's mouth. "Do not utter such blasphemy." Her eyes darted around. "Never mention this again. My mother has lost her faculties."

"Your mother is quite forward thinking."

"I agree. She . . . *drat.*"

A shiver crawled up Selena back. "What's wrong?"

"Our watchdogs found us."

"That was to be expected was it not?" Selena peered over her shoulder. The two jackals were prowling in their direction.

"I was hoping they'd be dense enough not to notice our departure."

"Ignore them. It's not like they can do anything in a public setting filled with women in trousers that do not restrict their movement. The men here are the ones who ought to be wary. Look at them all standing on the outskirts observing with disapproval yet not stopping us." Only Warrick and Saville had marched into the fray.

But before her words had even cooled, her sight was blinded by a coat being draped over her face. The scent of a familiar cologne of woody fragrance reached her.

He dared?

Arms circled her waist, and she was hoisted over a very hard, very muscled shoulder. The motion was so smooth, so quick, the only protest that left her lips a small gasp.

Yet the only objection or outrage on her behalf that she could sense came in a bout of hushed whispers that in no way helped her current predicament. Would no one come to her aid?

Where are your backbones, ladies?

Her own words finally burst forth. "Pig! Knave! Blackguard! Put me down!"

"In a moment."

"You best put me down right now, you watchdog, you beast!"

"You are making a scene."

"You are the one hoisting me up like a sack of potatoes!" Always thwarting her plans.

"Well, you are the prettiest sack of potatoes I've ever carried."

Selena resisted the urge to pummel his back like a madwoman. Had he ever even carried a sack of potatoes in his entire lofty life? But his steps were fluid, without any hesitation as he fetched her back to her house, lowering her only once they entered the hallway and the door slammed shut as though carrying the sack of potatoes—her—had been nothing but a walk in the park.

The butler scampered at their arrival, shooing curious servants away as well.

She ripped his jacket from her head and flung it to the ground. "Where is my brother and Theo?"

"I'm not sure. Your friend slipped away. Last I saw of your brother he was following in her wake."

"Good for her if she slipped away, you knave. I cannot believe you would cause such a public spectacle!"

"We were already in a public spectacle." Thick arms crossed over a heavy chest, drawing her attention to the solid wall that had so effortlessly supported her weight. "What are you up to, Lady Selena?"

Selena averted her gaze, shrugging off the sudden sense of conflict within her over whether to admire the man's body or meet his eyes. "Why do you think I'm up to anything?"

"I don't know." The frustration in his tone echoed off the walls of the front hall. "I have this feeling you are courting mischief."

"Did the trousers give me away?"

"Yes."

She couldn't help but peek at him, catching his gaze mere seconds before his eyes lowered to her trousers. The flash of annoyance gave way to a thrill of delight. A sliver of power. A surge, or perhaps more of an urge, a little nudge to tease him flared to life.

"I might be up to something."

A brow arched, even while his gaze remained steadfastly *there*.

"Well, more in *search* of something."

"We are all in search of something."

"How philosophical of you. Tell me then, what are *you* in search of?"

His eyes shifted back up before flicking again to her trousers before finally settling on her face once again. His lips pursed. "Peace of mind."

"I'm afraid you shall be searching for a long time." She gave a deliberate, mocking pause. "Then how about we help each other out?"

"I beg your pardon?"

"Do not sound so skeptical, Warrick." Selena smiled. Just how far would this man go in the name of his watchdog duties? "Cooperating could benefit both of us."

"That would mean *you* will be the one to help me gain peace of mind."

What was with that tone? "Why not me? I'm certain I can aid in that regard."

"When you are the origin of my turmoil in the first place?" His face turned grim. "Forgive me, but whatever deal or quid pro quo you could offer, no matter how I look at it, I lose."

"Interesting . . ." Her gaze tracked over his length. Had he grown wiser to her schemes since she last conversed with him? No matter. She was merely teasing him. If the earl did truly want peace of mind, he should become a monk.

Still, a distant sense of curiosity prevailed. "What will give you a moment of peace?"

"Only a moment?"

She nodded. "We are creatures that live in compounding moments, are we not?"

"I suppose we are."

"There you go with that skeptical tone again. You say I am the problem, correct? Well you must be aware that within every problem lies the solution."

That earned a slight twitch at the corner of his lips. "Are you saying that you are the solution to my problem that is you?"

"Exactly."

Dark eyes studied her. They almost appeared to be brooding with dissatisfaction. "I shall pass."

Selena wanted to laugh at his pinched expression. The urge to tease him heated a degree. "Are you sure? You seem to be in dire need of a few hours of mental repose. I can help you achieve a moment of peace in exchange for your help in finding what I'm searching for." Two beats of silence. "Are you not going to ask what I'm searching for?"

"I believe it's best not to know." He even took a step back from her. "For my peace of mind, you understand."

"How disappointing. I had just the thing in mind to relieve some of your stress."

His gaze turned dubious. "Now I'm terrified."

"But interested."

His eyes narrowed, and she laughed. The man looked so put out, she had half the mind to pinch his cheeks.

"What are you searching for, Lady Selena? Tell me before I change my mind."

She grinned at him. "Promise not to tell my brother."

"I give you my word."

"Not even the slightest hesitation." She considered the man before her. "Are you certain you will not tell my brother?"

"I gave you my word, didn't I?"

"I thought you were terrified."

"You've prickled my curiosity."

She hadn't even meant to secure his help. Didn't *want* his help. That would be a disaster. This man had been nothing but an obstacle in her way thus far. Always following her. Always in her way. Today was a perfect example.

And yet, the words left her before she could retract her tongue. "A secret women's club."

His face turned as blank as a sheet of paper. "A what?"

How can a tone say absolutely everything yet nothing at all? *More importantly, Selena, why did you say that?* But the command to be silent was further lost somewhere between her mind and her mouth. "What do you mean 'what'?"

"I'm certain I heard *secret woman's club*."

"You heard wrong."

"I heard right." He took a step closer. "You said a secret women's club."

She arched a brow. "Well, if that is what you heard, then that is what I must have said."

He stared at her. "I . . . have . . . no words."

She glanced back and forth. Save me, someone! Theo! She needed to rescue herself from her own treacherous mouth! Her mind raced. *In times of desperation, turn the tables.* "Phineas North, the Earl of Warrick, is rendered speechless. How marvelous."

Did that sound a bit too forced?

"How is that marvelous?"

Not too much, then. She shrugged. "I cannot say. It's just a *feeling* that buds from within. Also, I was merely jesting earlier. I'd rather not join hands with a jackal."

"Calling me a jackal when you are the princess of trouble seems rather pointless."

"If I am the princess of trouble then you must be the prince of brawn?"

"I beg your pardon?"

You are hopeless, Selena. Why did you just say that? Retract, retract, retract. "Forget it. I have things to do. Good day, my lord."

"Wait a minute, Selena." His gaze stabbed at her, threatening to pierce the veil of her soul. "I cannot just forget that you are searching for a secret club. Why are you searching for such a thing?"

"Does it matter?"

"Of course it matters. I'm responsible for your safety."

"But that is the crux of the matter, is it not? You *aren't* responsible for me or my safety."

"Take that up with your brother," he said simply. "Now, answer my question. Why are you looking for a secret club?"

"To thank them, of course."

"Thank them for what?"

She smiled and jutted out a leg, pulling at the fabric of her trousers. "For these."

"*They* supplied these godawful trousers?"

"I believe so."

"Then you are not sure?"

"There is always margin for error in any assumption."

"And let me guess—you wish to join this club once you find them?"

"Perhaps."

He pinched the bridge of his nose. "Is it your life's goal to send your brother to an early grave?"

"How heart stirring of you to conclude the only reason for me to search for this club is to annoy my brother. But then, given that he is my best and worst attribute, I can hardly blame you for your conjecture."

He cursed. "Forgive me, I did not mean it that way."

Selena waved his apology aside. She didn't need it. Neither

did she want his help. That would be a sure way for the man attach himself to her shadow even more. She should never have teased him. That was *her* mistake.

"As I said, I was merely jesting." She sent him her most cloyingly sweet smile. "Unless you want me to help you find some *peace?*"

"Saints, no."

She kept the corners of her lips hitched up, unwilling to show this jackal any sense of relief. "I suppose I won't be able to change your mind . . ."

"Correct."

"What a pity." *Do not overdo it, Selena.*

"No matter what you say, my answer will still be no."

Well, thank God.

What madness had overcome her to blurt out the existence of the club? Luckily, he had refused her ridiculous teasing. Good fortune had not forsaken her.

Yet.

A NIGHTMARE.

A living, breathing, nightmare. Why the devil had he promised to keep this a secret from Saville? The moment the minx had muttered *secret women's club*, all hope of peace of mind fled out the door. Those three words shot a chill through this heart.

Women. Plural.

And *they* meant secrets.

Which always meant more trouble.

All the exact opposite of peace of mind. In fact, every single word associated with "women" and "secret" and "club" could be pooled in a reservoir of unpleasantness that would plague him if he helped this mischief-maker find such a club.

His curse must be flaring up again. *Not* that he believed in curses. But then again, how else could three seemingly harmless words combined in such a nightmarish phrase wriggle their way into his life?

"Wait," he called when she turned to leave.

Her gaze locked with his.

"I'll . . ."—*You're going to shed more hair over this*—". . . help you. In exchange for a few hours of mental repose."

She stared at him.

And stared.

"So?" Warrick pressed.

"I . . ."

Well, well, well. "Who is the one speechless now, Lady Selena?"

"You said nothing could change your mind."

"I did say that." He'd meant it, too. However . . .

"What on earth happened to your mind? I mean, what happened to change it in the span of three seconds?"

"A man is entitled to change a decision on a whim." God help him. He sounded like his mother.

"Fickle or not, I said I was jesting."

"Yes, I recall you said something to that effect."

Her gaze narrowed on him, probing. "You truly mean to help me? As in *help*, as in *me*?"

He didn't. He'd rather forget about today entirely and all its promises and trouble. But . . . Lady Selena plus secret club that supplied Turkish trousers equaled trouble that London could not afford. He didn't believe for one second she just wanted to *thank* them when she eventually found them.

"Are you questioning my sincerity?"

"I'm more concerned about *why* you changed your mind."

"It occurred to me," right there and then, "that if I help you, I would not have to follow you about and hide behind London's lampposts."

That alone ought to bring him a measure of peace even as the woman threatened to rob him of every other ounce. But the more he thought about it, the more the idea seemed like the best course of action.

"I suppose you would find some solace in that."

"I do have one more condition, however," Warrick ventured. "A problem of my own I could use help with." He'd never have considered telling her about something as ridiculous as this if she hadn't told him about the club. But perhaps they could help each other. Perhaps in doing so, they could understand each other a little better. Perhaps then she might even take some pity on him and not make his life harder than it needed to be.

"Oh? What trouble ails the Earl of Warrick?"

"A family curse."

Her face went from amused to blank. "A . . . family curse?

Or perhaps everything was just wishful optimism on his part. "When you say it like that I sound like a madman."

"I'm not sure how I can help you with such a unique quandary."

Warrick furrowed his brows. Was she holding back a laugh? If so, she was doing it poorly. "Laugh if you must."

She pursed her lips, shaking her head.

He sighed. Wishful optimism or not, he couldn't retract it now. "This is my condition: find all the books you can rummage on family curses and summarize them for me. It should be simple enough." And keep her out of trouble for a while.

Her lips drooped downward. "You want me to *read up* on family curses?"

"Gather information."

"Are they different from each other? Do not tell me you believe in such superstitious things."

"I don't."

"Then why go through all this trouble to collect information on family curses?"

"One can never be too careful." He also treasured his head of hair. And in the case his family curse was real—which it absolutely was not—a man's only defense could be found in knowledge. If such knowledge even existed. But what better way to keep a mischievous princess out of mischief?

"You seem reluctant," Warrick said, studying her expression. "Surely this is not asking too much?"

"Just a touch, but I shall gather information for you." Her gaze assessed him from top to bottom. "What exactly is your family curse about?"

"That's a private matter." She would just advise him to marry if she knew, like everyone else. And he refused to bow down to something as ludicrous as a curse.

Her brow tracked up, disturbingly intrigued. "Do you have a witch in your family ancestry?"

"Do not be absurd."

"Then who would curse your family? Someone had to wave a wand of sage or something for there to be a curse, didn't they?"

"I don't care who waved what herb or chanted what chorus. Calamity has befallen me. I want it to end."

"Calamity, you say." More intrigue. "Do tell."

"No."

Her lips formed a pout. "So sour. Should I not know all about this curse if I am to do the research?"

"Aren't I also helping you find a club I know nothing about? And do not forget to provide me a few hours of repose." He looked forward to this most. And it seemed only fair in exchange for what he had to do.

"Speaking of which, what *do* you consider a peaceful moment?"

Good question. "I suppose anything that is pleasing and helps me relax."

"Elementary." She held out the palm of her hand. "Do we have an agreement?"

He clasped her hand in his. Why did he suddenly feel like an animal that had willingly walked straight into a cage meant to trap him? "We have an agreement."

"Splendid."

Warrick's gaze dropped to her trousers for what seemed the hundredth time, his fingers tightening when her hand would have slipped from his. "One more condition."

Her hand flexed in his grip. "Negotiations are over."

"One more."

"If it's about the club—"

"The trousers."

Her eyes widened. "What about them?"

"Never wear them again."

She froze, and Warrick stilled along with her. Were these words not reminiscent of the two traits he loathed the most? Demanding. Possessive.

"Not even in private?"

He cleared this throat, releasing her hand as though it had caught fire. "You can do what you please in private, of course."

"No need to sound so fierce. I was not planning to wear them again. In any event, we have an agreement, so do not follow me around anymore."

"I cannot agree to that."

"Such a good watchdog." She poked his chest with a finger, leaving a burning sensation in the wake of her stab. Warrick caught her hand. "Is it necessary to be so thorough in your *duty?*" she demanded.

"I am a very thorough man." *Especially when it comes to you.*

"But we are we partners now."

"That doesn't mean there are no longer fortune hunters lurking in the shadows." He released her hand and took a sensible step back. "I'm sure they shall retreat once the season is over."

"I suppose I shall have to put up with it until then."

"I would appreciate your effort. On another note, do you have any clues of his club of yours to aid in my search?"

"Only these trousers. They ought to have been manufactured in London. That should give you a good lead. Oh, and someone must have seen who placed the trousers before all the doors of Mayfair."

"Is that all?"

She nodded.

"Very well, I'll have my men inquire about the trousers."

"You're not doing it yourself?"

"I don't have that much time on my hands. You are an occupation that fills all my time." Warrick grimaced. "Not that I mean you are an occupation."

"Oh?" Small daggers appeared in her eyes. "Then what am I?"

"Saville's sister."

Her smile took on a forced quality. "Of course I am."

His back straightened—that was careless. He knew she was already prickly about her brother. Warrick quickly diverted the subject. "How did you come to learn of this secret club?"

She pursed her lips, but thankfully answered without a fuss. "I overheard two women speak of the club at the Everton ball, but before I could confirm their identities, they disappeared into one of the cardrooms."

"I see." Thank God for small mercies.

"I am curious. Why haven't you asked me if I have the betting book in my possession?"

The object of all his misery? "The book is nothing to do with me."

Let it be lost forever.

"I see."

"Do you not believe me?" Her tone was impossible to decipher.

"Oddly, I do."

"Good, because I have enough curses to worry about without having the book causing more trouble." His gaze probed hers. "You aren't planning to cause more trouble with the book?"

She shook her head. "The book already served its purpose."

If that was the case, why did he have a growing feeling that the book might be the biggest curse of them all?

Chapter Three

DREAMS WERE THE best part of sleeping. The icing on an otherwise spongy, comforting lemon cake. Sometimes they had a bit too much lemon, but mostly they were sweet. Never, at least in Selena's experience, had they been so syrupy that they bordered on shameless. Never had they been alarming.

Until she had a dream about him. *That* man. Warrick, her brother's best friend—rich, titled, the world at his fingers.

And in this rather frightening dream, he had kissed her.

If only that that had been the most scandalous part. But no, he had kissed her to distract her. His main goal? Stealing the betting book and running off right after, leaving her a bothered mess.

Like the knaves most men are.

She should never have made an alliance with Warrick, *and* she needed to get rid of that blasted book.

"Why are you scowling?" Theodosia asked with a small nudge to her arm. "We are supposed to be enjoying an evening of dancing."

Selena scoffed. "I'm agog at how little impact the Turkish trousers parade made. They should have made their debut on this dance floor, though there not many couples dancing."

Her friend lifted her shoulders in a small shrug. "Fabulous gowns will always trump trousers. And so long as the nights are filled with bright parties, jewels, and those fabulous gowns, the world could end, and the majority would not care. The world is truly strange."

"Strange . . . yes." Toss in a secret club, a family curse, an unlikely fellowship, and *strange* took on a rather stronger meaning. However, Selena didn't completely trust her alliance with Warrick, which was why she hadn't told him about the club's signature embroidered on the trousers.

Three days had passed since her brother had confined her to the house after the parade. Three days of being watched like a hawk until Selena thought she would die of stale air. Which was why she needed to get out of that house no matter the cost. She couldn't even breathe in there.

Oh, very well, it wasn't all *that* bad.

She supposed she could breathe just as well in the house as outside. What she couldn't do was search for clues about the club. She hadn't come up with a plan to find them either. Her sleuthing abilities were sorely lacking.

Was her best hope to receive a direct invitation? And if so, did that mean if she wanted to receive the holy pass, she would have to become *more* visible? Act *more* scandalous? Or poke and probe *more* amongst the ladies of the *ton*?

Though, upon reflection, it might be naïve to assume one had to behave scandalously to enter their ranks. After all, scandal served as poison to secrecy. The same for probing. Rumors might flare up.

Then should she appear proper? Who should she be? How should she act? These questions were giving her an ache in the temples.

"How troublesome."

Theodosia eyed her askance and guessed, "Still troubled by lack of clues?"

"Yes." Selena surveyed the crowd with interest. "That's why I'm here tonight. What about you? How did you give my brother the slip?"

Theodosia's eyes glittered with delight. She leaned closer to Selena. "I found a myself a girl who looks similar to me—a twin if you will—to take my place, cause him a wealth of confusion and throw him of my scent tonight."

Selena pinned her friend with a look of awe. "You truly possess a brilliant mind."

"You should take a page from my book if you wish to shake your watchdog."

"On the contrary, he is helping me find the club." In a way.

"When did *that* come about?"

"The day of the parade."

"Are you sure that's wise?" Theodosia clucked her tongue. "Incompetence seems to flow in that man's blood."

"Well, I can't seem to find a group of women hiding in plain sight, so birds of a feather."

Her friend shook her head. "That is different."

"Be that as it may, what more must a lady do to get invited? Honestly, I'm at a loss."

"Warrick might report to your brother. That would make it even harder."

"He promised not to, and I didn't tell him about the crest." *Yet.* "Perhaps I should let be what will be." Though the more she thought about her situation, the more she thought that Theodosia might have a point about this club. What *were* the club's intentions?

"And those are the words of a woman searching for meaning?"

"Those are the words of a woman accepting that meaning exists in her present circumstances as well as in her search for it." Selena's eyes widened as a light flickered in her mind. "*Present* circumstances."

"Ballroom," Theodosia said dryly.

"Exactly! Where would women of a secret club congregate at such an event?"

"I honestly cannot say."

"The cardroom."

"The cardroom? Why?"

"I seem to recall the women I overhead disappeared into a cardroom." Why hadn't she thought about this before?

Theodosia cocked her head to the side. "That doesn't mean much. They could just enjoy playing cards. Are you sure you are not grasping at straws?"

"Does my speculation seem so farfetched?" She didn't think so. At this point, even if she was grasping, she'd grasp with a smile on her face.

"Also, don't old women play cards? Oh, and married women whose husbands are cavorting around."

"What a ridiculous thing to say."

"My mother's words, not mine."

"Your mother truly is from a different breed of women."

"By the by," Theodosia drawled, her voice now dry as the desert. "How did you slip away from *your* watchdog?"

"Oh, that? As a determined woman does, I suppose. I marched straight through the front door and hailed a hackney."

"Are hackneys that readily available?"

"Fine, I sent for one ahead of time. Why do you ask?"

"Because your watchdog has been staring at you with blades shooting from his eyeballs since his arrival three minutes ago."

"*What?*" Selena head snapped in the direction Theodosia indicated with her chin. She had thought with her being confined to the house by her brother, he would drop his guard. Just a bit. Just so that she could steal a moment away from him. "Curse it."

Between the two of them—he with his family curse and she with his merciless presence—who was really more cursed?

Their gazes locked.

A shiver rippled along her nerve endings. She hadn't glimpsed his brawny body in three days, but she'd heard the low timbre of his voice those three mornings as she passed the dining room. However, she hadn't had the nerve to enter, their previous conversation too fresh in her mind.

Never wear them again.

The hair on the back of her neck rose. Every instinct pulled at her to approach him, but she remained frozen in place, unable to do anything but stare at him.

Amongst all her brother's friends, he was the only one not easily dismissed from her mind. It was those eyes. They weren't overly intense or outrageously indifferent. They were just . . . perceptive. In contrast, all other gazes appeared rather flighty. That was probably why her infatuation with him at the time had lasted as long as it did.

But it hadn't lasted.

Right.

All men were hound dogs, and that perceptive gaze had never remained on her long. Until now. Up until he'd been assigned as her guard dog, that gaze seemed to settle on older women. He had once even said so himself, and she had fostered a habit of giving her brother and his friends a wide berth when they were drinking at home after overhearing that snippet of conversation.

Ignorance meant bliss in some ways. But it was rather annoying at the moment. Should she tell him about the club's crest? He might be of more help if she placed a bit more trust in him.

"Are you all right?" Theodosia waved a hand before her eyes. "You've gone from pale to light pink to bright red."

Selena looked to Theodosia and patted her cheeks, breaking the spell woven by his gaze. "It must be the temperature of the room."

"If you say so," Theodosia said lightly. "What were we speaking about again? Oh, right, the cardroom."

Yes, the cardroom. "Old women and lonely wives aside, don't men like to play cards at *their* clubs? It makes perfect sense."

"I suppose it's not the worst assumption." Theodosia tapped her finger on her chin. "Cardrooms are usually where all the secret deals are made. At the very least it's worth looking into."

"Secret deals? How do you know that? Wait, you don't have to answer that. Your mother." Selena pondered for a moment.

"Since your mother is so knowledgeable, would she perhaps know about family curses?"

"Family curses?" Theodosia openly scrutinized her as though she were a newfound farm animal. "Why on earth would you want to know about such things? Do not tell me the Savages are cursed?"

"Not us, no." Selena peeked in Warrick's direction, his gaze still on her. Her cheeks heated up again. "It's him. He's the one with the family curse. In exchange for his assistance to find the club, I must help him gather information on curses."

Laughter curled Theodosia's lips. "You? Help a man break a curse?"

"What's with your tone?"

"Oh, no, nothing. It's all rather interesting, is all."

Selena cut her a look. "And I'm not helping him break the curse. He can break it himself. As I said, I am gathering information."

"In that case, I might know of someone who can help you with this topic."

"You do?" Delight filled Selena. "Who?"

"An acquaintance with more knowledge on these sorts of things. I shall send you his details in the morning."

"Splendid." At least she wouldn't have to read a book on the matter. Not that she would have gone that far—curses weren't real. It surprised her that Warrick would even entertain such a possibility.

"Shall we head over to the cardroom?" Theodosia asked. "You've put me in the mood to play a few hands."

Selena cast one last look in Warrick's direction before nodding. "Very well, but keep your eyes peeled for any clues."

WARRICK LIFTED HIS glass and took a swallow of spiced wine, his gaze tracking the dancers swirling about the black and white tiled floor of the Ashworth ballroom. There were only five couples dancing in total, which spoke volumes of how the mess of the betting book had escalated. Who would have thought misplacing a list with a bunch of heiresses' names would warrant this much trouble?

Very well . . . a list he'd had a hand in creating and transforming into the nightmare it was today. But still, he had a much more troubling and current nightmare to worry about. A nightmare that might cause more chaos than even that list.

What he wouldn't give for a bottle of French brandy, no obligation to get out of bed the next day, and the capacity to forget about that damn list and wagers for a few hours.

And her.

Forget about her.

But he was on duty tonight, and duty had a name: *Selena Savage.*

A name that represented a particularly sharp thorn. Always sticking and poking into his side. Three days ago, that thorn had grown ten sizes.

Despite his best intentions, despite having tried to get out of this role of protector, he'd been roped into a search for a damn secret organization. Even knowing the disaster that would come of this, he hadn't been able to say no. He'd sacrificed himself once again. And this time, he really questioned his choices in life. Unlike the times he merely flinched at them.

Selena was right—he was not responsible for her.

Yet he could not find the argument to wrench himself away from her. At first, guilt had driven him to agree to Saville's request, but guilt had certainly not driven him three days ago. Something else had. Something burning deep within.

Christ, those trousers . . . Another thing he couldn't wrench away from—the memory of the way they had clung to her legs as though they belonged on them. He had never seen Selena as anything but Saville's sister. An outspoken little chit that loved to bicker with her brother. Now, he saw her as something else. A woman. An outspoken woman that loved to bicker with her brother, certainly, but also one that had developed a dangerous charm.

Damn trousers . . .

Why did that memory have to call everything into question? Why did it affect him so much? What the hell was next?

These women had become more perturbing than the fortune hunters prowling the fringes of the ballroom when the list was exposed. They were all dangling over the cliff edge of chaos at each soiree, tea party, and musical.

He took another sip of mulled wine, his gaze tracking Selena where she conversed with Lady Theodosia as though she hadn't set a storm upon polite society. She was a vision in blue silk.

At least no Turkish trousers. A small mercy.

Her hair was piled atop her head tonight in a proper style.

I should have demanded she never again wear her hair down as well.

The entire mess was their own fault—him, Saville, Deerhurst, and Avondale. But mostly him. If he hadn't lost the list, so much chaos could have been prevented. Things might be different now. He understood why he and his friends had to keep an eye on the women with the aim of protecting them from unsavory characters. Yet the sight of Selena Savage three days ago had him willing to, if he could go back in time, lose that list all over again. A troubling thought.

He took another sip of wine.

Not bad. But not good either.

Oh Brandy, Brandy, wherefore art thou Brandy?

He had found the manufacturers of the trousers. Now, only one question remained: Did he tell her or not? He could bury the information and the manufacturer with a snap of his fingers. But would that stop her from marching into the streets of London to hunt them down herself?

No, it would not.

However, before he could approach Selena, another lady stepped into his path.

"Warrick, dear," Lady Ridgeland cooed. "You look like you're in need of a bit of attention tonight."

Warrick scowled. The chaos hadn't only brought fortune hunters from the shadows, but also called forth a different breed of females. Not that they didn't exist in the first place, they just moved from the shadows openly into the light.

This woman a perfect example. A huntress. Granted, the years had been kind to her, and she was still a beauty in her forties. But she was infamous for her affairs. She was also the Earl of Ridgeland's wife.

"You are mistaken, madam."

"Come on now." She leaned close—too close—as if she wanted to attract him with her scent, like a black widow attempting attract a mate. "I will make it worth your while."

A chill shot down his spine—the instinct of a male in danger—leaving a cold trail along his back. Warrick preferred to survive the proverbial mating ritual.

"I'm not in the mood, madam."

"How can that be? I'm offering you a night of pleasure on a silver tray. What man would turn down such a dessert freely offered?"

Him.

"I'm afraid I'm busy tonight," *and every night,* "madam."

"You don't look busy to me." She placed her hands on his chest. "Come now, Warrick, dear."

A bitter taste coated his mouth. It wasn't the first time she had approached him, but it was the first time she had been this bold. In other circumstances, he might not have minded, but he drew the line with married women. Though even if she hadn't been married, his mind only had space to occupy one woman at a time. He was a simple man in that regard. And that space had quite recently been claimed.

He shrugged off her touch, but not before he caught Selena's stare from across the floor. She looked away when their gazes touched, and Warrick inwardly cursed. "I'd prefer you don't test my patience. Go pester somebody else."

That beautifully aged face contorted, revealing the true woman behind the mask. "How dare—"

"Lady Ridgeland." Dare grinned as he sauntered over to them. "I see you have set your sights upon the one man you can never sway."

Warrick let out a light breath of relief, earning him a viscous glare from the woman.

"All men can be swayed," Lady Ridgeland said to Dare, her eyes never leaving Warrick. "The earl is merely playing hard to get."

Dare arched a brow at Warrick.

Damn it. "I don't play games."

Dare nodded, smiling at Lady Ridgeland while he flung and arm around Warrick's shoulder, finally drawing her attention, though there was a perceptible edge to that smile. "Warrick is not the best company tonight, but I hear the Duke of Mortimer has just arrived and is looking for some fun."

Lady Ridgeland eyed them a moment before striding off with a huff.

"I'm in your debt," Warrick said, inclining his head to the man.

"We males must stick together."

Warrick sent Dare a skeptical glance. "Mortimer is a male. Is he even attending tonight?"

"He is here, yes." Dare's grin widened. "But he is not looking for fun."

"Then why did you send that harpy his way?"

"He is more contemptuous than you."

Warrick grunted. He couldn't argue on that score. The duke was stiffer than a stick and extremely poised. Not one to tumble about with women of ill repute. He was also in search of the betting book and had shown that he was not a man to be crossed.

But that was about where Warrick's interest in him ended. Though he had wondered at the man's determination.

Dare patted his shoulder before removing his hand. "Be careful of Lady Ridgeland. She is not a woman who forgives or forgets."

"Are you speaking out of experience?" Warrick dusted off his chest where that woman had touched.

"God no, I value simplicity. But I've heard the tales. That woman is a complication that is hard to disentangle from once you allow her into your bed."

"Noted." Though Warrick had no intention of entangling with her in any way or form.

"You made quite the spectacle at the parade with Lady Selena," Dare remarked. "That must have earned you the slap of the century."

"You were there?"

"Of course. I would never miss the chance to see a group of women prancing about in trousers."

Why did he even ask such a question of a libertine like Dare? "It wasn't that much of a spectacle was it?"

Dare smirked. "No, the true spectacle followed after you left. Your little scene was the catalyst for others to retrieve their wives. Scores of women hoisted over their husbands' shoulders and swept off home."

"Bloody hell." This was the first he'd heard of that. At the time, he'd been too distracted to care about the consequences and he didn't follow the gossip rags. He'd acted out of instinct. No woman should be dressed like that and step foot outside.

His gaze shifted back to Selena. He froze. Where had she gone? She'd been there a few seconds ago.

His gaze tracked the crowd and found her just in time to glimpse her disappearing through the doors at the opposite end of the ballroom.

"What's over there?" Warrick asked Dare, pointing in the direction Selena had gone.

"Cardroom, if I'm not mistaken."

What was the wily woman up to now? Hopefully not something that required him to hoist her over his shoulder again. The shape of her curves had already haunted him enough. However, he could not help wondering whether she had witnessed that black widow trying to weave a perilous web for him. It shouldn't bother him. The touch meant nothing. Would lead to nothing. But he also didn't want any misunderstandings to arise because of it.

"Say, have you glimpsed Saville tonight?" Lady Theodosia was here so it stood to reason Saville should be here somewhere as well.

"I can't say that I have."

"Strange." Warrick handed his glass to Dare.

"What am I supposed to do with this?"

"Don't care," Warrick said as he patted the man's back. "There's a prickly thorn I need to pluck from my side."

Chapter Four

S HE FELT HIM—OR perhaps his scent wafted over to her, giving him away—right before he stepped into her path. Tall and broad shouldered, the earl was one of those men who command- ed the gazes of all women he passed. Whether he was aware of this was not clear, but any man would enjoy such attention. And usually, an indulgent smile played across his face. That smile was not present at the moment.

Rather, he looked annoyed.

At her.

She bit back a smile. The old *mission accomplished* ran through her head. But the mission had recently changed, and she needed to remember that they could be considered allies at present. As for how long this fellowship would last, only time would tell.

"You look vexed, Warrick. Whatever can you be displeased about?"

"You must take infinite delight in mocking me."

"I cannot deny that the urge flares to life in your presence." The previous night's dream suddenly flitted across the inner walls of her mind like a butterfly. Selena flushed.

Good grief! None of that! *Not now.*

It had been the first time she had dreamed of a man kissing her. And no matter how hard she hoped the scene would fade from her memory like most other dreams, this picture clung stubbornly to her mind. The shock of the dream kiss had been startling enough. Then came the betrayal . . .

"Do you believe in dreams?" Selena asked suddenly. "That they are warnings from heaven."

"No."

"But you believe in curses. How strange."

"I am careful of curses, there's a difference." He surveyed the card tables filled with activity. "Are you here to play cards?"

"Oh, no. I'm no good. I'm watching Theodosia play a hand while I study the players." She leaned closer. "Have you found information about the matter we have an agreement on?"

A short pause. "Yes."

"Well!" Selena cried, giddy with surprise and delight. "Spit it out."

His gaze flicked to the people gathered around them. "Settle down. The manufacturer didn't have much information. He received the order via a note with the instruction for delivery as well."

"So it's a dead end. How disappointing."

"It seems that way."

"And the note?"

"What about it?"

Honestly! "Did you not ask to see it?"

His brow furrowed. "Should I have?"

"Yes!" Selena wanted to box his ears. "The handwriting of the note could be a clue."

"Unless you plan to test the handwriting of every woman in polite society, which is utterly absurd, I don't see why retrieving the note is important."

"I still want to see it. What if I recognize the writing? I have many correspondents."

"Very well," he murmured, not seeming at all that enthusiastic. "I'll have my man retrieve it."

"Thank you." She eyed him askance. "I have a source for your curse as well."

"You do?" He looked startled—and a bit suspicious as well.

"You didn't think I could come through on my end?" Selena smirked. "I'll have you know I always deliver on my commitments."

"Curses are not your normal topic of conversation," he pointed out. "Which was why I was taken aback."

"Well, in any event, we can visit them tomorrow. As soon as I confirm their address."

"Yours source is a person, not a book?"

Selena nodded. "They are more of a source of a source, but yes."

"Very well. What about tonight? Have you found anything interesting about the secret club I should look into?"

Selena sighed. It was harder than she thought. "Sadly, no."

"And as expected, you cannot stay put for long. Can you at least let me know in advance when we plan to act on your impulses?"

"Then I wouldn't be acting on an impulse, would I?"

"Can you still send me a missive?" His hot eyes landed on her. "*Please.*"

Selena laughed. "Now where would be the fun in that?"

A scowl formed between his brows. "You sure are talented in setting and keeping a man on edge. There is a reason your brother is concerned for your safety. He is correct in protecting you."

"I wouldn't need protecting if it weren't for the lot of you." She blew out a breath. "If *you* hadn't written down those ridiculous flaws, things would never have escalated so far."

"I am aware of my past faults, Selena. No need to point them out so frequently."

"I'll stop once you find me this club."

"I have your word on this?"

Selena couldn't help the quirk of her lips. "No need to sound so skeptical. Of course, you have my word." Some extra motivation wouldn't hurt.

"It's best to still be cautious. There are still fortune hunters and rogues lurking about."

"So are you," Selena teased. "And we are getting on better than I expected." The last she murmured almost to herself, though, honestly, it was much too soon to really tell.

"I'm quite surprised myself." Those dark eyes glinted in the soft glow of candlelight.

Selena's breath caught. Why did that look remind her so much of her dream? She could feel a flush spreading across her cheeks and quickly looked away.

"Anyway," he continued. "What do you hope to gain from watching people play cards?"

A great question. She was searching for clues, but she had no idea what these clues might look like. Any woman in this room could be a member of the organization she sought. It was a good thing she hadn't set her sights on becoming a detective. Her sleuthing skills were truly dismal.

"I'm not sure what I am looking for to be honest," she admitted reluctantly, then followed with a defense, "But it's better than not looking at all."

"Why are you so set on finding these women?"

"Tell me, why did you and the rest of your gang decide my greatest attribute and my greatest flaw is my brother? Do I truly have nothing good or bad about me other than Saville?"

"Of course you have. We were just . . ."

"Foxed and alive with revelry?"

"Would you believe me if I said we were all scared of your brother?"

Selena nodded in thought. "I can certainly believe that. Though it still doesn't excuse you lot." And it still didn't make her feel better about the entire affair. Some things, once done, cannot be undone.

"You are right. There is no way for me to defend ourselves on that score. We are in the wrong."

"Let us not talk about that any more now." There were other, more important matters at hand. "I really must sharpen my detective skills."

"If you are thinking of seeking out a real detective, please don't."

She turned to him. "Why not?"

"My sense of peace."

A light chuckle left her lips. "Do not worry; I have no intention of going that far."

"Good. Your brother is already itching to send you to Fielding Park."

Fielding Park? She snorted. "He can try."

Come to think about it . . . Selena had first met Warrick at Fielding Park. She'd found him utterly enthralling with his bold, angelic features and hair the same shade as the deep hazel of his eyes. He had changed in many ways since then, but those two striking features still remained the same.

On the outside, Warrick might look the charming, pampered aristocrat, but Selena had more than once caught a glimpse of the cold, hard steel beneath his countenance. A wily, if a bit blundering, beast at his best; a lazy beast at his worst. Back then, he'd been so intimidating with his good looks and big size. Today, the only thing intimidating about the man was his presence in her dreams.

Silence filled the space between them. Not uncomfortable, but contemplating.

Warrick shifted beside her, inching a step closer. His lowered voice trailed pebbles across her skin. "Shall I escort you home?"

Selena blinked. "Now? I still want to observe the people in the room."

"I truly did receive the shortest end of stick between the two of us," he muttered, almost sounding petulant. "Not only must I watch over you, but I also promised to help you find a secret club I, you, know nothing about, while you dig for information on curses. I must have lost my mind."

"Will you hush? I am trying to concentrate on finding a clue."

Anything, really.

"But we haven't discussed the most important matter."

"And that is?" Selena asked, surveying all the woman in the room.

"When will you provide me with a moment of peace?"

Ah yes. What had he said about that? Anything that was pleasing. "You shall have it soon."

"I want three. Three moments of peace. Then I'll hush."

Demanding man. "Very well. You'll have three." Providing him these moments also provided her with them, after all.

"Then the first moment shall start now." He held out his hand. "Let's go."

Selena stared at that outstretched arm. "Will leaving the ball truly bring you that much peace?"

"Yes. It means I can go home, truss my feet up on my desk, and get skunk drunk without a care in the world."

"*That* is your idea of peace?"

He snatched her wrist and placed it on his arm, holding her hand in place with his palm. "Yes, because I wouldn't have worry about you."

"What about Theodosia? I cannot leave her."

Warrick motioned to the entry. A furious Saville strode through the doors of the cardroom.

Selena gasped. "Why didn't you say my brother arrived?"

The knave smirked. "Where would be the fun in that?"

"Beast." Selena grabbed the sleeve of his jacket and gave him a tug. "On second thought, I would prefer a warm bed right about now. Let's not delay your first moment of peace."

"Are you sure?" Amusement danced in his voice. "We should greet your brother, no?"

"Do not make me whack you over the head with my reticule, Warrick. If I can sense his foul mood from this distance, you must as well. A wide berth is best." Selena stilled for a moment as someone new entered the room, then she suddenly laughed. "Let me ask you something, Warrick. Are the rumors about you being chased by a woman brandishing a candelabra true?"

He cast her a suspicious look. "Why?"

She nodded toward the entry. "A woman with a candelabra just entered and she is heading our way."

Warrick glanced and curse. "Damn it. Not again."

She tugged at his sleeve again. "We had better hurry up, or you might also be on the receiving end of violence tonight."

He grunted, allowing her to guide them in the opposite direction to another set of doors. "Why do women keep brandishing candelabras at me?"

Good question. "You have that kind of face, I suppose."

"That is absurd."

Selena wasn't so sure. She glanced at one of the three candelabras on a nearby table. She had the same urge at the moment.

SOME THINGS A man couldn't explain.

Warrick clenched his fist to resist the urge to pat his face and trace his hairline across his forehead. Not only was he shedding hair, but his hairline seemed to be receding an inch a week—an exaggeration perhaps, but still a worry.

He loved his hair.

He didn't want to go bald.

And anyway, what the devil did Selena mean about him having *that* kind of face? What kind of face did a man have to have for a woman to brandish a candelabra at him?

No, this had to be down to something else.

Could it be about the list? This had been a thing that started to occur only recently, so that seemed a bit unlikely. Yet not entirely improbable.

Could it be the curse?

Surely not, though he could not disregard the fact that the harassment had started after he turned thirty, presumably activating this family curse.

The other option was that he *did* have that sort of face? Preposterous, if he may say so himself.

He didn't know which idea he resisted the most.

All of them.

Ardently.

This was what his life had come down to—too many inexplicable things. It made him uncomfortable. He needed those moments of peace. He wanted a lifetime of them, not just three. But for now, any would do.

A hand gripped his shoulder in a tight vise. "Running off so soon?" Saville's grating voice sliced between his shoulder blades, causing them to stiffen. "It seems everyone has set out to vex me this evening."

Warrick turned to his friend, shielding Selena's view. "Shouldn't you be more concerned with the reason you are here?"

"That little harridan hasn't noticed me yet. You, on the other hand, should escort my sister home. She has to gather her belongings for Fielding Park."

Selena snorted, stepping up to her brother. Never a good thing. "You'd dare to send me away?"

"I'm not *daring* to do anything. I just do it."

Her chin lifted a notch. Several notches. Warrick tried to step between the two, but her words were faster. "I'm not leaving."

"You are retiring to the country," a foxlike smile upturned his friend's mouth, "or you are marrying. Choose."

Curses stuck between Warrick's teeth. "Saville."

Selena stepped forward. "I choose neither. What will you do?" she challenged.

"That's not an option. My word is law."

"Saville," Warrick spoke in a low voice. "I shall see your sister home."

A mocking gaze met his. "Can I expect a proposal?"

Warrick back shot straight. "What are you talking about?"

"Yes." Selena prickled like a porcupine beside him. "What grave mood have you entered into now? Insisting I marry is one thing, but trying to pawn your friend off on me? Are you a revolting villain?"

"I share your sister's sentiments."

Her shocked gaze flew to his. "You do? This must be a first."

Before Warrick could break free from those bright eyes that locked on him with meaning, Saville snapped, "Is this a conspiracy?"

Then Warrick did something he had never done before: he shoved his friend back a step. "Consider your words before you speak, man."

"What are you doing right now?" Saville demanded.

Hell if he knew. "Do not lose your temper with us when we are not the ones who ignited it."

"What does it matter who ignited what? Escort Selena home. She is leaving for Fielding Park in the morning."

"Brother," Selena said. "If I retire to the country, will you join me? Theo will if I ask her. Shall all four of us shall embark upon a new adventure together?"

Saville puffed up. "Have you read the paper this morning?"

"What do you think?" she shot back.

"Well, today it's quite interesting. Lady Essex has run off with a Spanish lover after it came to light there was a wager about how many times Lord Essex could tup his mistress in one night. All rather scandalous."

"Saville," Warrick warned. His gaze tracked the crowd. Luckily, everyone's attention was on the card games. "That's no way to speak in front of a lady, even if she is your sister."

"What's the matter? It's in the papers for all ladies to read." His eyes settled on Selena. "I wonder why."

"I'm glad you wondered since your male brain seems to keep on forgetting. The blame lays solidly on your shoulders, brother dear. The list. The wagers. The reason I don't read the papers."

"You cannot blame the last on me."

"Of course I can."

Here we go again.

Selena poked a finger at her brother. "Since you are so curious, let me tell you. It all happened when I was a little girl, barely eight. My governess told me about a book she was reading. Her eyes lit up whenever she spoke of it. A fascinating tale of—"

"Get to the point, Selena."

"What a story killer, you are," she said. "Very well. I couldn't sleep on this night, so I decided to go in search of the book. It just so happened you were in the library that night as well."

Warrick had a nasty suspicion.

"Oh? What is so strange about that?"

"Yes, you were *reading* with one of the maids, your breeches around your ankles."

Warrick choked on a breath.

"Needless to say, it was that moment I became clear on what I can do without in life, and I could very much do without *that* picture. Even now, my brain hurts just thinking about it. I avoided the library like a plague after that, and also any sort of reading, since it all reminded me of your little affair."

"That . . ." Saville's voice trailed off. Another man left speechless by Selena Savage.

"For once in your life, brother, claim responsibility."

Saville glared at Selena. "Fine, I was wrong to use the library that way. And have I not been claiming responsibility for the rest?"

"You mean the list?" Selena asked.

"That list was drawn up by Avondale's mother."

"Blaming an old woman now?" She scoffed. "I've been curious for a while now. What contribution did *you* bring to the list?" Her gaze cast to Warrick. "What about you?"

Lord, I need a drink.

"I can't recall," Saville snapped. "Shall I gather Deerhurst and Avondale so we can hash this out?"

"Let's not do that tonight," Warrick protested. Or ever. He

hoped there would come a time when they didn't just rehash the debacle over and over. For now, it was best to let her vent her frustration on them until she was ready to forgive them. It was one of the reasons—he understood it now—why he would help her with anything she asked. Why he had allowed Saville to burden him with the title of protector, watchdog, and wetnurse. Though he'd only ever felt like the last.

In truth, he carried the weight of losing the list. He had grasped the pen that inscribed the words. But more than that, he felt responsible for this loss of self she seemed to be feeling. He couldn't recall who had spoken the words of Saville being her best and worst trait. But Saville wasn't even a trait to begin with. They'd been real blackguards back then.

"What better night than tonight," his friend said with a sullen look at them.

"Saville." Warrick reinforced his tone, making it unmistakably a command. "Let it go." *Let it all go*, he warned with his eyes. "Also, I'm here. I've been watching over her the entire time."

Saville shot back a warning of his own. "You knew she planned to sneak out tonight?"

"Are you asking about your sister or Lady Theodosia?"

Saville cursed.

"Don't forget who sparked your annoyance in the first place," Warrick reminded. "And don't forget who assigned me the role of guardian for this season."

"I am astonished that you are taking my sister's side. Weren't you the one who wanted out of this role three days ago no matter what? Since when have you become so close? You are even shielding her from my wrath." His eyes narrowed. "You've never done that before."

What the hell had wormed up Saville's arse tonight? His own temper would soon erupt if he didn't get out of this damn house soon.

"Close is not the word I'd use to describe it, but your sister and I have come to an understanding."

Saville crossed his arms. "And what understanding is that?"

"Rather than play cat and mouse, we coexist and mutually benefit from the coexistence. You might want to try it with your lady playing cards over yonder."

"And what are these mutual benefits?" Saville asked. He might as well have coated his voice with suspicion.

"I don't tattle to you, and she allows me to escort her safely to and from events," Warrick replied bluntly. He felt her gaze on him. Hot. Speculative. "It's a good deal."

"Bloody hell," Saville snapped. "I cannot believe you said that to my face."

"Neither can I," Selena murmured.

Neither could he, but that still didn't stop the pride swelling in his breast when he caught the look of delight in her gaze. Finally. Was this how it felt to champion a woman? Warrick had to admit, the feeling wasn't that bad. Not bad at all. A man could get addicted to this sensation.

The corner of his gaze caught the lady with the candlestick inching closer. She had hesitated when Saville joined their party, but she hadn't given up.

Of all the things he had to deal with.

Someone pinched his arse.

Warrick jerked forward, a curse leaving his lips even as he whirled around to catch the culprit. Could someone please explain to him what's the matter with the woman of the *ton* and why they are targeting him?

"What's the matter?" Selena asked.

Confound it! They escaped again. "A bug bit me."

Confusion clouded her face. "A bug bit you?" Her eyes darted back and forth, searching the air. "What sort of bug? I hate bugs."

Saville laughed, a knowing glint entering his gaze. "A bug, you say?"

"If you hate bugs, then we had better leave at once," Warrick said, sending his friend a threating look. "We will discuss this more another time."

As for tonight, all he wanted to do was escort Selena home and practice peace of mind with a bottle of liquor. Any would do at this point. It wasn't too late to salvage this night. He could still return home and forget about women pinching his arse, ladies brandishing candelabras, and her.

He could forget, even if just for a moment, all about Selena Savage and the look that flashed across her heart-shaped face when he chose her side over her brother's.

Yes, let him forget it all.

Chapter Five

THE SCENT OF alcohol hit her the moment Selena stepped into his bedchamber. Raw. Intense. Overpowering. Much like the man himself, at times. Her gaze fell on that man sprawled on the bed like a starfish, light snores indicating he was still in a deep sleep. Had he enjoyed his "peace of mind" this much?

"Well, this is a new sight . . ."

With Saville as a brother, she had come across all sorts of drunken scenes over the course of twenty years, each scene more pitiful than the next. Warrick, on the other hand, didn't look all that pitiful. Granted, this position did give off a dash of hopelessness, but for the most part, it rather highlighted the powerful contours of his body.

Her gaze drifted over the broad, bulky expanse of his bare chest. A set of symmetrical muscles sculpted his abdomen.

How did a man get muscles like that?

Selena would have appreciated the sight more if the entire room hadn't reeked of spirits. The smell must be coming straight from him. She tore her gaze away from his body and strode to the windows, whipping open the drapes and allowing sunlight to pour into the chamber.

A groan came from the bed.

She glanced over her shoulder and snorted. She'd waited all morning for this stinky man to respond to the three missive she had sent until her patience had run out. Theodosia had sent the name and address of a person with knowledge on curses and wrote that he expected their arrival today. And Selena wanted that note from the manufacturer. She'd thought perhaps Warrick had business which had prevented him from responding to her, but this . . .

Was this the scene you found when pulling back the proverbial curtain on a modern man?

How . . . *eye-opening*.

She could hardly blame him, she supposed. The earl had had a tough few weeks. Selena thought back to Warrick's predicament with the candelabras. Just what did those women have against him? What must a man do for woman to attack him with a candelabra? But then, he seemed just as baffled.

She approached the bed, tilting her head to the side to examine a half-dead Warrick. She had teased him when she said he had *that* sort of face. He didn't. Rogue locks fell over his brow, giving him a more rugged look than usual. Still handsome.

There must be more to his story than met the eye.

Lovers scorned or the consequence of the wagers on the pages they'd released?

I should have stuck it out and read through the betting book.

She stabbed the earl's cheek with a finger. "Warrick, wake up."

No response.

She tapped again, her finger grazing over light stubble that coated his face. Prickly. Her finger trailed upward to poke at his forehead.

Not as brainless as she'd first thought. Not *that* bright either, though, or she would have that note from the manufacturer in her hands by now. But he had stood up for her last night, and that had cleansed a margin of displeasure she had felt toward him since he had become her watchdog. She had *felt* protected for the first time.

She poked harder.

A hand snaked out to snatch her wrist and jerked. Selena catapulted forward, landing on a hard, solid chest. The same chest that was very, very naked. The smell of brandy ought to have burned her nostrils but was chased away by the shocking warmth of his skin.

"What are you doing?" Selena demanded.

"What are you doing?" He peered at her through small cracks in his eyelids. "Selena?"

"Are you expecting someone else?"

He wiped his eyes. "No. Is that really you?"

"If not me, then who else? My twin?"

"The dream you," he said in a gruff voice, blinking a few times. "Always bloody dreaming."

Her eyes widened. Always dreaming? What on earth did *that* mean? Had he dreamed about her too? How shocking would that be, especially if his dreams were as wild as hers?

Her cheeks heated. "Are these the ramblings of a man half-asleep?"

"You aren't real."

"I assure you, I am very real."

He stared at her. "If you are real, what are you doing in my bed?"

Good question. Selena stilled, her eyes widening as she considered the implications of his question. Wait a second. "If I am a *dream*, why am I in your *arms*?"

The shackles of his arms around her instantly disappeared, providing her an opportunity to scramble from the bed.

Warrick sat up. "Would you be there in reality? Christ, my temples are killing me." He glanced at her and seemed to take in his surroundings properly for the first time. "What are you doing here in my bedchamber?"

Selena took a moment to gather her wits. She inhaled focus and exhaled the feel of his body beneath hers before she returned her gaze to him. "You were supposed to meet me this morning. It's already past noon."

He grunted. "Who the hell let you into my chamber?"

"I let myself in," Selena said, trying hard not to stare at his chest. "Your servants did not stop me. They even pointed the way."

"I'll fire the lot of them."

"Don't be so hasty. Rather ask yourself why they had no problem lending me a hand to find you."

"Was it a footman with red hair?"

"How did you know?" Clarity came in a flash. "Is he one of your foot soldiers meant to keep an eye on me while you are"—her gaze roamed the bed—"out of commission?"

"He still shouldn't have sent you to my chamber," Warrick growled.

"Perhaps he was worried. You looked rather corpse-like when I entered."

"Nothing excuses your presence here, Selena."

"Oh, settle your feathers. I shan't be ruined over this minor thing."

"Strictly speaking, you are ruined right now."

"Strictly speaking, ruination follows discovery. Rest assured, even if your servants are not trustworthy, no one shall believe I entered your chamber of my own accord."

"What a flattering thing to say."

"Are you always such a grump when rising from a near-death experience?"

"A bottle of brandy is not enough to send one of my feet into a grave." He massaged his temples again. "Where are you dragging me off to again?"

"To gather information on curses. I cannot believe I'm saying this, but we should be able to find out how to break this family curse of yours today." She gave him an assessing look. "Given your state of being, I'm starting to believe this curse exists."

"Thank you for the compliment."

What a grump!

"I meant to ask you last night, but what did you do to that

woman for her to keep attacking you with a candelabra?"

"Hell if I know. I've never met her before."

"That can't be right. Why would she attack you then?"

"I'd love to know the answer to that as well."

"You must have done something." Selena tapped her chin thoughtfully. "Either to her or someone she knows."

"I have never done anything to warrant such attacks."

"Then can it be the curse?"

"Lady Selena." He gave her a hard look. "Please wait for me in the drawing room while I wash up."

Selena sighed. "Very well, I shall go. But first tell me what this curse of yours is about." She was dying of curiosity.

"Will you leave if I tell you?"

She grinned at him. "Of course."

He let out a long-suffering breath. "If I don't marry by thirty, calamity will befall me."

Selena nodded her head slowly, digesting this newfound information of the Warrick family. As curses went, it was rather sensible. Marry or you shall be punished. Quite like it was for women, only their curse was called spinsterhood.

"You do realize you could marry and the curse would be broken."

"Would you surrender to a curse?"

Fair point. "Well, I would hardly call your recent bad luck a calamity," she tried to soothe. "This bad luck might be good luck in disguise."

"That's a theory I cannot support." He dragged a hand through his hair. "How is all this good luck?"

"Well, individually, each incident these past weeks might seem like bad luck, but if you consider the bigger picture, it might be a good thing they happened."

"And what is this bigger picture?"

She lifted her hands into the air. "How should I know? That's for you to discover, just like searching for meaning beyond my name and title is mine."

"There is nothing wrong with your name or title."

"I know there is not, and yet there is still meaning beyond them, don't you agree?"

"You win. I can't debate with you this early in the morning. Not while my head is threatening to split open. Just remember, some titles you can never rid yourself of no matter how much you try. As unfortunate as it may seem, you will forever be Saville's sister."

"I am aware," Selena said. "The significance of that title I both loathe and love at the same time."

"A lady's search for meaning." His lips inched upward. "You should write a book."

"Lord no, that sounds exhausting, and my penmanship is atrocious. Even *I* struggle to read what I've written after I've written it. You write one—an earl's search to break a curse. I'm sure it shall be a smashing success amongst the women of the *ton*."

Warrick rose from the bed and went to ring the servants' bell, and all thoughts of meaning fled from her brain.

Dear Lord, Lord, Lord.

The man's back was just as solid as his front.

She gave a small cough into her hand. "Anyhow, I shall take my leave and wait for you downstairs."

If she didn't leave soon, not even the cavalry would be able to pry her eyes from the earl's bare back. The man had a body that would have any woman salivating. He also seemed to possess no self-awareness. Wouldn't a normal gentleman have covered up by now?

She marched to the door.

"Selena." His strong voice stopped her escape just as her fingers folded over the doorknob.

She glanced over her shoulder and almost gasped at the heat dancing in his eyes.

"Don't ever enter my chamber alone again."

HE MUST BE crazy.

Why else would he agree to call on a stranger about a family curse he didn't fully believe in but couldn't deny because of all the peculiar incidents happening to him?

This morning was a prime example.

Selena Savage. Alone. In his bedchamber.

Bloody, bloody hell.

He could still remember her soft body sprawled over him. Even after that, her proximity in his bedchamber, two feet from his bed, was deuced unnerving. Had she not felt any nerves dancing over her own skin?

How could she be so cavalier and enter a gentleman's chamber?

Was it just him?

He had briefly escaped in drink, his wish to forget all his woes fulfilled, yet his biggest woe had returned tenfold the next day. He should never have overindulged. Without her, that momentary peace of mind always collapsed the instant he opened his eyes the next day. With her . . . his brain could not keep up with the speed of her wit. Otherwise, he might have questioned why he'd been dragged to the house of God knew who and was standing in a hall that smelled of vinegar and a copper undertone he couldn't entirely place.

The butler returned. "This way, please. Doctor White is expecting you."

Doctor?

Warrick scowled at the woman beside him as they followed the short, stocky man. They were shown into the study, and a tall, wiry, grey man rose from behind the desk when they entered.

Selena curtsied. "Doctor White, thank you for taking the time to see us."

"Of course. My niece said you have quite an interesting case." He motioned for them to take a seat.

Niece?

His brain wasn't ready to deal with this, whatever this was. Warrick stared at the man across from him as he lowered into a seat beside Selena. The action was so measured, it was almost painful. Why were they calling on a doctor? He wasn't sick. Or diseased. Or bloody rotting from the inside.

"What exactly is the problem?" Doctor White asked.

Warrick turned to glance at Selena.

"My companion . . ." she gave a light cough, "wishes to break a family curse. I was informed you might be of help in his matter."

"I see," Doctor White said, steepling his fingers.

Warrick's temples flared in pain. Did the doctor really see? He doubted that. And yet the man stared at him calmly, studying him.

"When did it start?" the doctor asked after a moment, directing the question to Selena. She, in turn, looked to him in question.

Warrick rubbed his forehead. "A few months ago."

"I see." The doctor reached for the quill and scribbled something into a notebook. "Has this curse affected anyone else in the patient's family?" Again, he directed the question at Selena.

What was the man's problem? And *patient?*

"Not that I'm aware of. Perhaps older ancestors."

The doctor nodded. "And how has it been affecting the patient's life?"

Annoyance stirred. "I'm not a bloody patient," Warrick snapped. "And how do you think it has been affecting me? It's a family curse—calamity will befall any man of my clan if we don't wed by thirty. I turned thirty a few months ago. Now bad luck follows me like a damn lost puppy I once tossed a scrap of meat. How do I get rid of that damn puppy?"

"You should have just wed," Selena muttered from beside

him.

"I refuse to have my life dictated by a curse. I want to break it."

"You believe in this curse?" the doctor asked.

"No."

"Yet, you are here seeking help to break it," the doctor said, scribbling some more notes.

Put it that way, he sounded as if he belonged in Bedlam. Warrick clenched his fists, glaring at the man with his pen and paper.

"I see the problem," the doctor said, "but there is no easy treatment for your problem. We have to do some tests."

"Tests?" *What bloody tests?*

If anyone thought for one minute he would subject himself to the whims of this charlatan, they were sorely mistaken.

A small sigh came from beside him. "Theodosia, you really are too much."

Ah, so her source was Lady Theodosia, that mischievous wench. He should have asked for more clarity before he set out today.

The doctor looked over to Selena. "Are you his caretaker?"

His entire body jerked in reaction to that question. He glanced at her slowly. Their eyes met. A sudden sparkle lit her gaze, sending a shiver of warning down his spine.

She turned back to the doctor. "Why yes, he is my ward."

I am being punished, aren't I?

"I see." The doctor put his quill down. "His condition is quite sensitive. But it may soon become quite dangerous for you alone to manage. I suggest you consider sending your ward to a care facility in the future."

Warrick bristled. Wait a bloody minute.

Selena nodded thoughtfully. "The family curse. . ."

"I cannot be sure. He is suffering from some form of delusion. If you want help, we shall have to do further tests to get to the root of the cause."

"Oh?" That *oh* contained so much intrigue that Warrick wanted to throttle the woman. "Delusion? Is this treatable?"

Delusion my arse! Dear God, could this day get any worse? The only delusion he suffered was that Selena would be of any help. She was born to torment him. In person, and these days, in his dreams as well. He couldn't even tell the difference between what was real and what was not.

The doctor nodded. "Treatment will include—"

Warrick leaped from his chair. "No treatment is needed."

"Sir, I suggest you calm down."

"Do not tell me to calm down, you quack. I am calm. Extremely calm. What I'm not is delusional." God forbid this man strap him into a chair with needles poking into his head. Wasn't that what these sorts of charlatans called testing? Warrick sent a warning look to Selena. "We're leaving."

She nodded, rising from her chair. "Thank you for your time, doctor. I think it best if I escort my ward home for the time being."

A sound of disgust gurgled from the back of Warrick's throat. *Thank you for your time?* This was time wasted that he could never get back. Time he could have spent sleeping. In peace.

Warrick marched from the charlatan's house, his temper growing with every step. His belly growled, reminding him he hadn't had breakfast yet. He needed sustenance or he might just explode. His tempter never fared well on an empty belly.

The moment they entered the carriage, Warrick turned a heated look to Selena, "What the devil is the meaning of this, my dear, sweet guardian?"

"I can explain."

"I'm all ears."

She sighed, picking at the fabric of her skirt. "Firstly, I didn't know this would happen. Theodosia said she had someone who could help with information on curses."

"So you told your friend about my private matters?"

"This is no common quandary, Warrick, so I asked for her

help. But do not worry. She won't breathe a word about it to anyone."

"But someone else—Doctor White—now knows and thinks I'm a lunatic."

"I give you my word, I was just as surprised by all that as you were."

Warrick ground his teeth. "It rather sounded as though you were enjoying yourself."

"Honestly, once I got over the shock of the situation, I could not help but see the humor in it." The corner of her lips turned up slightly.

"Humor, my arse."

"I admit, Theodosia did us wrong."

"If he charges us for the consultation, you are paying the bill."

"If there is a bill, rest assured, I shall pay it," she said serenely.

"Good."

"But do not think to use this as an excuse to weasel your way out of retrieving that note from the manufacturer," she continued.

He snorted. "I won't. *I* uphold my deals. One of my men should have already retrieved it while we were wasting our time at this quack's house."

He glanced away from her, silence settling over the carriage. Warrick had to admit that the quack had done one thing for him. Any lingering thoughts of Selena in his embrace this very morning had evaporated like smoke, along with the confusing feelings they'd produced. For a moment, he'd forgotten who he was dealing with—the princess of trouble. Well, no longer.

"Will you forgive me?"

He glanced back at her, meeting big, clear, imploring eyes.

"Just this once, please?"

"Fine," he muttered, not able to withstand that look. "You truly are a vexing creature."

"Of course. We vexing creatures live for vexing beasts like you."

"Remind me why I ever agreed to this nonsense?"

"If you are talking about our agreement, then you agreed because you are in dire need of peace."

"And what did I get today?"

One thin brow rose in question. "Did you not find your peace last night after we left the ball?"

"Well, what's the point of peace if you only shatter it the next day?"

"Come now, Warrick. Today was a failure, but all is not lost."

"That is a matter up for debate."

A smile upturned her lips. "If it's just a matter of wedding, you ought to break the curse by finding a wife. You have to find one eventually, anyway, don't you?"

He smirked. "Now that I think about it, you did agree to help me take break it."

Smart as a whip, she caught his meaning instantly and retorted, "Gathering information is hardly akin to marriage."

"Marriage could be a form of information gathering," he challenged.

"Not in this lifetime," she tossed back. "Though I must admit, it was a rather novel experience playing your guardian, even though it lasted only a minute."

He actually laughed. Of course the brazen minx with think that. He, on the other hand . . . "I can't bloody think on an empty stomach."

"You know, I can understand why you are rebelling. I wouldn't want to marry just to appease a family curse either. I'd stay a spinster all my life. Perhaps I shall anyway. I could raise an exotic animal or two. They are much less troublesome than a husband, I'm sure."

"Your mouth truly is a masterpiece," Warrick remarked.

"Are you telling me to keep it shut? What if I don't want to?" She grinned, a smile that hit him dead center in the chest.

Warrick dragged a hand through his hair. He thought he could remain calm in her presence, but he couldn't. The nerves all over his body were sparking with aggravation from her teasing.

Well, he wasn't the only one that could be on the receiving end . . .

He leaned toward her until their noses were almost touching and their breaths mingled. "Then I have no choice." *I'll shut it for you.*

"What are you doing?" she breathed.

"Hell if I know." Then his lips found hers, swallowing any and all words that might have followed his. Madness claimed a man many times over the course of his lifetime, but this was probably the maddest thing he had ever done. And this kiss . . . her lips molding beneath his, so much softer than he'd imagined . . .

Sharp teeth clamped down on his lower lip. The pain sent a jolt through him. Warrick pulled away to meet two stabbing eyes.

"I asked, what are you doing?"

Warrick brushed his lower lips with a finger. He tasted blood. "I'd have thought the answer was obvious."

"You cannot think on an empty stomach, but you can kiss on one?"

"Hunger can make a man lose his senses, so please forgive me." His lips pulled up in a smirk. "Just this once."

Chapter Six

The next day ~ Theodosia's Garden Party

SELENA LATCHED ONTO her prey and marched straight toward the person her gaze had fixed upon. While her and Warrick's little adventure to the "doctor" had provided her some amusement, the consequences had led to a kiss! Did her friend realize what influence that had on her sleep?

Of course not!

"Theodosia!"

"Ah, Selena, you've arrived."

Selena grabbed her friend's arm and pulled her off to the side so that they were out of earshot of the rest of the attendees. "Have you gone mad? Sending us to that doctor's house! You knew very well the earl is not sick."

Theodosia laughed. "I see your visit had the intended effect. Aren't you happy? You got back at Warrick for all the trouble he's caused."

Yes, then he got her back in a much more striking way. A kiss which had kept Selena up all night. What sort of man mutters *hell if I know* and then kisses a woman? What sort of woman enjoys it before realizing she shouldn't and then ends the kiss with a bite? Though, quite frankly, it had been thoroughly satisfying.

But now, she was stuck with the knowledge that a real kiss

from Warrick was even better than a dream kiss from Warrick!

However, the true problem wasn't so much the kiss itself but rather that it had come so naturally to accept his kiss. Perhaps because he had kissed her in her dreams already. She couldn't rightly say.

"Who is that doctor anyway?" Selena asked. "He said his niece mentioned us. That is you, isn't it?"

Theodosia waved a dismissive hand. "He is a distant relative. A bit of a hermit. Everyone finds him strange, so they just avoid him."

"I see crazy is a family trait of yours."

"Everyone has odd relatives, I'm sure. Our family just has a bit more than our fair share." Theodosia waved at Leonora, who stepped onto the lawn. "Was the earl very angry?"

"Yes." But he was also hungry and hungover.

"One a scale of one to ten, how much did his temper flare?"

"I'm not sure." How annoyed must a man be to kiss someone out of vexation? Selena couldn't even begin to measure that. "I cannot say it was high, but it certainly wasn't low. Rather average, I suppose then."

"That's a bit disappointing."

Selena shrugged. "He must still be rather put out, since he didn't join my brother for breakfast today."

"He shall get over the matter soon enough."

Yes, but she didn't want him to avoid her. That was inexpedient for their arrangement, was it not? He hadn't even handed the note from the manufacturer over to her in person. He sent that red-haired footman.

While Selena found this half amusing, she also felt a bit bad for the earl. She didn't mean to have fun at his expense. Perhaps she should send him a gift? Maybe a box of tea. Was there one that promoted health and good hair growth? He seemed to have a preoccupation with his hair.

"Oh, and happy birthday. I had a maid send your gift up to your chamber."

"Oh?" Theodosia's gaze lit up with interest. "Why not hand it to me personally?"

"Well, it's not appropriate to hand it over in public."

Theodosia's eyes widened. "What scandalous present did you get me?"

Oh, nothing much. "A book."

Theodosia's smile slipped. "Not a big, journal-like book?"

"Yes, exactly so. The very one you've always wanted, in fact."

Her friend pulled a face. "Forgive me if I don't thank you for this present."

"No thanks are needed. You having this book kindles such relief in my heart, and that is enough for me." She sighed contentedly before changing the subject. "By the by"—she rummaged through her reticule to retrieve the note Warrick procured and handed it to Theodosia—"do you recognize this handwriting?"

Theodosia scrutinized the neat, impeccable script. "I cannot say that I do. Most women have pretty penmanship."

"Not me."

"I said most." Theodosia handed the scrap of paper back. "This was written by one of the club members, I presume?"

"I believe so," Selena said. "But it's a dead end. Warrick was right. There's no way to figure out whose handwriting this is without comparing it to the handwriting of every woman in polite society."

"They might not be from polite society," Theodosia said with a thoughtful tap on her chin.

"Now that would be shocking."

"Would you still join them if they are not?"

Selena shrugged. "That would depend on what they are about." Of course, she knew no person or club could give her the meaning she sought, but it would bring her a step closer to finding her identity within this world.

"Good. Motive is everything."

There is nothing wrong with your name or title.

She froze. Why would those words come and haunt her now? Of course, Warrick wouldn't understand her plight. Not completely. Perhaps it was simpler for men. They had the most advantages in the world, didn't they? They didn't have to worry about things like *meaning*. Why yearn for more if you already have it all?

So, she would find the club, ask the members why they hadn't invited her. If she had the chance, she would join. Then she would forge an identity that would move her beyond the shadow of her brother.

Her motives were pure.

A certain kiss came suddenly to mind.

Selena ruthlessly pushed the picture from her mind. Kissing her to shut her up. What kind of motive was that? And that mocking tone afterward. The man had a way to set her teeth on edge with his choices.

"Selena! Theodosia!" Lady Leonora sauntered over to them and exclaimed excitedly, "An only women tea party! How novel. Even the servers are all women."

"That's the point," Theodosia said with a smile. "All the male servants have been dismissed for today as well."

"You father is quite lenient," Leonora murmured.

"He's been dismissed as well."

Selena laughed along with Leonora.

"Well, you are certainly not shying away from the gossip sheets." Lady Harriet, recently wed to the Marquess of Leeds, joined them. "Your name shall be sprawled across the paper tomorrow. It is quite refreshing indeed. Who knows, perhaps soon we'll see men dismissed party after party."

Theodosia grinned. "I'm surprised your husband allowed you attend without him."

"Oh, he is skulking in the carriage with a book," Harriet said drily.

Selena laughed. Leeds was obsessed with his wife, especially when it came to matters of safety, though this could hardly be considered a risky event. "I am not surprised."

"I wish I could snatch a protective husband such as Leeds," Leonora said. "It's enough to make one's heart flutter."

Selena's snort followed Theodosia's.

"You don't agree?" Leonora asked. "Do you not want to find husbands?"

"It's not that I don't want a husband," Selena said. "It's just that I'm not *looking* for one. I shall find myself first and then find a husband."

Harriet nodded. "I quite understand. Your entry on the heiress list claimed both your best and worst attribute to be your brother. If that is not depressing, I don't know what is."

"Exactly."

"Those entries don't carry much meaning, do they?" Leonora asked. "Given your brother's temper, it's only natural that his friends wouldn't want to provoke it by saying anything more specific."

True . . . Warrick had alluded to that much as well.

"I agree," Harriet said. "Besides, my husband adores my laughter and that was my biggest flaw, as you recall."

"Well, I for one, can tell you that Saville is a fire-breathing dragon," Theodosia muttered. "He is also the reason I decided to host a female only tea party. Do try the punch. It has a delightful kick."

Leonora lifted her glass. "I can attest to that." She glanced at Selena. "If what those rascals said about you bothers you so much, just ask another man's opinion."

Selena accepted a glass of punch from a passing server. "I'd rather not. They leave a rather sour taste in my mouth these days." She took a sip. Sweet. "Let's change the topic, shall we? I've had enough of wagers, lists, and the opinions of men."

"Fair enough," Theodosia said, clinking glasses with her. "Why don't you ask if anyone here has received an invitation?"

"Oh, right, has any of you been invited to a secret women's club?" If they had, she would know for certain that this club was toying with her.

"No," Harriet said.

Leonora shook her head.

"Apparently none of us meet their requirements, whatever they are." Selena took another sip of punch. Still the only leads they had were the note, the crest, and the trousers.

"And you wish to receive an invitation?" Harriet guessed.

Selena nodded.

"How brave," Harriet responded. "Leeds would explode if he found out I joined a secret organization. I shall tease him to death if I receive such an invitation."

"Your husband is the type that would lock you in a tower and toss away the key," Selena said.

"Tease and run," Theodosia suggested.

"Tease and run . . ." Harriet bit her lip in thought. "I shall have to try it."

"Don't take Theo's bad advice, Harriet," Selena said. "Your husband has long legs. Be sure you can outrun him before you start teasing."

"And run far way," Leonora supplied with a chuckle. To Selena, she said, "Perhaps these women are still observing you and everyone on the list."

"Or," Theodosia said slyly, "perhaps they are a bunch of old crones having fun." She nudged Selena with her shoulder. "You'd have to wait a few years to qualify."

Selena rolled her eyes. "It's not always the destination that matters, rather than the journey there."

"So long as you know what you want," Theodosia said with a small smile.

"I wish I could be more like you in that regard." Selena swallowed another sip, surveying the women bustling about the garden. "I shall figure out what I want along the way."

"I, for one, can absolutely relate," Leonora said. "The future is uncertain and all we can do is seize all moments as they come."

"Didn't you want a protective husband like Leeds a moment

ago?" Theodosia arched a brow lined with amusement.

"Well, that's but one character trait, and it's optional. Then again, is it? Should it be mandatory? What other traits do I want in a man? I'm *so* indecisive."

Selena laughed.

Unable to decide what she wanted—she could certainly relate to that. What did she hope to gain by finding or even joining this club? Was it that important? What traits did she want in a husband? Did she want to marry or not? If not, what happened to her then? If she did, what would happen to her *then*?

All these questions clamored for answers. But what if she made the wrong choice when she did answer them, when she did choose her path?

What if she lost more than just her identity?

So many decisions . . .

WARRICK WATCHED AS Saville peeked through the window of the carriage stationed outside Lady Theodosia's house. He should never have been swayed by his friend, who had lured him out of the house on the pretense of visiting Tattersalls.

Crazy fool.

Instead, he found himself in the one place he did not want to be—once again following Selena Savage. These siblings really knew how to rile a man.

But enough was enough.

Yes, he had his portion of blame to share when it came down to that deuced heiress list, but that didn't mean he had to pay for it with his sanity. It also didn't mean he had to spend his entire life atoning for it. They had all made a mistake, but what was done was done.

The moment the betting book was stolen from White's, the original record lost, there was no honorable way to fulfil the wagers. Even if the book was retrieved, he would not allow it to come back into play. Either White's ripped those pages out, or he would bloody burn the book until there was nothing left but ashes.

That was *if* the book was ever found. Warrick had his doubts whether those heiresses would relinquish the thing.

Either way, he was finished. It was time to move on. Selena in his bedroom, Selena dragging him to a charlatan's house, and Selena kissing—no, *him* kissing Selena had been the eye-opening jolt he sorely needed.

He stared at Saville peering out the window, shaking his head slowly. "After today, your sister is all yours."

"What do you mean?" Saville asked offhandedly, craning his neck to peek down the street when a carriage passed them.

"I'm done with my role of protector to your sister."

"Why?" Saville asked without giving up his view of the street. "We agreed. The women on the list need protecting."

Warrick gave a rare snort, the kind he needed only around the Savages. "If those women need protection, I am the Pope. Whoever approaches them with ill intent, they are the ones in need of protection."

"Have you forgotten what happened to Deerhurst's wife?"

"That was all Cromby. He's been dealt with. Besides, he serves as a useful example to any miscreant who dares follow in his footsteps."

"So, you're saying Selena doesn't require protection."

"I'm saying you can manage your sister all by yourself."

"Lady Theodosia—"

"Has six brothers," Warrick finished for him.

"And where are they? None of them are in London."

Warrick shrugged. "Perhaps word hasn't yet spread to where they are, or perhaps they aren't worried. And if they aren't worried about their sister, then neither should you be."

Saville sent him a look. "Why are you such a grump? Has your family curse claimed more of your hair?"

Warrick scowled. "Blackguard."

"And weren't you the one who heroically stood up for my sister in the cardroom just the other night? Nearly brought me to tears."

"It nearly gave you heart palpitations. Take care or that temper of yours or it will send you to an early grave." Lord knows, they could all use a reprieve from it.

Saville tapped the window with the tip of his finger. "I lost my temper at the Ashworth ball, I'll admit, but you were still going on about how you were the guardian and so on and so forth."

"I've changed my mind."

"Just like that? Did my sister get your hackles up again? What did she do now?"

Warrick looked away. He chose not to answer that, lest his friend's temper explode in this terribly confided space.

Saville chuckled. "Fine, do as you wish. After today, I won't force your hand."

That was easy. Almost too easy. But he wasn't about to question this boon. "Thank you."

Saville diverted his attention back to the window. "This is ridiculous," he muttered. "Why the devil would she host a tea party and not invite any men?'

Warrick's brow inched upward. "*That* is what you find ridiculous?"

"Why? Don't you?"

"I find it more ridiculous that we are hiding in a carriage peeking at a lady's house."

"You are right," Saville sneered. "Men should not hide in carriages. We are better than that."

Are we? Warrick had his doubts.

"We should be in there, in the thick of things." Saville squared his shoulders and adjusted his cravat. "Come on, let's go."

Warrick massaged his temples. Another habit he developed

when with a Savage. "Go where?"

"Staying in the carriage is getting us nowhere. We should slip into the house and spy from a room that gives us a view of the party."

God above. "No. Absolutely not."

"Why?"

Because I am avoiding your sister. Because if he entered that house . . . he might falter.

Again.

But he couldn't tell his friend that. Not without getting into the *why* he was avoiding her. And what Warrick didn't have was answers for his friend. Saville and Selena might bicker constantly, but when it came to his sister, Saville threw punches first and asked for explanations second. And if he didn't like the explanation . . .

What could he even say?

I'm helping your sister find a secret club. Oh, and she entered my bedchamber alone while I was sleeping off a night of drink. Forgive me for yanking her onto me. I also kissed her.

No.

Warrick would rather not stare down the barrel of a forced marriage that would ensure both parties a miserable outcome.

"Why the devil do you want to spy on a gaggle of females, anyhow?"

"What's with you lately?" Saville countered. "Did Selena curse your existence? Throw kitchenware at you? Cut up your favorite waistcoats?"

"Of course not. I'm not *you*."

Saville's glare spoke volumes. "I'm choosing not to respond to that."

"So you *can* choose not to respond to something. Well, if you make this choice more often, I doubt your existence will be cursed, you will have kitchenware tossed at you, or your waistcoats will be cut up."

"Why, thank you for your sage advice."

"I live to impart sage advice to my friends."

"You really have a singular talent for vexing me." Saville slouched back into his seat. "Fine, the reason I'm snooping today is not to spy but because it's Lady Theodosia's birthday." He motioned to the package beside him. "I wish to give her a gift."

"Drop it off at the door."

"This is no ordinary birthday gift," Saville said. "It serves as an apology gift as well.

This caught his attention. "What did you do?"

Saville gave an exaggerated sigh. "We might have had some words at the card game. By the by, have you seen this crest?" Saville handed him a slip of paper he retrieved from his pocket.

Warrick studied the sword entwined with roses. "What is this?"

"An organization of some sort operating in the shadows. Mortimer asked me to keep an eye out for it."

Warrick froze.

Why did that sound so familiar? What was it with these Savages and shadowy organizations?

"Isn't Mortimer searching for the betting book?" And now this?

Saville opened the carriage door and jumped out. "So far as I know, yes."

Warrick studied the drawing, brows furrowing. "What else did he say?"

"Can't recall. Why? Do you recognize it?"

"No." But a suspicion formed in his mind. What were the chances there were two secret organizations that two people connected to the betting book were searching for? And if his suspicion was correct, why was the duke searching for a club run by women? No matter how Warrick looked at it, this did not bode well for anyone.

He handed the slip back to Saville. "The design is not particularly original." This had nothing to do with him, he reminded himself.

I'm done.

Saville nodded. "Are you joining?"

Warrick clenched his fists.

I'm done.

She was Saville's sister. He'd known her since she was a little girl. Some lines should never be crossed when it came to your friends. Some lines, when you crossed them, served as a gateway to crossing more lines. She had crossed a line when she'd entered his chamber. He had crossed a line when he'd kissed her.

He might cross a line again. She might too. What would they be then? Just two people recklessly and endlessly crossing lines back and forth?

"Well?" Saville pressed.

Warrick pinched the bridge of his nose. If he didn't want Saville to kill him, he had to stay as far away from Selena Savage as possible. But if his suspicions were correct and the crest belonged to Selena's club . . . could he stand back and watch whatever catastrophe was bound to happen? Though, if he were wrong . . .

Let me be wrong.

"I'll come." Warrick exited the carriage to follow his friend. "But I'm not setting foot in that garden."

"Wouldn't want to you to, old friend. I'm merely dropping off a gift in person, that's all."

They hadn't taken three steps when a man said, "I was wondering how long the two of you would hold out."

Warrick followed Saville's gaze to another man stepping from a coach a few yards beyond theirs. He nodded "Leeds."

Leeds inclined his head toward them. "Are you heading inside?"

"Figured the house is bigger than the carriage," Saville remarked.

"Do you mind if I join you?" Leeds asked. "My carriage is quite cramped as well."

Saville grinned. "The more the merrier."

"No more than quarter of an hour," Warrick warned his friend. "Then we leave for Tattersalls."

"Deal."

Should he have known better to make a deal with the devil? Probably.

Chapter Seven

"WHAT'S THE MATTER?" Selena cocked her head when Theodosia's brow wrinkled into a frown as a maid whispered something in her ear before scurrying off. She had a suspicion that the furrow between her friend's brows had something to do with a man, fair-haired, and surnamed Savage.

"Your brother is here."

"That rogue . . ." Why on earth would he be here? She had made it clear when she left the house an hour ago this tea party was for women *only*. "Did he dress in a skirt? I told him anything with breeches was not allowed."

"I'm not sure. He is not alone."

Oh, surely not . . . "Warrick is here as well?"

Theodosia nodded, and Selena's heartbeat accelerated. He didn't have the nerve to hand over the note from the manufacturer himself, but he could show up with her brother at an event where neither was invited nor belonged? Could it mean he had news?

No.

That could not be. He would have sought her out privately if he'd found a noteworthy lead. Or sent his lackey. That was if he were still of a mind to help her search for the club. She'd already decided to send him tea as an apology gift. Though, in all fairness, Theodosia should be the one apologizing.

"I wonder what they want," Harriet murmured, "or if they ran into my husband."

Theodosia pursed her lips. "They have not requested an audience, but apparently your brother brought a gift."

"A gift?" That surprised Selena. "Saville has never bought anyone a gift before. Not even me."

Theodosia's eyes widened. "Truly?"

Selena nodded. They weren't affectionate that way. "I send him the bills of my purchases and he sends me grumbles, birthday or not."

Theodosia shook her head. "He and my eldest brother would get along famously."

"I'm surprised your brothers haven't returned to London," Leonora murmured. "They are depriving London of their handsome faces."

"Oh stop," Theodosia muttered. "The longer they stay away, the better for me. My parents have been keeping news under wraps, but it's only a matter of time before they descend upon London anyway. Shall we go see what the men want, or shall we ignore them until the party is done?"

Leonora nodded to one of the drawing rooms that faced the garden. "That would be them, I expect."

Selena squinted in the direction of the house. Sure enough, two, no, three silhouettes could be seen shadowing the windows.

"Is that Leeds?" Selena asked.

Harriet groaned. "He must have grasped the opportunity and latched onto your suitors."

"They are not our suitors," Selena and Theodosia blurted at the same time.

Leonora laughed.

"This is ridiculous," Selena exclaimed, as she marched to the house. "I'll go chase them off."

These men . . . could they not give them even half a day's reprieve? And just when she'd been having a very interesting conversation with Leonora. Clearly, there was no need for their protection at an all-women's tea party. Yet they still dared to encroach? Honestly, if Warrick could send a footman to deliver an important note, Saville could have sent a footman to deliver his gift. Or he could deliver it and *leave*. Then again, having lived with her brother's shamelessness all her life, his behavior ought not come as surprise.

Warrick, on the other hand, had no reason to be here.

And Leeds . . . well, that was Leeds. Ever the opportunist.

By the time she entered the drawing room, flanked by Theodosia and Harriet, the men were calmly seated, as though they had no care whatsoever that they were supposed to be anywhere else but here.

Theodosia's cold gaze swept over the men. "Men are not allowed at this party."

Saville nodded. "We are not at your party; we are in the drawing room."

Utterly Shameless.

Selena's gaze fell on Warrick. Their gazes met fleetingly before he glanced away. Selena blinked. Was he *ignoring* her?

"If you haven't noticed," Theodosia crossed her arms, "all the men in the house, servants and family, have been dismissed for the party. You're the only ones here."

Warrick rose to his feet. "I'll wait in the carriage," he directed at Saville before nodding at the ladies and striding from the room.

Selena's gaze tracked his back in astonishment. Not once, but for that brief instant, did he even look at her. Selena had never been so blatantly ignored in all her life. This man . . . this man had just given her the cut direct! Was he *that* mad?

By Jove!

She would not be so glaringly disregarded! Her feet stormed after him even before her brain finished the thought. She grabbed him by the elbow, pulling him to a stop. "Why are you ignoring me?"

He refused to look at her.

"Are you not even going to look at me?" Her eyes narrowed

on him. "Are you never going to look at me again? Are you certain you can manage that?"

He remained stubbornly silent.

"I suppose we can mime our words with our hands," Selena said gratingly. "Or we can communicate with the written word."

His jaw was tight, his composure forced, and his hands fisted into tight balls. Selena let go of his elbow, her arms falling back to her sides. "I never took you for a man who would ignore a person in such a blatant fashion."

Those dark eyes finally settled on her.

Selena's heart did a little somersault in her chest. "A clenched jaw. Stiff posture. Fisted hands. Your entire body speaks how severely annoyed with me you must be. Not to mention the fact that you gave me the cut in there."

"I'm not annoyed with you."

"Aha! He speaks. You are not annoyed with me, you say, but you are annoyed. Plus, you were so obvious in your disregard. Who are you vexed with if not me?"

He unclenched his fists, flexing his fingers to relax them. "I'm not annoyed with you, Selena, I'm annoyed with myself. More so now that I've given in and entertained this conversation."

Rude man. "Is it because I took you to a charlatan's house or because you kissed me?"

He stared at her without a word.

"Because I bit you, perhaps?" Could it be that?

He still gave her nothing.

"All of them, then. What must I do to make you forgive me? I was planning on sending you tea as an apology."

"I have enough, thank you."

"Does that mean you are not going to forgive me? I've forgiven you, and this is a *special* tea."

He arched a brow.

"It aids hair growth."

His face frosted over.

Why must the man be so rigid? "Come now, Warrick, what

must I do? I will do anything you want." She paused, lowering her voice. "If it's about the kiss, it didn't bother me that much."

The corners of his eyes crinkled. She'd caught his attention. "The kiss didn't bother you?"

"No," she said simply. "It was a moment of madness. I understand."

So long as it never happened again. Because this was Warrick. Saville's friend. A previous girlhood infatuation. One of the men who had turned her life upside down and had her questioning her very existence in this world.

She studied his face as she waited for his response. Warrick had been in her world longer than he had not. She supposed that was why the betrayal she had felt when she had learned about what he and her brother had done had been no less than her anger toward them.

Had she still not let that hurt go?

"A moment of madness," he finally repeated.

Why did she sense that his mood had plummeted even more? "Was it not?"

"So, me kissing you didn't bother you?"

"I said as much, didn't I?" Selena smirked. "It seems to have bothered you."

His gaze searched hers and a slow smile creeped across his face, so suddenly it seemed wholly out of place from the mood he emanated mere moments ago. "You said you'd do anything as long I forgive you?"

Selena paused. "Within reason," she said slowly.

"Define *reason.*"

"Not too difficult to accomplish. Not too strenuous. And nothing that requires me to use a weapon."

He snatched her wrist, pulled her swiftly into the nearest room, and backed her against the wall. Heat rose to her cheeks. "What are you doing, Phineas?"

"What I want is simple." He leaned in close. "It is nowhere near laborious and requires no weapon whatsoever."

"What do you want?" Did she honestly want to know?

Yes. Yes, I do.

His gaze burned into hers. "I want my kiss to bother you."

Selena blinked.

"So I'm going to do it you again until you are damn well as bothered by it as me."

Her breath hitched. Before Selena could utter even one word, her lips were covered by his. For a second, the world froze, and all she could feel was the probing of his tongue demanding and claiming entrance. Her heart thudded, drowning out all other noise until she could hear no sound but its pounding beat. She could almost taste resentment in his kiss, the frustration. Whether it was because she teased him, bit him, or refused to have him ignore her, whatever had triggered this sensual onslaught, Selena could not find the reason to push him away.

In truth, she loved the way he was bothered by her. The way he responded when he was teased by her. She rewarded his delightful responses by sliding her hands to the back of his neck. She wanted to bother and tease him even more. Day and night.

A throat cleared.

Selena's eyes shot open, and she pushed at Warrick even as he took a hasty step backward. Leonora stood a few feet away, staring at them in astonishment, her cheeks glowing bright red. This . . . This . . . "It's not what you think," she blurted and wanted to slap her forehead. Because it was—it was exactly what her friend thought.

"I'm not thinking anything." Leonora slowly retreated a step.

"He's helping me," Selena said, straightening her gown, "with finding the club we spoke about earlier."

"No, I am not."

Her gaze flew to his, Leonora all but forgotten. "You aren't helping me anymore?"

"No."

"Because of the doctor incident?"

"No."

"The kiss?"

"No."

Selena's mind raced. "The hair growth tea."

"*No.*"

"Then why?"

He dragged a hand through his hair. "Because I agreed in the first place against my better judgment."

"Which you have now miraculously recovered?"

"Yes," he bit out.

He just stole every sense from her body and now this? "You just wait, Phineas." Selena turned on her heel and marched from the room. She couldn't think with that distracting scent, that face, and the frustration that suddenly stabbed her chest.

"What do you mean by that?" he called out after her. "Where the hell do you think you are going?"

She kept walking, her back straight.

"Selena!"

Call all you like, you rotten rogue. She could also ignore him. She would be as tight-lipped as though her mouth had been sewn shut with embroidery needles.

DISASTER LOOMED.

He could feel it in his bones. He should never have followed Saville and Leeds into the house. The moment he saw a maid open the door, not a butler, and no footman in sight, he should have run.

Now she was the one dashing off, leaving him with parting words that brought an odd tightness to his chest.

"I wouldn't if I were you."

Warrick stopped his pursuit in it tracks at the soft voice. He spared a glance at Lady Leonora, whom he had forgotten about.

Right.

They'd been caught kissing.

In. The. Act.

Christ.

This was why he hadn't wanted to run into Selena. Why he'd tried his best to hold back. One look, one word from her was all it took to draw him in and provoking this sudden lack of control he found himself exhibiting. But her earlier words had triggered the beast inside him. The kiss hadn't troubled her? Truly? While he had been extremely pained by not *only* their kiss but his reaction when their lips touched?

He suddenly understood what she meant by feeling insignificant. A truly ghastly feeling, that.

She thought he'd kissed her out of anger. So had he. But the truth was even more shocking. Deep down, he just couldn't help himself. He *wanted* to kiss her.

Badly.

Madly.

And utterly incomprehensibly.

He had wanted to unravel the threads that tangled Selena up. He'd just hoped to God that he wouldn't unravel along with them. But the moment he had—as he'd feared he would—he'd panicked. Which led to the current circumstance of being caught in the act. And his dread hadn't subsided yet. With each passing second it seemed to grow stuffier right at the center of his chest.

But before he could deal with that, he first had to deal with Selena's friend.

"I trust you will keep this matter a secret?"

Lady Leonora inclined her head. "I will. However, if I were you, I'd allow some time for Selena—and yourself—to cool down."

Warrick nodded. "Noted. If you will excuse me."

"Of course."

Warrick strode from the room. He probably *should* give her time to settle her temper. As well as time for his own body, which still throbbed with heat, to calm. He cursed his own thoughts.

Hadn't he moments ago said he was done? What the hell had happened to his resolve?

You know what happened.

She happened.

At the very least, he ought to apologize, shouldn't he? Perhaps he shouldn't have been *done* in the first place. *Confound it.* He needed to clear his head.

He nodded at the maid that stood at the entrance of the door, striding through the door she opened and hurrying down the three steps before marching to Saville's carriage. Forget Tattersalls, forget Saville.

Saville could walk home.

He wrenched open the door of the carriage and froze mid-enter. Two pools of blazing fires stared at him from within. "What are you doing? This isn't your carriage." Selena's voice was dark.

"I clearly remember arriving in it."

"Well, I'm leaving in it."

Warrick studied her fiery eyes for a moment before inclining his head. Very well, it seemed he'd be walking home. "Then I shall take my leave another way."

"Wait!" She leaned over to press against the door he started to shut. "Come in."

"I don't think that's a good idea." Had she come here instead of going back to the party because she gathered he'd return here? Was that what her *you just wait* meant? One look at her narrowed eyes, and Warrick decided not to ask.

Against his better judgement, he entered and settled in across from her. "Selena—"

"I thought I could keep silent," she interrupted him, and Warrick shut his mouth, staring at her. "But I am once again reminded that it's not in my nature to do so. I'm furious and want to yell at someone."

"Your friend suggested we give each other space to cool down."

"Leonora? What else did she say?"

"She promised to not breathe a word of what she witnessed."

"Of course. She is my friend, after all. But I don't need space at the moment. I need answers."

"By all means, shout if you must." They should not be alone together, but leaving was also not an option. The woman before him as looking for a fight. He had an inkling that she would chase him down the street, with or without a candelabra, in her current mood.

"Are you really not going to help me anymore?"

Warrick dragged a hand through his hair at the question. He'd expected it, but how to answer? He still had men inquiring after the club. He hadn't called them off yet. In fact, the moment his suspicion formed after Saville showed him that drawing, he knew he wouldn't.

But that was different than helping Selena find a club that had now become even more suspect than before. Then again, if he stopped helping her, she would venture off on her own again. He lost, no matter what. However, the club wasn't the root issue here. There was a bigger and more terrifying problem that they were currently glossing over and ignoring: all the lines they had crossed.

"I'm still searching for your club," he finally admitted.

"Then why . . . you know what, never mind. Let's not delve into your reasoning."

"You know my reasoning."

"The kiss."

He stared back. "Did it not bother you at all?" It had been bothering him so much that he'd been acting hot one moment and cold the next.

"Which one?"

"Don't play coy."

She arched a brow. "Who is the one playing coy today?"

"I'm a man. I don't act coy."

"Well, neither do I. I don't have the patience."

She lifted the palms of her hands. "In any case, if a kiss bothers you so much, why did you do it?"

"How was I to know it was going to bother me as much as it does?" Warrick retorted, then stilled.

They both looked away.

"Well," she said after a moment, tapping the window with her finger, just like her brother had done earlier. "This is rather anticlimactic. I intended to yell at you and perhaps punch you one or two times, but now I've lost the urge. In any case, since you loathe the idea of helping me so much, you don't need to trouble yourself anymore."

Warrick turned to study her. "I beg your pardon?"

"The best thing to do is simply go our separate ways." She pursed her lips. "Perhaps space is what I need after all."

Warrick had never been at a loss for how to respond as at that moment. They were both like little children playing tug of war, but neither gaining any ground. He suddenly laughed. "It seems we both have conflicting feelings on the matter."

Her brows drew together sharply, but then slowly smoothed. A small smile followed. "It seems that you are right."

He shouldn't ask, but, "Where does that leave us?"

"I'm not sure." She lifted her chin, meeting his gaze. "But I do know we made a deal. Shall we continue to honor it?"

"Let me ask you this first: Did you know about the sword and rose crest?"

Her eyes widened.

So she did. "You never told me." A wild guess formed. "You never told me because you never intended for me to accept the deal, did you?"

"Honestly, at the start, no. I blundered that day. You didn't allow me to retract my blunder."

"I see." So their deal had been an accidental one. "Given all that, you're still willing to honor the deal?"

"I am." She scooted to the edge of her seat. "How do you know about the crest?"

Warrick had half a mind to withhold the information. Tease her a bit. He cleared his throat. "I have my ways, and I'm still debating whether it's in my best interest to continue with our deal. You are certainly quick to change your mind."

"Fickleness is within the repertoire of a woman's character, didn't you know?"

"True, but then glossing over a woman's fickleness is certainly within the repertoire of a man's character, don't you agree?"

She settled back into the seat and stared at him intently. There was something new about her gaze, a cautious assessment that had his nerves prickling.

"It troubles me," she continued after a moment.

Warrick was taken aback. "What does?"

"The first kiss," she clarified. "And today's one. I'm not unbothered."

"They . . . bother you, too," Warrick repeated dumbly, then cursed at himself for sounding like an undeveloped infant who couldn't yet understand words.

"Yes. Kissing you troubles me. It troubles me that I didn't push you away. It troubles me that I liked it. It troubles be because no matter what, I can't seem to escape you, neither can I forget the content of that list boldly claiming space on a scrap of paper written in your scrawl."

"Selena . . ." Words failed him.

"It troubles me because I trust you and I don't trust you at the same time."

The corner of his eye twitched.

He didn't like that. He didn't like that at all.

"So since we are both so troubled, let us call what happened between us a transaction between friends," she suggested. "We are at least that, are we not?"

Warrick exhaled a deep, lengthy breath. *Friends*. He liked the term better than guard dog. "I'd like to believe that we are."

"Very good," she said, reaching for the door of the carriage. "If you decide to continue our deal, let me know."

Warrick started. How clever of her, turning the tables on him. Whether she meant to or not, *teasing* him. Snatching any upper hand away from him. He now sorely doubted he'd ever had it to begin with.

Perhaps he was on a journey of self-discovery as well—Lord knows, it didn't seem *he* knew what he wanted either—a quest to find out what the devil he was supposed to do with about this curse, about this woman, about this deuced knot tightening in his chest.

He said the only thing he could at the moment. "Send my apologies to Lady Theodosia for intruding."

Her brow furrowed, and he thought she might say something, but she then she gave a small nod before she left him alone in the carriage and made her way back to the party.

Warrick threw his head back against the seat and shut his eyes.

He sighed. What a bloody disaster.

His eyes snapped open.

Why hadn't she pressed him about the crest?

Chapter Eight

SELENA RESISTED THE urge to cover her nose as she jumped from the carriage that stopped before an alehouse. The most recent—and unexpected—clue had led her here. It was a breakthrough in her search for the elusive organization that had been quite effective in slipping through her grasp.

"So, this is the place Dare allegedly saw the crest." Selena glanced at Leonora. "Just how did Dare"—a notorious rake, a seemingly frivolous character—"find the mark on your Turkish trousers?"

Leonora smirked. "Just how did you and Warrick manage to lock lips together?"

"Very well, I won't ask."

"I'm surprised the earl did not escort us."

"You heard him yesterday, he said he wouldn't help me." Then everything else happened, though Selena still was unsure exactly what it was that had happened. Things between them had taken an awkward turn, but she'd dropped the gauntlet on his side. And her brain might as well have turned into a mushy stew because of that man. "Plus, didn't you advise him to give me space?"

Leonora shrugged. "I told him not to follow you so that you both can calm down."

"Well, I suppose we're still calming ourselves." She had

calmed the moment she sent him the tea this morning. He, on the other hand—well, it would depend on how well he received her gift. Her cheeks flushed as she recalled how she had blurted out to him all that had bothered her. Why had she said all those things? The more she thought about it, the more embarrassment flushed her face. She'd even admitted she enjoyed his kisses.

She patted her warm cheeks.

Those two kisses, brief as though they were, were more than tempting. They were downright dangerous. With each one, those old, familiar feelings of admiration and sweetness had exploded back to the surface. Luckily, she hadn't confessed to any of that. She had thought her innocent childhood passion had long faded. Could it be that it had only been buried to once more resurface?

That couldn't be, could it?

Bah! This was driving her crazy. Which was why it was best to move on before she made an irrevocable mistake. Like acting on impulses that would only leave her heartbroken and disappointed in the end.

"Shall we go in?" Leonora asked, looking over the street with curiosity.

Selena nodded. She had been skeptical about this lead. However, since she wanted to find the club, every lead, no matter how small, no matter where it came from, should be investigated.

She wondered if Warrick knew about the alehouse. He'd discovered the crest, so he might have discovered more clues she wasn't aware of. She should be annoyed, but then, she'd hidden things from him, too. Unless he decided to fully commit to helping her, she refused to count on him for anything.

"I've never been to an alehouse before," Leonora said.

"Me neither."

Bright light spilled into the room from the open door and windows, chasing away the dim shadows as they entered. The smell of smoke clung to the dark, varnished wooden tables and stools, but they looked clean.

"It's not as stuffy as I imagined," Leonora remarked.

"That's because it's broad daylight. I imagine the moment the sun sets the scene changes." Selena's gaze flicked to all corners of the room, from the wooden beams crossing the ceiling down to the scuffed floorboards, looking for any sign of those roses entwining a sword. Her eyes darted to a sword—without any roses—hanging on the wall above the bar.

Interesting.

"This seems rather . . ."

"Unsophisticated?" Leonora offered. "It's not quite what I imagined the lair of a secret club run by women would look like."

"Perhaps it's not their lair but a property they own."

"Why would they own an alehouse on the docks?"

"Good question," Selena said. "Let's go find a seat." They sauntered over to a table and settled in. "Did Dare mention anything else about the crest?"

"If I'd known you were so interested in the topic I would have dug deeper. Should we send a missive for him to meet us here?"

"*No.* The fewer people know about who and what I'm searching for the better. We are already not supposed to be here. Let's not tempt fate by adding a rake to the mix."

"A handsome rake."

That remained debatable.

A big, bulky man with a scar down the outer corner of his left eye approached them. "What can I get ye, ladies?"

Selena glanced at Leonora, who nodded with eagerness. She turned to the man. "Two pints of your finest ale."

He gave them each a silent look-over before nodding and heading back to the bar.

"Heavens," Leonora whispered. "That is one scary-looking man. Do we dare ask outright about the symbol?"

"Wait a bit. It's best to scout the place and the people first. The barman might look frightening, but he doesn't seem hostile."

"I suppose you cannot judge a man by his scars. Did you see the way he looked at us? Are the cloaks too much? We should have borrowed clothes from our maids."

"It's too late now." Selena's gaze flicked over the few cus-
tomers scattered in various spots throughout the place, her eyes
skimming over a man in a shadowed corner of the room. He
seemed to be looking in their direction, but his face and eyes were
half obscured by a cap, so she couldn't be sure.

How eerie.

She suddenly wished she'd brought along that jackal, Warrick. She hadn't realized up until this very moment, but while she
had thought it annoying to a certain degree, Warrick tailing her
around London had provided a level of reassurance which she
certainly didn't feel at present.

"Say, if you started your own secret club, where would you
hold your gatherings?" Leonora asked, her curious gaze sweeping
the room.

Selena tapped her chin in thought. A good question. White's
and Boodles were private clubs but not secret, so they had their
own fine establishments set up. But if you were to host a secret
one . . . "I suppose I would hold them under the guise of a charity.
That way, my members and I could hide in the open."

"Perhaps this club is doing the same," Leonora suggested.

"Seems reasonable."

"Then what charity gatherings do you suppose are held at an
alehouse?"

"Injured war veterans?" Selena proposed. The scarred man
brought over their ale. "Excuse me," Selena asked while reaching
for her beer. "Are there any charities that gather at your
establishment?"

Sharp eyes met hers, and a chill slithered down her spine.

"No," he said bluntly before turning and walking away.

Selena blinked at his back.

"Such direct rejection," Leonora murmured. "Do you think
he's lying?"

"I truly cannot say." Selena murmured. "He didn't hesitate in
his answer. Perhaps our assumption is wrong. It wouldn't be the

first time."

"Perhaps he shall warm up to us." Leonora picked up her glass and studied the bubbly content. "I've never had beer before."

Selena took a sip. "Not bad."

"Rather refreshing," Leonora agreed. "Even if we don't find any clues for you, this at least is a novel experience."

Selena's gaze moved back to the mysterious man in the corner. He still seemed to be looking in their direction. Was she imagining things? There was something about him that niggled at the back of her mind. Something important.

Other than him, there were only three other people in this place. No one else paid them any mind. She was just being overly suspicious, she decided.

"Selena!"

Selena turned back to Leonora at her sudden exclamation of glee. "What is it?"

Leonora pointed to the bottom of her empty glass.

Selena's eyes widened. "You already finished it all?"

"Focus! Isn't this the emblem you are searching for?"

"Let me see!" She snatched the glass from Leonora. Sure enough, there it was, etched on the bottom of the glass. She glanced at her full glass before gulping down the entire contents in one go. Her eyes fixed at the bottom until a clear imprint of roses and a sword appeared.

"Who is drinking too fast now?" Lenora asked dryly.

Selena swallowed the last sip, her mind still racing as she stared at the link she'd been hoping to find. "This is . . ."

"The exact same as the one on the Turkish trousers," Leonora finished for her.

Excitement unfurled in Selena's breast along with a small feather of trepidation. She had never been this close! But what would happen if she truly found the club? The location was rather unexpected . . . "Do you think this means the club owns this alehouse, or do they run a charity through the establishment, or do they use it for other purposes?"

"I'm not sure, but whatever their connection to this place, asking the barman about it will rouse their suspicions of us."

Selena's gaze followed Leonora's to the man who served their drinks. He stood behind the bar, eyeing them with an expressionless stare. Another shiver shot down her spine. She had to agree with Leonora. He was one scary man.

And Warrick was not here.

They hadn't informed anyone of their whereabouts, and for the first time that made Selena nervous.

She couldn't believe she was about to admit this, even to herself, but she missed him. Not so much the man, but certainly his presence and the security it provided. She had let them both off easy with a claim of friendship. But Warrick had never been her friend. He was her brother's friend. And she knew he'd never seen her as anything but her brother's sister. Then he kissed her, and she kissed him back, and now the relationship had moved into uncharted territory.

She no longer knew who he was to her just as he didn't know who she was to him, but she did know she missed him.

She gave another quick look at the barman, who resumed his duties.

"We might have stumbled onto something," Selena said softly.

"Are you nervous?" Leonora asked, matching her tone.

Selena nodded. "Whatever we stumbled onto, let us hope we can stumble right back out."

"You lowly blackguard!"

Warrick was rudely awakened by the door slamming against the wall, and Saville, who burst into his bedchamber, his face flushed with anger. What was with these siblings, entering his chamber as they pleased? No, the better question was what was wrong with his servants allowing them to enter in the first place? There were rules in households. Show the guests to the parlor. Inform the host. How damn difficult was that?

He squinted that the fire-breathing Saville. "What did you just call me?"

"You kissed my sister!"

That one sentence was like a cold bucket of water splashed all over Warrick's face and jolted him from his sleepiness, yet also left him paralyzed.

Saville ripped the covers from the bed. "Do you dare deny it?"

Warrick rubbed his temples as he sat up. How the hell had Savile found out? He couldn't know for certain. "Where did you hear such a rumor?"

"Rumor, my arse! I saw it with my own eyes."

"Impossible."

"Impossible because I couldn't have been there to see it with my own eyes, or impossible because you didn't kiss my sister?"

"If you had seen it with your own eyes then you wouldn't have waited to only be picking a fight with me now," Warrick pointed out.

"You bloody knave. I see you are not denying it." A finger stabbed in his direction. "At first, I thought I was wrong. But why would my sister exit a drawing room, minutes before you, face flushed?"

"*This* is what has you so up in arms?"

"I also saw you enter my carriage and Selena exit it. No matter how I look at it, you kissed my sister."

"You gather that from just those two scenes?" Warrick shook his head and fell back onto the bed, shielding his eyes with his forearm. "Leave me in peace, man."

"I haven't even told you the best part."

"And what is the best part?" Warrick hated asking.

"I have kissed my fair share of women, and I have keen sense of intuition. More importantly, I know how a woman's lips look after a passionate kiss. Are you still going to deny it?"

Warrick lifted his arm and stared at his friend. "No. You are right." Every ounce of frustration of the past twenty-four hours poured into his reply. "I kissed Selena." *There, he'd said it. Make with it what you will.*

"You blackguard!" Saville lunged at him. He barely had time to roll over before his friend's heavy body slammed into the mattress next to him. A punch landed on the left side of his jaw.

An involuntary grunt left him. "Damn it!" he cursed. "Why can't you act like an adult?"

"Why did you kiss my sister?"

"Go ask her yourself!" Warrick snapped back. "Why did she kiss me back?"

"That's a good question! Why would she return a kiss from a cad like you?"

"Could it be because she enjoyed my kisses?"

"Kiss*es*?" Saville exploded, and several punches rained down, each blow's impact drawing out another grunt of pain. "You kissed more than once. You are a dead man!"

Devil take it. "Can we discuss this like adults?" Warrick tried to crawl away but was anchored by Saville's weight.

"Of course we can," Saville growled. "The moment my fists are satisfied, let's talk."

"You crazy infant." Warrick shoved at his friend. "Let go of me."

"Once I have my satisfaction."

"Satisfaction, my arse!" With a quick roll, Warrick hooked his friend's torso and flipped them both to the floor, hitting the ground with a thud. He pinned the struggling man, hoping to reign in those vicious fists. "Get a hold of yourself, man! It's not like I ruined her."

"You dare use that term to my face. You better get your affairs in order. The bride price will be a queen's ransom!"

"Bride price? What nonsense are you spouting?"

"Your marriage, of course." The corners of Saville's lips

turned up into a smile that made Warrick's skin crawl. *"Brother."*

"Don't say something you'll regret, *friend.*"

"You refuse to take responsibility for my sister?"

"For a kiss? You must be mad."

"What do you mean I must be mad? If word gets out, she will be ruined! Just a whiff of a rumor is enough to cast suspicion onto her. You know that!"

"We weren't caught. No one will ever find out." Not exactly true.

"Who is the ridiculous one now? I didn't see you, but I still caught you."

"That's only because I didn't deny it." And Saville knew it.

"And why the hell didn't you deny it?" Saville started thrashing and managed to toss Warrick off to the side. "I didn't want to know!"

Warrick rolled to his knees, prepared for another onslaught of fists.

"Then why the hell did you come barging into my chamber leveling accusations in the first place? You and your sister are more alike than you know!"

Saville froze, but his eyes had turned to flame. "What did you just say?"

Warrick froze along with him.

Confound it.

Two steely eyes burned into him. "My sister was in your bedchamber? *This* very bedchamber?"

"It's not what you think. She wasn't alone."

"Oh? And who was with her?"

Me . . .

"There were servants all over the house." God, a lame excuse if there was any.

"Warrick." Saville's voice dropped to a dangerously low tone. "I expect a proposal by the end of today."

"You have high expectations for a lowly blackguard."

A leg shot out in a sharp kick. "Don't give me that rubbish!"

Warrick blocked Saville's boot and shoved it away from him. "What rubbish? If you violently attack me in my own chamber don't think of asking for favors."

"What favors? This is your duty! As a man. As a friend."

"You speak of duty? Did you offer marriage to any of the chits you kissed in the past?"

"I've never kissed an innocent one."

"Are you sure none of them were innocent?" Warrick challenged.

"This isn't about me," Saville bit out between clenched teeth.

Warrick shrugged. "I have no problem turning the tables."

"We are talking about my sister."

"And what does *she* want? Have you even asked her?"

"She kissed you, so she must have already decided."

"She would beg to differ."

"Are you speaking for her now? Is that how *close* the two of you have grown?"

"The point is that if you love your sister, you wouldn't try to force her into a marriage she is not prepared to accept."

"This is the way of the world. Love and happiness have no bearing on matters of money, reputation, and duty. You bloody know this already!"

Yes, he did. But then, who decided these societal rules in the first place? Perhaps he was tired of these rules. Perhaps he'd read too many idealistic novels. Perhaps that was why he kissed Selena, caught up in a moment that would work in fiction but not reality.

Whatever the case, on a normal day, hell would have to ice over before he coerced a woman into a marriage she didn't want. With Selena . . . hell, Heaven, and the universe combined would have to turn into icicles before he offered for her hand.

He valued his life, after all.

Saville threw another punch, this one smashing into the corner of his eye. "I will kill you."

"Better you do it than her," Warrick growled, temper erupting at having been caught off guard. He cursed when Saville grabbed a fist full of his hair and yanked. Damn it, Saville didn't play fair.

If that's how it is . . .

Warrick threw several punches of his own and tried to twist out of that painful grip. Blackguard. He turned his head and bit down on the arm that refused to let go of his hair.

A curse rang through the chamber. "You damn dog!"

Warrick bit down harder.

A throat cleared loudly at the door.

Both men stilled, heads whipping to the sound. Four men filled the doorway.

What the hell?

A red-haired man stepped forward. Cameron, his footman. "My lord, we sent for help."

Warrick scowled. *"Help?"*

"Gentlemen." A tall man stepped forward. "I am Marcus Hunt, Bow Street Runner." His gaze flicked between the two men, their position. "I hesitate to ask, but I've learned as a Runner that not all things are what they seem, so I'll ask this only once. Is everything in order here?"

What. The. Hell?

Only then did Warrick realize his and Saville's limbs were tangled up like a couple of snakes.

He leaped to his feet—or tried, at least. A miscalculation. Saville was still frozen, his cooperation incomplete, leaving Warrick's back to hit the floor.

Deuced embarrassing.

Not the sort of brawl any man wants to have witnessed.

"A minor scuffle," he said and rose to his feet, a bit more cautiously this time. "No harm done."

"Speak for yourself," Saville exploded. He, at least, managed to rise with grace even though his tone still contained a sharp edge of pettiness. He covered the side of his face with his hand, hiding his mouth from their unexpected audience, and mouthed, *pistols at dawn.*

"Are you serious?"

Saville pointed at him. *"Choose,"* he mouthed, *"your second."* Only then did he drop his hand.

Bloody hell.

Why hadn't he just denied Saville's accusation? He should have denied it until his last breath. Until even he believed he hadn't kissed Selena. That was how strong his denial should have been, damn it.

"My lord," Cameron spoke up after Saville had shoved his way past his footman and Mr. Hunt and stalked from the chamber. "We also received word about Lady Selena."

Warrick sighed.

What did that little she-devil do now? It didn't matter. Whatever she was up to now could not be worse than what had transpired in his bedchamber here today.

"She went to an alehouse, my lord."

She did what?

Chapter Nine

THE FIRST TIME Selena ever found herself in a fix—stuck in a tree after picking apples in the countryside—she had been scolded for several hours on end by her brother. The two of them may not always have seen eye to eye, but her brother had always been there to get her out of scrapes. He had always been there for her, period. Always him. Their mother had decided to embark on a new life, but Selena didn't blame her for that. She'd had Saville and that was enough.

Until the list of heiresses that he and his friends had created was exposed. For once, he had been the one who had caused the trouble. However, instead of helping her as he had done in the past, he had brought in Warrick.

Recalling those moments of his past protection, Selena's current anger and sense of betrayal was partly over the list, but mostly over her brother's abandonment. She had felt deserted by the very man who ought to have shielded her.

Warrick had been right about conflicting feelings.

So many conflicting feelings.

Because she had also experienced a sense of relief since she hadn't entirely wanted him to protect her. She wanted to stand on her own. But then he'd gone and enlisted a proxy, confusing the matter further still.

Her feelings were deeply in conflict this very moment,

though in this case they were about Warrick, hoping he would walk through the door, and at the same time wishing he would not.

He didn't.

And again, that feeling of inner turmoil surfaced.

Selena straightened when the barman approached with another two beers and set them on table.

"We didn't order these," Selena said, glancing at the big man with frank suspicion.

"Nevertheless, they're for you." He reached for their empty glasses. Only then did she notice the scars that crisscrossed his hands. "Don't go anywhere. Wait."

Selena watched his back as he strode off. Just what situation had they gotten themselves into? She turned her wide eyes to Leonora.

"Don't go anywhere? Wait?" Leonora's face mirrored hers. "Should we make a run for it? I can run pretty fast, but his legs are longer."

Selena agreed. "I'm not sure how far we would get."

"Aren't you scared?" Leonora asked in a hushed voice.

"A bit," Selena admitted truthfully. "But I'm also curious."

Leonora's eyes widened in disbelief. "About what?"

"Why we should wait."

"Perhaps he caught onto us. I mean, we did ask him about charities, and we weren't exactly inconspicuous when inspecting our glasses."

"Speaking of which . . ." Selena carefully lifted her beer to peer at the bottom. No emblem. Highly suspicious. "You might be right."

"This is not good, Selena. What are we going to do now?"

"Don't fret," Selena reassured even while her own heart thundered. Could it be a mere coincidence? She didn't believe so. Odds were that they were finally going to meet whoever was in charge of this club. This was what she had wanted. Also, "We still have our driver and footmen outside. We shall be fine."

But for the first time since she started her search, Selena experienced a sense of crisis. These women, she knew nothing about them, nor did she know anything about the club. Though after today, it was clear that it was no ordinary club of women gathering and discussing the demise of the world hierarchy. And this time, neither her brother nor Warrick was here to save and protect her. Plus, she had dragged Leonora along.

Selena calmly took a sip of her beer. In a time of panic, never let the panic show. She'd learned that in all her years testing the boundaries of her brother's temper. "I wonder if we know anyone in the club."

"I suppose we shall be surprised by the reveal."

"Would you join if they invited you?" Selena asked.

"That shall depend on what happens here today." Leonora shifted in her seat, reaching for beer as well. "What about you? Will you join without evaluating the benefits?"

"Honestly, I never thought about benefits. Only finding the club and joining."

"But you must have your reasons."

She did. Although they were growing rather hazy of late. "They seem to have lost some of their valor."

"A situation like this will do that to even the best of motivations."

Selena chuckled. Had she been too caught up in her reasons that she ignored a bright red flag? She took another small sip. "The beer is good though."

Her friend nodded. "It's better than mulled wine."

Selena noticed a man enter from a backroom and whisper into the barman's ear. A moment later, the scarred man approached them again. "Come with me."

Selena and Leonora shared a look before rising.

Well, I suppose the time has come.

"What if we don't want to?"

The man just stared her, his penetrating gaze her answer.

A girl had to try.

The door of the alehouse slammed open, drawing her attention, and two looming figures stepped over the threshold leisurely, sharp eyes taking in everything of their environment. One of those figures' gaze fell on Selena and didn't leave.

"Warrick?" Shock, delight, confusion all wrapped up in that one word. She didn't recognize the other man, who wandered off to inspect the place.

He hadn't forsaken her yet.

"The moment I take my eyes off you, you run amok," Warrick said, striding over.

She had never appreciated more the sight of . . .

A gasp flew past her lips as she took in the cut on his lower lip, then the bruise on his cheek. "What happened to your face?"

"I'll tell you later. First, I want to know what you are doing at a bloody tavern."

"A lead brought us here."

He nodded. "The rose and the sword."

Selena's brows furrowed. He'd picked up on it quicker than they had. "In any case, the barman," Selena pointed at the empty space beside her, and then blinked. "Where has he gone?"

Leonora shrugged her shoulders.

Warrick glanced around the room. "The big one? He left when we entered. Why, what about him?"

"He told us to follow him."

Warrick's face turned grim. "And the two of you were just going to blindly do as he said?"

"We couldn't fight him off, now, could we? I believe he was going to lead us to the head of the club, or at very least a representative."

His gaze turned more vigilant as his eyes darted from the backdoor to her. "Damn it, you are as reckless ever."

"We must find him," Selena pressed. "He could be the final piece of the puzzle to finding these women."

"It's too late."

"Why?" Selena asked. "He couldn't have gone far."

"I arrived with a Bow Street Runner." He pointed to the man he'd arrived with, currently inspected the overhead sword. "Do you imagine they will risk being exposed now? A damn alehouse of all places. . ."

He was right. Anyone who valued their secrecy would be long gone by now. However, "Why are you here with a Bow Street Runner?"

"It's a long story."

"Does it have to do with why your face is beaten to a pulp?"

He sighed, glancing to Leonora and back. "I suppose I ought to warn you, your brother knows we kissed."

"What? *How?*"

He looked away. "You should ask him about his intuition and sharp eye. But I didn't deny it when he accused me."

Selena bristled. "Are you mad? Why wouldn't you deny it? Who admits to such things?" She could not believe this.

"Unfortunately, your brother knows my tells." His eyes, filled with some unreadable emotion, lifted to hers. "He demanded we marry."

Selena couldn't contain the shock jolted through her body. *Marry?* "That is why you should have denied it even if he didn't believe you!"

"Damn it. I refused, all right?"

"You *refused?*"

Confusion marred his brow. "Shouldn't I have?"

"Of course you should have!" She pinched the bridge of her nose, drawing in a deep breath. "It's just my brother . . ."

"Was furious, yes." He stepped closer and said in a lowered voice, "I can handle Saville. No need to worry that you will be leg shackled to me."

"That's not what I am worried about!"

"It's . . . not?"

Selena froze. *It's not?* Wait. Did that sound like she wouldn't mind if he hadn't refused? She shook her head. "I mean, that is *exactly* what I am worried about!"

A snort. "Like I said, there's no need to worry."

Selena bit down on her lip. "Whether you can handle him or not, Saville won't just leave it at that. What aren't you telling me?" She reached out to his bruised face, her hand hovering over the discoloring skin before she retracted her arm. "Does it hurt?"

"No," he said softly.

"Liar." Her brother had a nasty temper. "Out with it. What aren't you telling me?" she asked again in a sterner voice.

His gaze shifted to the runner. Selena followed his gaze, not surprised to find the man standing guard at the door and her friend laughing at something he'd said. She hadn't even noticed when Leonora had wandered off. Warrick glanced back at her, lowering his voice to whisper, "He challenged me to a duel at dawn."

"That is madness," Selena hissed back. "I won't stand for a duel." What if Warrick got hurt? Not that her brother was a crack shot, but the danger of a duel was all too real regardless. She couldn't allow this to happen. Wouldn't allow it.

"I can handle your brother," he reassured.

"So you've said, but Saville is willing to openly point a pistol at you and fire, he's that stubborn."

Warrick suddenly smiled, catching Selena off guard. "A trait that runs in your family."

"You should worry more about what runs in yours."

He chuckled.

"Honestly, have you forgotten you are cursed? Bad luck follows you around like a lost puppy you tossed a scrap of meat to, or did you forget?"

"I understand your concern, but I promise you, I can handle your brother."

"Everything good here?" the Runner asked as he and Leonora strode up to them.

"All good." Warrick nodded at the man. "We're leaving."

Selena looked at Leonora, whose once worried features were vibrant again with a knowing smile. How was it that every time she conversed with Warrick she forgot about everyone else? Her face flushed.

"What's wrong?" Warrick asked.

She turned back to him. "What do you mean?"

The back of his hand pressed against her cheek. "You're suddenly red." His gaze flicked to the table. "How much beer did you drink?"

Leonora laughed. "Oh, it not the beer."

Selena glared at her friend. "It's just the heat."

"Yes," Leonora agreed, her eyes sparkling. "The *heat*."

She patted her cheeks. "And we had two beers each."

"Quite right." Leonora's grin inched upward. "The beers also helped with the heat, I think."

"Let's go," Selena said, back rigid. *Leonora, you just wait.* She stole a glance at Warrick, her brow furrowing as they fell on those wounds again. He was here. He had come for her.

Brother . . . you just wait as well.

Dawn, the next day

WARRICK ONCE THOUGHT that if a man had good friends, even if life turned to utter hell, it would still feel like a supreme paradise. He wasn't so sure about that anymore.

"Is this what years of friendship has boiled down to?" his second, the Earl of Deerhurst, nagged from the chair beside the desk in his study. "A duel?"

Warrick reached for the wooden case that held his pistols. "He is the one who issued the challenge. I'm honor bound to accept the challenge."

"That's horse shit and you know it."

Warrick ignored Deerhurst's remark and opened the case, inspecting the pistols. Of course he didn't want to duel with one of his friends, but Saville would never let him off. If this was the only way to calm his friend's temper, so be it.

"So not only are you two fighting, but you have also dragged the rest of us into this mess as well."

"What the devil am I supposed to do? Saville needs an outlet for his rage. I am it."

"It's easy," Deerhurst said. "Ask for Selena's hand."

Warrick's brows sprung to his hairline. "Why does everyone believe *that* is the answer? Pressuring two unwilling people together?"

"This isn't about applying pressure. She still has the right to refuse. But you'd have at least offered. Let Saville deal with his sister's choice."

"What if Saville threatens her into accepting? What then?" Then there would be no way he could back out in any way or form.

"You believe that chit can truly be pressured into anything?"

No . . . "Nevertheless, I'm not giving that madman such an opening. He'll ruin their relationship."

"He is right to be angry," Deerhurst pointed out. "What the devil possessed you to kiss his sister?"

"I am aware," Warrick bit out. "But it's not like I committed a grave sin."

"You are, however, still meeting him for a duel."

"He issued the challenge. He must retract it." He was going to do exactly what Saville was doing—stubbornly point a pistol at one of his closest friends—in the hope that friend wouldn't pull the trigger.

It wasn't that Warrick couldn't understand his friend's anger. If he had a sister, he would do no differently. Well, the brawl in his chamber was too much, but he'd probably also call for pistols at dawn if a man who confessed to kissing his sister refused to take responsibility. But this wasn't about responsibility.

This was about Selena.

About what she wanted.

He hadn't wanted her to know about the duel with her

brother. There was no hiding it, however. Saville would have confined her by now—lock and key—and with that big mouth of his, he would have bellowed all his misgivings, cursed Warrick's ancestors, and declared his stance.

"Forgive me for asking, but do you have feelings for Selena?"

Feelings for Selena? Selena Savage?

"You did kiss her." Deerhurst crossed one leg over the other. "There must be some sort of attraction."

"When has attraction been a reason enough to marry?" Men get lost over attraction, but they didn't marry because of it.

"Some men would argue it's better than marrying with no attraction at all."

"It doesn't matter. It was a mere impulse on my part."

Deerhurst's arched brow accused him of lies. "Two times the impulse?"

More than that, an impulse that hadn't waned. "Is that so hard to believe? How many times did you kiss your wife before you offered marriage?"

Deerhurst coughed into his hand. "This is not about me. And I did marry her in the end."

"Good for you."

"Does Selena not return the sentiment then?"

He didn't know what she returned or didn't return, but she *had* been bothered, just like him. "I haven't asked her."

"Then answer me this, do you still feel guilty because of the list?"

Warrick ignored him, but his heart felt the jab.

"It's fine to feel guilty. It's not fine to let it ruin your life."

Warrick placed the pistol back into the case. "It's not ruining my life."

"So you *do* still feel guilt."

"Wouldn't you?" he countered.

"I feel the things I need to feel and then I let them go, especially if what I feel does not serve me or my family. There is no point in losing hair over something that has passed."

Warrick lifted a warning gaze to his friend. "Leave my damn hair out of this."

"Fine. There is no point in losing sleep over past matters," Deerhurst amended with a smile.

"I sleep like a log. Dead to the world."

"Very well, then why does it look like you've lost weight—"

"I have not lost one ounce," Warrick growled.

Deerhurst chuckled. "What about your mind? Not lost that?"

"Fully intact."

"Then it must be your heart."

Dear God in Heaven. "The organ in my chest is beating just fine." Warrick set the pistol case down. "What are you getting at, Deerhurst? That I've lost my heart?"

"Haven't you?"

"It's still very much in my possession."

"Then why the hell did you admit to the kiss? You could have taken the truth to your grave. Both your graves."

He had been questioning this as well. Maybe he'd admitted it so that Saville could keep them apart, keep them from crossing any more lines. Or maybe he admitted it in hopes he would force them together.

He couldn't tell which.

He didn't care to know either.

"Without a confession, speculation remains speculation," Deerhurst went on. "He would have doubted his own imagination after enough time had passed. Perhaps a part of you wanted him to back you into a corner."

"Perhaps I did." Warrick sighed, letting his head fall back, shutting his eyes briefly before turning back to Deerhurst. "Perhaps I just wanted Saville to beat me to a pulp and come to his senses on trusting a friend to play guardian over his sister."

"If that is the case, you certainly succeeded."

Truthfully, he himself couldn't get as far as believing his reasoning. But after he found Selena at that alehouse, embroiled in this club affair, agreeing to follow questionable a barman to an unknown location, he didn't regret his choice in admitting to the kiss if it led to her protection.

Selena needed to be locked down. Not in the way one would cage an exotic creature, but more to save it from falling into the hands of the people who would. Maybe she wouldn't see the difference, but he certainly could.

Christ, just thinking what could have happened to her set his heart in a wild frenzy.

The undeniable truth of the matter was Saville had the right to keep a tighter leash on his sister. So he would duel with his best friend. And then perhaps things would return to the way they were before.

Another lie. Nothing would return to the way it was before.

Warrick rose to his feet. "Let's not tarry. I don't want forfeit on account of being late."

Deerhurst nodded. "My carriage is outside, ready."

Warrick followed Deerhurst out the door and straight into his ride to whatever fate awaited him and his friendship with Saville. It wasn't until the carriage lurched forward that the measure of calm he'd held onto started to crack.

I am doing this for her.

For her.

Selena Savage.

A woman who dared to challenge them all.

And it was all so she could search out, and potentially find, what she had lost amidst the aftermath of his mistake. Deerhurst hadn't been wrong. Guilt still stabbed at him. But not as much anymore. And by his actions today, he hoped all would be forgiven and he could finally move on from this matter.

Of course, he had no intention of shooting Saville. Saville, no doubt, had every intention of putting a hole in his heart. If he survived, was it too much to ask—too selfish to hope—that he might receive a kind thought, perhaps even a bit of sympathy, from Selena?

Warrick's lips lifted.

Lord, oh, Lord, this truly was the most laughable situation he had ever found himself in. That damn curse. Even if he did aim his pistol at Saville—a true aim—he would probably still miss his target. With his luck, he might very well die today.

At least he would die with an acceptable head of hair still intact.

Deerhurst eyed him. "Nervous?"

"No." Warrick glanced at his pocket watch. "We should be arriving shortly."

Deerhurst peered through the curtains, pausing before a furrow formed between his brows. "This doesn't seem right. We are nowhere near the designated point."

All the blood left Warrick's limbs. He ripped open the curtain. "Where the hell are we going then?"

"I'm not sure." Deerhurst rapped on the roof. "Stop the carriage."

There was no response and no sign of the carriage slowing.

Warrick scowled. "What the hell is the meaning of this?" He called out, "Driver! Stop the carriage or these pistols will be used on you."

No response.

Warrick turned his gaze to his friend, eye blazing. "Is this your doing? A ploy for us not to duel?"

Deerhurst lifted his hands in surrender. "I give you my word, I had no hand in this."

"Avondale?"

"He is working on calming Saville down."

"If not you the two of you, then who—"

Dear Christ.

There is only one other person who knew about the duel and would be mad enough to interfere.

"Selena."

That damn Savage had done it again!

Chapter Ten

SELENA ARRIVED AT Putney Heath right on time and watched as a hundred different emotions along with various shades of color flashed across her brother's face when she exited the carriage. When last had she found such satisfaction from glimpsing those particular expressions on full display one after the other? Rage, astonishment, disbelief, more rage, concern, disapproval, more rage, and frustration. She smiled at him, but no brightness reached her eyes. This was a determined smile. A *just you wait, brother* smile.

Ah, satisfaction, indeed.

She nodded at Avondale, who stood beside her brother, confusion written all over his face.

"What the devil are you doing here?" He growled, his fists clenched by his sides. "Get back into the carriage and return home!"

"I'm afraid not, brother. This duel is because of me, is it not?"

"How did you even know the duel would be held here? Wait, how did you even know about the duel?" His face contorted. "Warrick tattled on me, didn't he?"

"I wouldn't call it a tattle," Selena said as she allowed the cool morning air to soothe her mood, and she made her way further into the field. "You weren't hiding it all that well either, bellowing this, roaring that. You do realize the walls of our house aren't that thick?"

"So you decided to take action? That kiss must have been damn good for you to rise this early and cheer the man on."

Selena laughed. How funny! "Oh, I'm not cheering Warrick on."

"Then what the hell are you doing here?"

"Why, I'm here to take his place. I am, after all, Warrick's second."

If he hadn't exploded before, Selena thought he might after those words left her mouth.

Several curses flew from her mouth. "This is no joking matter, Selena!"

"Oh, I am not treating it as a joke, brother." She motioned for a footman to retrieve her pistols. "I came quite prepared."

"Don't you dare give her those pistols!"

The footman hesitated, but still cautiously brought the case over. Selena smirked. "He's on loan from a friend." Lady Leonora to be exact. "He does not take orders from you."

She could practically see his proverbial feathers bristle. "Women aren't allowed to duel."

"As far as I am aware, men are not allowed to duel either. Does this make us sibling outlaws?"

"My arse, we are sibling outlaws! Get yours back into the carriage and return home. Right. Now."

"As a second, I can't do that."

"Calm down, old chap." Avondale stepped forward, clapping Saville on the shoulder. "Lady Selena, Warrick and Deerhurst are supposed to join us. Do you perhaps know where they are?"

She sent the man a grin. Smart. "Otherwise occupied. That is why I am stepping in."

"Deerhurst is Warrick's second, not you," Saville bit out.

"You are mistaken, brother." Selena smiled. "If the earl is anything then he must the third."

Avondale shook his head. "You still cannot take Warrick's place."

"Oh? And why not?"

"It's not dueling etiquette."

Selena inhaled a deep breath and retrieved her pistols from the box the footman held. She took a place ten yards from her brother and pointed the pistol straight at him. "I don't care about dueling etiquette. I should have challenged you to a duel instead of cutting up your clothes weeks ago when I first learned what you did."

"This is madness," Saville growled. "Put that pistol away."

"It occurred to me yesterday. When we were children you were always the hero who could vanquish any of my muddles. This one, however, you are the cause of. But instead of helping me, you pawned me off on your friend. *Now* you wish to act all tough and mighty? Just because something did not go the way you imagined?" There was an edge in her voice she seldom employed. "I think not. Pick up your pistol and duel."

Avondale cursed.

"What do you mean pawn you off?" Saville demanded. "I've done my best to shield you from the consequences my actions brought."

"You? You mean Warrick." She gave a slight shake of her head and met her brother's gaze. "It doesn't matter anymore. Let's get his duel over with."

"Fine, you wish to duel, sister," he retrieved his pistol. "Let us duel."

"Saville," Avondale said in a low voice, "call this off."

"Why? If Selena is so adamant, who am I to decline her request?"

"You are angry. You shouldn't make rash decisions in this state." Avondale turned to her. "You are more rational than your brother, Lady Selena. Please stop this."

"I think you are mistaken, Avondale. I am beyond furious with him." Believing he could command her to marry because of a secret kiss. Beating people up. Demanding satisfaction by duel. "He issued this challenge, not me."

"It's not my fault you kissed my best friend. Any normal man would react the same."

"A kiss is a kiss. I'm sure you've done worse. Besides, you're the one acting as though my reputation is in tatters. This could have been a secret between us, but look what you've done, look who you have dragged into all of this. If my reputation does fall into disrepair, it's all your fault. So yes, I quite want revenge." Her pistol never wavered. "Shall we?"

"Let us get this done with," Saville growled. "There is no use in arguing with a woman in a childish temper."

Selena grit her teeth. If she hadn't been angry before, that sentence was enough to tempt her to pull the trigger before the count.

Avondale let out a helpless sigh, but took position to Saville's left, a frown carved onto his face.

"On the count of three?" Selena suggested.

"By all means."

"*One.*"

Selena didn't waiver. Neither did Saville.

"*Two.*"

He held steady. So did she.

Avondale cursed. "This is madne—."

"*Three.*"

Two shots rang out.

Selena jolted, half expecting her body to explode into pain. Her brother might not be the best shot, but that didn't mean he couldn't hit a target. Not that she believed he would shoot her. His whole attitude was that of a male deigning to indulge a female.

That angered her most.

A loud curse rang out through the clearing in the wake of the two rapid fires. Saville dropped to his knees, clutching his arm, blood trickled through his fingers.

"Oh," Selena murmured, heart galloping at a neck break pace. "I didn't miss." Of course, she hadn't meant to really *shoot* him, either. She merely wanted to vent some of her anger.

"That's all you have to say for yourself?" Saville wailed. "You didn't *miss*? You bloody shot me!"

"Why are you so surprised?" Selena asked, still rather surprised and in a bit of shock herself. "Isn't this the point of a duel? Plus, I've always been a better shot than you."

"I didn't fire the pistol at you. I purposely missed! Did you think I would shoot you? A woman? My *sister*?"

"I'm a crack shot, brother. It's a scratch, I assure you." The blood caught her a bit off guard, but she didn't exaggerate her ability.

"You . . . you . . ."

She lowered her pistol as Avondale hunkered down next to Saville. "Let me see." He inspected the wound.

Selena's stepped closer a few feet then stopped again. "Why are acting as though I've dealt a deadly hit?"

Avondale tore a strip of cloth from his clothing and wound it around her brother's arm. "It's not deep."

In the distance, a carriage approached, and Selena spared a swift glance over her shoulder before looking back at her brother. Her heart did a little somersault.

That would be Warrick.

Would he be angry at her for stealing his duel? Probably. But she refused to regret her decision. He had come to her at the alehouse, the least she could do was save him from her brother. Warrick might have kissed her, but she hadn't pushed him away. Her honor needn't be defended. Even if it did, she could defend her own.

Her brother, however, glared at the carriage with the ferocity of a rising sun.

Selena turned, her thumb stroking over the metal she still gripped in her hand. The moment the horses came to a halt, the door swung open and Warrick jumped from the carriage. His eyes immediately met hers before dropping to the pistol in her hand. "What happened?"

"Good," Saville growled. He rose from his crouching position, still clutching his bandaged arm. "You are here. Now the duel can proceed."

Selena leveled a glare at her brother. "Shall I shoot you in the other arm?"

"You shot your brother?" Warrick strode over to her and took the pistol from her hand, a finger brushing over the fringes of her palm before she could evade him.

Shivers.

"As your second," Selena breathed, half-succeeding and half-failing to sound stern. "I stepped up in your stead. The duel is over."

"Who made you my second?" he asked in a shushed voice. "What possessed you to do such a thing?"

She pointed at her brother. "That devil possessed me."

"The duel is *not* over," Saville bellowed. "Are you not even going to look at me? I demand satisfaction!"

"Enough," Avondale said. "You've already been shot by your own flesh and blood. Do you want to die today?" He turned to Selena. "I'll bring him home. You head out first."

"What? I should be troubled by this little wound?"

Selena watched as her brother withdrew his hand from his wound, bringing the bloody palm to his face. "This . . . This . . ."

His body dropped to the ground.

"Honestly!"

All eyes turned to her. Selena shrugged, almost helplessly. "In the past, once or twice, he has fainted at the sight of blood."

Avondale, hunched down, almost having dropped along with her brother, motioned Deerhurst over. "Collect Saville's pistols. I'll send a man for the doctor."

Selena nodded. "Don't worry, he'll be fine. He survived almost removing his finger with a knife dining one evening."

"That's good to know," Deerhurst muttered, placing a hand at her brother's neck to feel for a pulse.

Would it be appropriate to roll her eyes at the moment?

"Come," Warrick said. "I'll escort you home."

She was about to decline, but when she met Warrick's gaze, those unnamable emotions again flashing in their depths, Selena thought better of it.

She nodded.

Back straight, she marched to the carriage Warrick had leaped from. Her brother might display his feelings all over his face, but Warrick carried them a bit deeper. Having seen all the men's looks and "not" looks when they all were on the scene together, it was what true friendship—no, *commitment*—looked like.

She wanted that.

But between them? Between Warrick and Saville?

Had she only made things worse?

WARRICK STARED AT the rows and rows of books that lined the shelves of the Savage library before reading a passage from the one he selected, *The Starry Night*—a book he'd already read three times. What a hell of a morning it had turned out to be. He cast a gloomy look toward the window. It had started raining after they returned from the proverbial battlefield between brother and sister.

He didn't want to think about how he could have prevented this particular mess had he been more on guard, but also could help but wonder if this was what was meant to happen. With Selena taking charge in such a bold way, Saville ought to settle down. *Ought to . . .* though he could never tell with this friend of his.

"Oh, there you are."

Warrick lifted his head to meet Selena's gaze as she strode over to the sofa and plopped down next to him. "Saville's wound has been taken care of?"

She nodded. "The doctor gave him a bit of laudanum when he woke up, and he fell asleep again. I'm sure he'll be up and shouting in no time, however."

"Nothing can keep your brother down for long," Warrick agreed.

"Truer words have never been spoken.

"Should I leave?" Saville wouldn't want him here when he woke up, and he didn't want to cause any more discord between the siblings.

"Do you want to leave?"

No.

"In any event," Selena continued when he didn't respond, "I'm not in the mood to be yelled at alone. So stay. Let's provide each other with some much-needed distraction. The mood has grown quite morbid in this house."

Warrick tugged his cravat to loosen it a bit. "Well, you did shoot your brother. Something I still can't quite bring myself to believe yet."

"I'm sure it shall settle in soon," she said. "Truthfully, I'm still in awe of it myself."

"You seem rather delighted."

"Not entirely, although I did feel the anger that's been simmering for weeks begin to melt away the moment he cried out in pain."

Warrick quirked his lips. She made one hell of a sister. She would make one hell of a wife.

He stilled.

The sudden thought startled him. Also made him ponder . . .

She would *make one hell of a wife.*

But he'd already had a humiliating fight with Saville exactly because he had said *no* to the prospect of marrying her. Yet the allure of that single thought made his heart contract now. Beside him sat half the problem, but all the answers to releasing him from his curse.

He shook his head at that last.

He would never marry Selena just to break a curse. And no one had yet bothered to ask what she wanted.

He studied her through lazy eyes. Now that her brother and several of their friends had learned of the kisses, she might be feeling a different way than she had at the tavern when he told her about everything that led up to today. It wouldn't hurt to make a wild suggestion.

"You could marry me."

Her head whipped to his. "I can *what?*"

He laughed. "I see I can still shock you."

"Shock in an understatement, so I repeat, *what?*'

"Marry . . ." He pointed to his chest. "Me."

"If that's a proposal, it's the worst proposal I've ever heard of."

He shrugged. "It's a suggestion."

"A poor one."

"Poor?" He cocked his head to the side. "I've never been called a poor choice before."

"Well, that's because I know what you would get out of wedding me, but what would I get out of wedding you?"

He arched a brow. "Wouldn't we just be getting each other?" A novel idea, really. It also didn't sound half bad. Getting each other—on second thought, that sounded rather . . . well, wilder than the suggestion to marry, quite honestly.

She crossed her arms. "You'd also get my dowry."

"Keep it. I have my own blunt."

"You'd be breaking your family curse; I'd be receiving one."

Warrick laughed. "Savage, Selena Savage."

She grinned at him. "But am I wrong?"

"In calling me a curse? Absolutely."

"Have you ever considered that you are the one giving your curse its power?" she pointed out. "Take back your power."

Interesting. "I have not considered that, no. How would I be giving it power?" All he wanted to do was erase it from his family's books so as not to bother future generations.

"You are consumed by it. All your attention is focused on it."

"I merely mention here and there," Warrick said thoughtfully. Perhaps a tiny bit of preoccupation. "Should I simply forget about it then?"

"Redirect your attention to something else."

"I could do that," he murmured. A new preoccupation might have already formed. A wild one.

He cleared his throat.

But in that direction lay even more frustration, no doubt. Much more intrigue, though, much more than a family curse. And perhaps she was right. Perhaps he gave the curse power by refusing to dismiss the damn thing from his mind, by allowing it to take over his thoughts. However, when the evidence of it was so clear, letting it go became harder and harder.

She plopped back against the pillows with a sigh.

"I see the princess of trouble has many troubles today." Warrick relaxed into the sofa a bit more himself. Trouble seemed to be the word of the day.

She snorted. "Why would you think anything is troubling me? I am exceptionally trouble free as I am slouched here."

"Not true. You have a small line that draws together between your brows whenever something is nagging at your mind. Not enough to be a frown, but slight enough to take note."

She eyed him askance. "How observant of you."

"Being so has become a habit of necessity."

She scrunched her face into more lines. "Spotting my frown lines has become a necessity?"

"Of course." Everything about her had become a necessity to learn. "How else am I to decipher what unruliness you will get into next?"

"Your commitment to your task is admirable, but I'm still quite worry free."

"If you aren't worried, then what are you?" Warrick asked, curious.

"Woolgathering."

"A haunting prospect."

"Yes, I have the same thought when I contemplate anything

regarding my brother."

So did he. However, "There are better ways to pass the time."

She sent him one of those smiles that on any other day would have warned him of imminent catastrophe. For him. "Do tell."

He tossed the book onto her lap. "Here, read something. It will be edifying I daresay."

She poked at the book. "Read? Please, I've never read a book in my life. I'm not starting now."

Ah yes, the Saville incident in this very library. "Suit yourself."

"Talking would be edifying too," she said after a moment.

Oh? "What would you like to talk about?" Warrick asked, his gaze dropping to where she picked at her dress.

Her eyes met his. "You refused to cave to my brother's demand to marry me."

"I did."

"Perhaps you do have a bit of brain to go with your brawn after all."

"Did you just insult my intelligence?" He had a lot more than *a bit* of brain to go with his brawn!

"Forget it." Her tone took on a teasing note. "If you have to ask me that, then I must be mistaken."

His eyes narrowed on the little minx. "Says the woman who doesn't read."

"What does reading have to do with intelligence?"

"Forget it. If you have to ask me that, then you've answered your own question."

She huffed out a breath before suddenly picking up the book. "But I am curious about the types of books *you* read. What's this? A thrilling tale of mayhem?" She opened the book at a random spot.

"On second thought . . ." He tried to snatch the book away, but she was one step quicker and leaped from the sofa, book in hand.

"Now I'm even more curious." Her gaze flew over a paragraph, eyes widening. *"Oh, how dearly I love you, John . . ."* She looked at him. "You read *romance?*"

Warrick groaned. "I don't read romance."

"I'm pretty sure this book," she glanced at the spine, *"The Starry Night* is a romance book."

"It's not. It's about a woman who finds herself in debt and yet manages to save her family from debtor's prison."

"Are you sure it's not a man who saves her and her family? The very same John who almost had her and her family imprisoned but then falls madly in love with her. He redeems himself and they live happily ever after."

Warrick's lips quirked. "I thought you said you didn't read."

"I thought you said this wasn't a romance," she countered.

"I suppose there are elements, *elements,*" he repeated at her look, "of romance in the story. But that's not what the story is about."

She cocked her head. "Then what is the story about?"

"Redemption."

"Well," she tossed the book back at him. "Redemption or not, I passed when Leonora gushed over the book. I'll pass now as well."

Warrick considered her, a thought suddenly occurring to him. "So this is why you took the advice of Lady Theodosia and dragged me to a charlatan's house? Because you would not read a book?"

"Research requires combing through a great many books. I'd rather slit my wrists."

"What about the betting book?"

"I could not even get through one page without falling asleep."

Warrick watched her closely. "Then you have the book in your possession?"

Her gaze flew to his. "Why do you ask? I thought you didn't care whether I had it or not?"

He shrugged. "Pure curiosity, nothing else."

"Well, stow your curiosity. You shall get no information from me."

"As you wish." The book was the last thing on his mind anyway, and the further it stayed away from White's, the better. He'd grown quite averse to betting books in general.

"What is the big deal about a kiss anyway?" she suddenly asked, settling back into her spot. "I'm sure my brother has stolen tons of kisses from innocent ladies."

Simple. "Because it's you. And because it's me."

"Yes, but what if I had been the one to steal the kiss?" She raised a brow. "Would that have made a difference?"

"No." Warrick met her gaze. "It would still be you. It would still be me."

"Yet everything else would be different."

Warrick furrowed his brows. "I'm not sure what you mean."

She leaned in close. "The intention would be different. Perhaps even the outcome."

"What the devil are you saying?" How would it be different? *Please, demonstrate.*

Chapter Eleven

SELENA'S LIPS HOVERED over Warrick's, her gaze teasing his with sparks of laughter. The infatuation she'd had for this earl back in her childhood had begun with another such moment where their eyes had met and held for more than five seconds. Both then and now she had fallen into a daze. Only that time, he had been the one teasing her, and his gaze had been full of humor and not expectation. This one hinted at secrets and shared intimacies. Two things she thought she'd never experience with this man.

But it was the expectation that gave her pause.

She slowly pulled back.

No longer a naïve girl who would have twirled at a request for marriage from him, Selena didn't need to take days to realize that an infatuation had blossomed, as she had when she was young. She recognized the burgeoning signs instantly. If she wasn't careful, a real feeling might sprout, a budding attraction that could at any moment bloom into something else. Not something more, just something else.

A kiss.

A touch.

A scandal.

This much she had gathered with their second kiss. A third would be a mistake.

Dark eyes flashed. "It's dangerous to tease a man this way."

Keep your cool, Selena. "I know. Am I not allowed?"

He leaned forward, imitating her earlier behavior, and she scooted farther away, putting a less tempting distance between them. "If you are willing to take the risk, you can tease, but only if I'm allowed to tease you back."

"We shouldn't be teasing each other in the first place," she muttered more to herself than as a warning than him.

The way she wanted to abandon all resolve both confused and vexed her. She had not come this far just to be robbed of her common sense with a past-and-perhaps-recently-returned fascination. No matter how tempting and handsome he looked. She would not be swayed because he read romance novels, though inside her heart gave a little scream of admiration. What men read romance novels? *She* didn't even read romance novels.

"Agreed," he said. "It's not the appropriate time with your brother lying wounded in bed."

"Your reasoning . . ." She gave a burst of laughter. "Never mind. We should probably *not* give into this basic nature of ours again."

"Right." He nodded slowly. "We shouldn't."

"Not very convincing, Phineas."

"I can't help myself." His eyes took on a sharp glint. "Especially when you say my name."

"That is not an answer that . . ." *that a woman who also can't help herself wants to hear . . .*

"What answer were you hoping for, *Selena* . . .?"

Argh. *I give up.* She pressed the back of her palm against her forehead. "This conversation is making my head spin."

"My head has been spinning for a while now," Warrick responded in a low voice, and Selena had to will her body not to shudder. "I feel this sudden, absurdly strange attraction between us. I am uncertain what to do about it since you refuse to wed me."

Dear God, Warrick confessed to feeling an attraction toward

her. Her pulse leaped. Dear God, dear God, dear God. "I am not ready for marriage, so stow your attraction."

"That might not be an option."

"Marriage or stowing your attraction?"

A brow shot upward. "Do you think it's something I can put back in a box? In my experience, ignoring a problem doesn't make it go away. It only makes it grow bigger."

He was right. And before she could think any better of it, she asked, "Then what do you suppose we do if we can't ignore it?"

"Cut it off completely. That is the only way."

Her brows furrowed. "How do you mean?" Surely not what it sounded like . . .

"We cut ties, Selena. At least temporary ties. You don't wish to marry me, and I can't make heads or tails about how I'm feeling. This is the best course of action."

Ah. Exactly what it sounded like. "I see."

His gaze narrowed. "You do not intend to make it easy for me to put distance between us, do you?"

"I'm not sure. So many things have happened these past few days, I am also a bit unnerved. When I said you should change the focus away from your curse, I didn't mean it should be on me instead." Familiar feelings of conflict rose within her, and the heat within her cooled.

He ran his finger along the spine of the book, an almost lazy action. "You're the only other direction worth looking at."

And then the heat started up again. "This is a rather bold style of flirting, my lord."

"My lord?" Both his eyebrows shot up. "This must be the first time you've ever addressed me in such a formal fashion."

"Is this not what you want?" Selena asked. "There are more ways than one to put distance between two people."

He nodded thoughtfully. "Noted."

"What exactly do you note?" Selena asked curiously.

"That distance can be achieved in many ways. My lady."

"My lord, I must admit, this particular distance is quite novel.

I might just lose my head again if we keep this up."

He chuckled. "It takes a brave woman to admit that she loses control in the presence of a handsome man."

She snorted. "What handsome man? This conversation has taken a turn."

"Since it has taken a turn, why not lean into it?"

She snatched the book from him, that finger trailing up and down the spine of the book wholly distracting. "Are you punishing me for a stealing your duel?"

He titled his head a fraction, studying her with unsettling thoroughness. "I'm not the punishing sort." He leaned back into the sofa. "However, I am curious. Do you wish to be ruined?"

She arched a brow at that. "Are you referring to my many reckless acts?" A shrug. "I never intentionally set out to ruin myself, so no. I do not wish it."

"Then, do you want to marry me?"

Selena stilled. The man certainly knew how to cause a girl to pause! "No."

"You hesitated." He smiled.

"You caught me off guard!"

"I did? Are you sure? Wouldn't you have blinked if you were caught off guard? Like this," he blinked two times. "You clearly paused."

Blinking? How ridiculous! "Not because I'm unsure of the answer."

His gaze turned curious. "Why else would you not deny it straight?"

"Why are you bringing up marriage again?" Selena shot back. The man wanted her to expire from a racing heartbeat, didn't he? Honestly!

"I merely wish for you to consider the option, Selena." Something flickered in his face. "You do have options. And unfortunately, you won't escape having to have a thorough discussion with your brother on the subject."

"His opinion doesn't count."

"Ah, well, he will beg to differ." He shook his head. "He might not let the matter go."

"You are right on that score," a growl came from the library door. "I *won't* let this matter go."

Selena jolted, but quickly recovered to narrow her eyes on her brother's thunderous face. "What are you doing out of bed? You should be resting."

"When there is a wolf in my house?" This face turned even more thundering. "I think not."

A sigh came from beside Selena. "Now I'm a wolf?"

"Yes!"

Selena thought sparks of lightning might shoot out of her brother's eyes any moment. "Do not be a prude, Saville. A little kiss will not do me any harm."

"A little kiss?" He glared at her. "A peck is little. Was the kiss you shared a *peck*?"

She crossed her arms over her chest. "I'd rather not talk with my brother about kissing."

"You won't talk with your brother, but you don't mind shooting him," Saville bit out darkly.

All the guilt and remorse she may have felt tapered away further with each word that left his mouth. "You were grazed. Why are you sulking over a scratch?"

"You still aimed a pistol at me and shot with the intent to hit me, even if it did end up being a graze!"

"You know that's not true." Where remorse had fled, annoyance began to take its place. "I apologize for shooting you." She lifted her palm in the air. "There, I've apologized. Do you feel better now?"

He gave an unnecessarily loud snort. "I suppose a sincere apology is too much to hope for."

Hah! "Thankfully we understand each other."

But instead of backing down, his eyes took on another glint. "Not only did you shoot me, you cost me a friendship."

Selena jumped to her feet in protest at that lightning strike. "I beg your pardon? *I* cost you *what* friendship?" How dare he accuse her of such a thing? "Do not be ridiculous."

His gaze skipped from her to Warrick. "Please see yourself out."

Warrick nodded and rose to his feet.

Was Saville being serious? Was Warrick just going to leave like that? "You are best friends!" Selena snapped, turning to Warrick. "You are just going to accept this?"

"Unless you've changed your mind about wedding me."

Selena had no words to offer.

A kiss was not nearly enough grounds for her to make such a decision. Even though her infatuation might once again have sprouted, and she couldn't help herself teasing him, it might also once again go away. What would happen then?

Besides, shouldn't a proposal at least be romantic? How could a man who read romance novels treat a topic such as this as casually as one conversing about the weather over tea?

Warrick gave a curt nod. "Then it's settled."

Selena stared in shock as he strode to the door. Was he truly going to cut ties just like that?

"This is what you want?" Their entire conversation had been a mix of teasing and testing each other's boundaries. She hadn't really taken his suggestion of distance seriously.

"This is what you need." He cast over his shoulder at her, and once again, she caught a flash of veiled emotion in his face. "What we all need," he finished before stalking from the library.

Just like that.

It was done.

Over.

She turned to her brother. "Are you happy now? I hope you enjoy this happiness. *Alone.*"

She marched from the room without looking back.

SOME THINGS ARE hard to take your eyes off of once you notice them. Like the sun setting over the fields in the countryside. Two dogs mating on the side of the road. A little girl with an innocent face transforming into a beguiling woman. Or, in the immediate vicinity of the spot Warrick had chosen in White's, a new betting book.

Something akin to disgust—a palpable aversion—rose from deep within and gathered between his brows in the form of a scowl. It distracted him from his task at hand—writing a letter. An apology. What the devil did one say to a woman after kissing her, hinting at marriage, and then walking away, completely cutting ties?

He had made another mess.

Could he just blame his bloody curse? Perhaps he might feel better about the entire affair that way. But then again, perhaps not.

For the last several hours, he had poured over their conversation again and again. Each time he did he wanted to slap a hand over his face. Why the devil had he made such a suggestion? Marriage! And then walking out on that last claim. And how did each conversation between them always oscillate between banal, serious, and teasing, then back to serious, back to banal, back to teasing?

Ah, hell.

He had not wanted to put pressure on her. He hadn't wanted her to run away, and he hadn't wanted the weight of a proposal hanging over them. So instead, he had run off and left an overhanging cloud of more confusion. But wasn't it all the same?

He rubbed his temples. "Christ, I don't know what I'm doing anymore."

And now on top of that . . . why did they have to open another betting book? Why not do away with the practice altogether? Even as the question moved through his mind, the answer already shifted along with it. The book of wagers was as much a part of the club's blood as the rigid control over member selection. One incident would not change this.

Perhaps two? Should he steal the book?

No. That wouldn't change much, either.

It would take a bloody miracle, and perhaps a few lifetimes, for them to do away with the practice. He alone could not change anything, but he could be a start. A start of what, he couldn't say. That remained to be seen.

"Warrick."

His gaze shifted from the book to settle on the Duke of Mortimer, who motioned to the seat across from him. "Do you mind?"

"Go ahead. Though, I warn you, I'm miserable company tonight." So miserable that nary a word wanted to flow.

The duke took a seat, crossing one leg over the other. "Does this misery have to do with the new betting book?"

Warrick arched a brow. "Why would you say that?"

"You've been staring at it as though it might burst into flames any moment."

Well, yes, he supposed that was true. "It's a bloody sore sight."

"I agree with you there." Mortimer motioned for a server to bring him his usual drink of choice. "Some men, some establishments, never learn."

Warrick cast another moody look in the direction the book. "In this case, there is no entertainment to be had in learning from what happened here."

Mortimer nodded. "One would think that as advanced beings we could find better pastimes, but alas." He nodded to the blank sheet of paper. "You seem stuck."

"I am," Warrick said, a new idea taking shape in his mind. "Now that you're here, you can help me with something,"

Mortimer arched a brow. "Certainly, what do you need help with?"

"Who are the top reigning eligible bachelors in London?"

Mortimer's second brow joined the first. "The top reigning

bachelors in London? Eligible?" He gave a thoughtful tap on the table with his finger. "Off the top of my head, I'd say it would be you, me, Saville, Dare, Wrath, Cassidy, and Mandeville."

Warrick scribbled down the names and drew lines for columns.

The duke murmured his thanks when a server brought over a bottle of cognac and two glasses. He poured them each one. He pushed a glass to Warrick, who nodded. "What are you doing?"

"Creating a list."

"A list? Why does this scene feel familiar?" Mortimer's normally calm voice held a note of amusement.

"If you are going to nag me," Warrick lifted his head to him, "leave." He'd had enough nagging the past two days from his own friends to last him a lifetime. He didn't need it from others.

"I don't nag."

"Good," Warrick said, paused, and shot the man a speculative look. "What would you say is your biggest flaw?"

"You should ask my mother."

Warrick's lips quirked, watching as the duke swirled the drink in his hand, almost lazily. "I'm asking you."

"Well," the duke gave a moment of thought, "my mother claims that I am too obstinate."

Warrick nodded, jotting down *mulish*.

"What about you?" Mortimer asked.

"Receding hairline."

Mortimer chuckled. "The plight of many a gentleman."

"Now . . ." Warrick wrote down *titled* beside all the names in the column he labeled "Best Trait." All except one. Next to *that* name he wrote another. *Selena.* Next he jotted down Saville's worst trait.

The duke peered over. "Infantile?"

"It's a recurring theme these days." He paused in his scribbling to think, staring at the names of the men in his bold scrawl. "We all know Dare is a libertine. Wrath is, well he is . . ."

"Cold."

Warrick nodded as he continued writing. "Mandeville has an aggressive nature."

"Cassidy is in love with himself."

Warrick would take Mortimer's word for it. He scribbled it down and sat back to eye his work.

"Forgive me for asking," Mortimer spoke, "but are you certain you are creating this list for the right reasons? I heard about the duel at dawn today."

Warrick wasn't surprised. "Those ears of yours are admirably sharp."

Mortimer shrugged. "That, and I have my eyes on the heiresses."

"Because of the betting book?" Warrick asked, considering the man.

"Amongst other things."

Warrick cocked his head. "Is your interest in the betting book not a bit too much?" He'd thought this for a while now.

"The club charged me with retrieving it," Mortimer answered. "And once I start, I'm like a dog that's got the scent of a bone. I won't stop until I get my bone."

"How self-aware of you."

"Being titled isn't my only good feature."

"Humility is certainly not one either."

"Ah yes," Mortimer murmured. "What is this 'humility' you speak of?"

Warrick laughed. Amusement finally poked through his sour mood. "Do you have any leads on the book yet?"

Mortimer's lips quirked. Not in amusement, nor in annoyance. It was one of those in-between smiles that couldn't be placed. "No. I suspect the ladies are alternating the book between them. It's impossible to guess who has it or who will be next in turn to collect it."

"Have you thought about asking them for the book?"

"Would they hand it over?'

Maybe. Probably not. "I suspect that depends on their mood,

as well as the reason for wanting the book back. I suggest finding a reason other than 'White's charged me.'"

Mortimer nodded thoughtfully. "What reason would be acceptable?"

"The truth." Nothing else. "Those females will smell a lie before it's had a chance to form on your lips."

"White's commissioned me—truth."

"It might be White's truth, but it's not yours."

A low chuckle, followed by a rare smile. "Why wouldn't that be my truth?"

"A duke hired by a gentleman's club to look for a betting book. Even I don't completely believe it." Whoever believes that must be as witless as a post.

"Is that so strange? I'm a member."

"You might be a member, but your bloodhound determination to find your bone, on the other hand . . . one must wonder about your motivation."

Mortimer nodded slowly. "I see."

Warrick put the quill down and glanced at the betting book.

"You are going to secure that in the new book?" Mortimer asked.

"Yes." He glanced back at the duke. "Will you stop me?"

Mortimer shook his head. "I wouldn't dare."

"Much obliged."

"However, it bears reminding that you didn't create the list of heiresses," Mortimer said as Warrick rose to his feet. "Whatever guilt you may be feeling, don't be too consumed by it. What's done is done."

Yes, Avondale's mother had created the list, he thought as he strode to the table where the new betting book rested. However, he had participated, his scrawl had accompanied their fun, and he had lost the list. And it was time to put it in the past.

Now his handwriting once again accompanied a list, one of his creation. And he would, once again "lose" the list. The impact would probably be minute, but this wasn't about impact. He couldn't find the words for a letter, so let this be his apology. Not just for his part in the original list, but also for the look in her eyes as he walked away from her, her brother, and the mess he had created.

Let it be the beginning of his redemption.

Chapter Twelve

S ELENA HADN'T SEEN Warrick in six days, thirteen hours, and— she glanced at the pocket watch clutched between her fingers—twenty-five minutes. Her behavior would surely be considered disturbing to some, keeping track of time in such a manner. And certainly, she found her constant attention to the watch rather alarming, too, but after watching Warrick stride out of the library with his back straight and without so much as a backward peek after his last words, her awareness of every hour, minute, and at times even seconds in a day had become a torturous burden she could not escape from.

He had also stopped following her.

Or rather, he'd stopped a while back, when they'd come to their agreement, but he hadn't resumed his lurking after that day in the library. Every day she went out for a stroll on Bond Street. Not once had she caught a glimpse of his hulking body behind any of the lampposts. She didn't know if he still had servants following her. She doubted he did. She hadn't spotted his red-headed footman anywhere either.

Theodosia tapped a finger on the watch, drawing Selena's attention away from the ticking hands within the golden case. "I don't think he will come."

Selena returned the watch to her reticule, where a crumbled note that had been delivered to her earlier that morning lay nestled. "He will come," she said with more confidence than she felt.

He *had* to come.

She didn't believe—couldn't believe—that he would cut ties so cleanly. The man must still be observing her movements from the fringes, mustn't he? No, she dared him *not* to show his face today. He'd receive word one way or another that she'd revisited the alehouse, and he'd rush over. Like the last time.

"We've been waiting for three hours." Theodosia peeped through the carriage window, pulled up outside The Rose. "Why not wait inside? Leonora said their ale is good."

"The place belongs to those people."

"Those people? You mean the club you desire so desperately to join."

"I'm not desperate." Her fingers worried the material that held her pocket watch. Could she truly claim such a thing?

"Determined, then."

Selena glanced at her friend. "I've decided to take your advice."

"That's a terrifying thing to hear. What advice are you taking exactly?"

"Finding out what the club is about *before* I join."

"Oh, that. Indeed, good advice if I say so myself." Theodosia's voice was dry as sand. "What changed your mind?"

"I'm not sure. This place, I suppose. What secret club owns an alehouse on the docks?"

"Perhaps the women love beer?"

Selena wasn't so sure, but then, she couldn't rule it out either. Also, there was the note she'd received the morning . . . which she hadn't shown her friend yet. So, she couldn't blame her for her impatience.

"Forgive me for pointing this out." Theodosia leaned forward a touch. "You detest Warrick. Why are we attempting to lure the earl to us? Has your youthful passion perhaps returned?"

Selena ignored the dangerous question. "I never detested

him. I was annoyed by him for a time, but there was no detesting."

"Then what is this about?"

Selena picked at her reticule. "We have unfinished business."

"Then why not call on him? Why go to this length?" *Why drag me into this*, her eyes demanded.

"I did call on him. He refuses to see me." *And you are my friend, you must support me without question*, Selena answered with a look of her own.

"Is that even possible?"

"Yes, apparently." It was as though the two kisses they'd shared meant nothing. But for that, she hated to admit, the blame lay on her shoulders.

Do you wish to be ruined? Do you wish to marry me?

Her heart beat a little faster, and then skipped when she thought of how she'd been barred from searching the house for him. She could perhaps slip past one footman but not the seven who had been on guard.

"He shall come around."

Selena shook her head. "I'm not so certain anymore." She'd practically pushed him out the library door with her remarks. However, she hadn't truly believed he would hold such a stubborn stance! How ironic. She finally had the distance she wanted at the start but now all she wanted to do was close it. Even if she couldn't, even if she failed, she still, had to try. This was one of her last, dramatic resorts.

"You're not certain that Warrick would forgive you for whatever you did?" Theodosia snorted. "I find that hard to believe."

"Believe." Selena forced a light smile. She was starting to believe as well. "There were some things between us," *like his kisses, his unromantic marriage suggestion, him*, "that were worthy of deeper attention, but I pretended otherwise."

Theodosia arched a brow, but she didn't question her. "Then drop the pretense."

Selena peeked through the window again. "Easier said than

done."

"Why? It seems to me that you enjoy the fellow helping you find your club. Just continue to do what you were doing."

"You seemed to have forgotten about my brother and the duel . . ." *amongst other things.* "I fear we have reached a point of no return."

"And yet we find ourselves in a carriage in the hope that Warrick will appear," Theodosia pointed out. "Besides, doesn't coming to a point of no return just mean you have no other choice but to forge onward? See where the path you are on leads you."

Yes, but, "What if it leads to marriage?"

"So what if it does? What if it doesn't? There is no use dwelling on such questions since they will answer themselves eventually. You decided to partake in this journey. You decide how it ends. Period."

Could it be that simple? "See." She grinned at her friend. "I knew there was a reason I brought you along. You always set my mind at ease."

Theodosia nodded. "Now it's your turn to impart some advice." Her voice turned serious. "What do I need to do to get rid of your brother?"

"Why not see where fate leads you?"

Theodosia gave her a flat look. "Do not make me laugh. Our situations are *not* the same. I have no previous affection to draw from like you. Your brother makes my skin scrawl."

"Quite frankly, if you want to get rid of him, leave London."

"*That's* your advice?"

"My brother rarely changes his mind once he is set on a task, or mission in this case. And won't your brothers arrive any day now?"

Theodosia scowled. "Drat them."

"And if you do decide to retire to the country, take the book with you," Selena suggested.

"The betting book?"

She nodded.

"Has the Duke of Mortimer paid you a visit?" Theodosia asked. "It seems he's speaking to the heiresses."

"No," Selena murmured. "But I suspect he might be looking for the book for personal reasons."

"Why? Did something happen?"

"No, it's just a hunch." One formed after receiving the note. Selena almost handed the note to Theodosia but held back. She didn't want to show the note to anyone else *before* she showed it to Warrick.

"Well, I shall consider it. Lord knows, the sea air might be just what I need to set my mind at ease."

The door to carriage was wrenched open, and Selena's heart thudded as she sat up straight.

"What the devil are the two of you doing?" A familiar voice accompanied by an unwelcome countenance demanded.

Her smile drooped. "What are *you* doing here?"

"I'm your damn brother and I followed you here. It's been three hours. My arse hurts from waiting around. What are the two of you up to?"

"As usual, you are a joy," Theodosia murmured. "And who says we are up to something?"

"Don't take me for a fool." Saville ducked into the carriage, but before he could take a seat beside Selena, she stretched sideways to block him. "This spot is taken."

He sent her a begrudging look as he settled next to Theodosia instead.

Selena crossed her arms, returning her brother's look. "Are you here to badger, scold, and curse us?"

"Is that not *your* favorite pastime?" he countered.

She huffed out a breath. "I've moved on to different hobbies, if you must know."

"More inappropriate ones, I imagine."

"At least *I* have direction," Selena snapped. "What do you have?"

Saville snorted. "Direction? Did that direction lead you here?"

"Why yes, it did. Thank you for asking."

Theodosia clapped her hands twice. "Let's not bicker in such a confined space, please. Warrick is not with you?"

Saville scowled. "Why would that villain be with me?"

Theodosia arched a brow. "So the rumors are true. The two of you are in the midst of a lovers' tiff."

"What lovers' tiff? That cad crossed the line!"

"By that account," Selena said in his defense, "I crossed the line as well."

"He should have known better," Saville growled.

"Because he is a man?" Selena demanded.

"Yes!" A short pause. "No. That's not the reason."

Selene arched a brow. "Are you certain? You don't seem so sure about your answer."

"Damn it, he should have known because he is *older*."

Theodosia burst out laughing. Selena wanted to as well, but she couldn't find the humor. "Older means wiser then?" she asked instead.

"Older means more life experience."

"Then why are you acting like a child?"

"Don't call me a bloody chi—" He cut off suddenly and cursed. Saville cleared this throat and continued more calmly. "So, why are the two of you here? Are you waiting for someone? Does it have something to do with the new list that appeared in White's?"

Selena jolted. "What new list?"

"Yes, do tell," Theodosia murmured.

"A list of the most eligible bachelors," Saville said, adding in a sour note, "and their flaws."

"What about their best attributes?"

A grunt. "If you could call *titled* a best attribute, then yes," he said, "but I do understand your past resentment better now."

"How intriguing," Theodosia said. "Are we to assume *your* name is on the list? What's your flaw? Shall we take a guess?"

"Infantile," Saville said without preamble. "They called me infantile."

Selena did laugh at this. She wanted to kiss whoever compiled the list. "They must know you quite well."

"I already know who created the list. Your lover."

Her lover? Did he mean Warrick? Selena refused to fall for such a paltry trick. "I do not have a lover."

A snort. "Kissing friends, then."

"There is no such thing." And if there were, she'd be supremely intrigued. But kissing never stayed at just kissing. It evolves. Into dreams. Fantasies. Longing.

Theodosia shook her head. "I never took you for a prude, Saville."

"Whose side are you on? Or do you also believe there is nothing wrong with walking around and kissing people?"

Selena rolled her eyes.

"You truly have to ask that?" Theodosia responded. "Well, I shall answer in any case. I am on the side of independence and free will."

"The side of rebellion, then."

Selena wanted to boot her brother from the carriage. However, like a stubborn barnacle attached to the bottom of a ship, it would be near impossible to brush him off. It didn't matter anyhow. The only thing that did matter, the only thing that was a true bother . . .

Her heart constricted.

He hadn't come.

WARRICK LOWERED THE cap over his brow as he watched the carriage pull away and disappear into the distance. He waited until he could no longer see them before entering the alehouse. She had tested him today, and she would have been happy to discover that her ploy had worked.

Only, perhaps not in the way she would have wanted. Had she entered the tavern on the other hand . . .

"Why didn't she enter?" Warrick muttered in thought. That day should have left an impression on her, supported her confident belief that he would show up when he was needed. But today she hadn't entered. Realization struck. She hadn't been certain he would follow her.

Doubt had already formed in her mind.

He sighed.

Six days.

Six days he had painstakingly avoided her. Emphasis on the pain. He remained uncertain where, how, or when he had become so attached that he'd had to resort to full out avoidance yet still lurked in the shadows to catch a glimpse of her.

When had he turned this pitiful?

That look in her eyes before he'd walked away . . . Lord above, that look haunted him. Followed him around like a damn ghost refusing to enter the light.

Keeping his distance was for the best. He was not all that good to begin with, starting as many fires as he put out. And after all he'd done to harm her, what woman would attach herself to such a man? But that didn't stop him missing their interactions.

Or perhaps just missing her.

His gaze found the man in a shadowed corner. While he'd been watching Selena, he'd also glimpsed a familiar figure enter.

Warrick narrowed his eyes and strode to the man seated in a darkened corner at the back. "You were here that day as well, weren't you?"

The Duke of Mortimer lifted his head to meet his gaze. "Keen observation, Warrick."

"You followed Lady Selena today?" A wild guess.

"Not quite."

"Not quite?" He paused in thought. "You believe she has the betting book."

He inclined his head. "I believe it's in her hands at the moment, yes."

"It's not."

The duke arched a brow. "You know this for a fact?"

Warrick plopped down and signaled for a beer. "Is that the same barman from the other day?"

"No," the duke said. "He hasn't shown up since then."

Was that so? "Suspicious business."

Mortimer inclined his head. "Very."

"I know she did have the book at one time," Warrick offered after a moment. "I also know she hates reading."

"So she passed the book along already."

Warrick narrowed her eyes on the man. "What *are* you doing here, Mortimer? You don't strike me as the sort of man to visit taverns such as these just to keep track of a lady who may or may not have a book you were asked to retrieve."

"Should I have sat in a carriage or stood next to a lamppost for three hours then? I'd rather spend my time more comfortably."

"When you say it like that, you make it sound as though I belong in Bedlam." Warrick's tone couldn't hide a sour note. Mortimer still hadn't given him any response that would even remotely answer his question. This must be part of the real reason he was hunting the book.

"What about you?" Mortimer asked. "I thought you'd laid the matter of Lady Selena to rest."

He had. He did. "Curiosity."

The arch of a single brow was filled with a question: *Are you sure?*

"Believe what you like," Warrick muttered.

"It's a pity she hates reading," Mortimer remarked. "You wrote quite the love note."

"I made a list. Hardly a love note."

"Do you have any regrets? You must have heard that Mandeville's tumbler exploded in his hand when he read your assessment."

"Proving my claim, no? That must have infuriated him even more." Warrick thanked the server when she brought his ale. "As expected, neither the list nor the wagers has left the walls of White's."

"We are not as sensational as the heiresses." Mortimer gave him an unreadable look. "Forgive me for pointing this out, but you look like hell."

"Well, thank you." He knew just how hellish he looked.

Mortimer's gaze flicked to his head. "Your hair seems—"

"Be careful now," Warrick cut him off while meeting his gaze. "Or I'll be meeting you at dawn."

"Still itching for the duel that was taken from you?'

He even knew that much. "That's right."

Mortimer chuckled. "I only meant to say I've never seen a head of hair as disheveled as yours." A small pause. "You said your biggest flaw was your receding hairline. It's not. Your hairline is just fine."

Warrick brushed lightly over the strands of his hair and grunted.

"If you don't believe me," Mortimer went on, "look at the hairlines of most of the men at events. You have nothing to worry about."

"I'll be sure to have a look next time."

Mortimer shrugged. "In my humble and perhaps unwelcome opinion, your biggest flaw is that you allow the people you care for to treat you as a sheep when your true nature is that of a wolf."

"A wolf you say . . ." Warrick took a big swallow of beer and almost spat it out at the duke's next claim.

"You are searching for a secret women's club."

Warrick set down his glass with a thump. "How the hell did you know that? Wait, you know about that group as well?"

The duke nodded, tapping his finger on the table. "I gathered that was why Lady Selena showed interest in this particular establishment. They weren't hiding their interest either."

"Don't tell me *you* are searching for the club as well?" What an unbelievable and terrifying prospect.

"I am a man of many interests."

"Most men are." A brief silence followed where the two men stared at each other. Warrick took another swallow of beer. "Lady Selena wants to join the club."

"I surmised as much."

Warrick's gaze swept over the interior of the tavern and settled on the sword hanging above the bar. "My instinct tells me they are trouble. And not the good kind." Was there even a good kind?

Yes.

Her mischief.

"Your instinct would be right," Mortimer informed him. "There is nothing good about them."

This was not the response Warrick was hoping for. For once, he wished he was wrong, that his instinct was just an excuse to hold onto a rope he should long ago have released. The last thing he needed was a real reason to return to her side, because he knew he would cross the line again. And she would cross it along with him. There was no denying it anymore—he was a bad influence on her. He indulged her and brought her over the line with him. He was too soft when it came to Selena Savage.

He cursed. "How the hell do I get her to give up this madness?"

"I'm sorry," Mortimer said. "I don't have the answers you are looking for. I'm no good with ladies."

Warrick glanced over to the duke's stiff posture. He could believe that. He sighed. "I just want her to be happy."

"That, I can understand." Mortimer's face turned thoughtful. "I suppose I ought to take your advice."

"About?" He couldn't recall that he ever imparted advice.

"Asking for the book. Explain my reasoning. Perhaps we can come to an agreement."

Ah, yes, he did say that. He didn't give a farthing about the book or the duke's reason for wanting it. "I wish you all the luck."

"Aren't you going to warn me off talking to Lady Selena?"

Warrick's brows furrowed. "Why would I do that?"

"Seems a theme amongst your friends so far."

"Yes, well, they are rather protective." Warrick smirked. "I suppose most men would feel threatened when a predator approaches their wife or fiancée or sister. Especially when the predator's intentions are unclear."

"Fair enough."

"You do have a way of infuriating people," Warrick pointed out.

"So my mother tells me."

Warrick chuckled. "Are you attached to your mother's hip?"

"It would be more apt to say she is attached to mine."

Another laugh. "On your case to take a wife?"

"Isn't it the life's goal of every mother to see her offspring married off?"

"Cannot argue that point."

A companionable silence settled over them, but Mortimer's words from earlier still stewed in Warrick's mind, poking at the center of his being. Did he allow the people he cared for to treat him like a sheep? One particular friend came to mind. A friend who had herded him straight into a pen that he might never escape from.

Allow.

Mortimer wasn't wrong.

He had allowed Saville to rope him into "protecting" his sister while he "protected" Lady Theodosia. And Warrick had permitted it in spite of his reservations. He had given in to many things.

He'd acted the sheep when his true nature, perhaps, was that of a wolf. No, not a wolf . . . but rather . . . a lion.

"I'll be damned."

He was a lion. A lion with a great bushy mane.

Not a sheep.

Perhaps it was time for him to roar.

Chapter Thirteen

The next morning

SELENA CLUTCHED *A Starry Night* in a death grip as she flung open the door of *that earl's* bedchamber. His absence over these past days irked her in a way not even her brother had managed over the years. So now she refused to sit idly by and wait for this jackal to come to his senses.

What senses?

Now seeing Warrick sprawled in the center of the bed in nothing but his breeches had all but robbed her of her own. He on the other hand . . . not even the door slamming against the wall of his chamber had woken him!

Things had taken an unexpected turn this last week. The duel. A rekindled infatuation. And Warrick finally cutting the cord that had tied them together on her brother's request.

But looking at him there, she could no longer deny or pretend. She found this rascal earl attractive, and she wanted to hunt down the meaning of the attraction between them. But she couldn't do that if he kept her at a distance.

Selena's eyes drifted over the length of his body.

All strength.

Her gaze narrowed. Even the soft vibration of his snores mocked her, indicating a man in the grip of a peaceful slumber.

Honestly!

The book flew from her fingers, an impulsive toss aimed at his mighty chest. She didn't even stop to admire the sight, anger once again flaring at this restful picture. The book, however, had other ideas, and landed just south of where she aimed.

The earl shot up with a grunt-like oath, cupping his nether regions. "Hell and damnation! Who courts death?"

"'Tis I, Selena Savage."

"Selena?" Her name spat like a curse from his lips. "What are you doing here?"

"I could ask the same of you. Has drinking become a new hobby of yours?"

He fell back onto the bed, curling into a ball. "Get out."

"Why? Have I disturbed your *peace*?"

"I'm not joking, Selena." He managed a glare through a face contorted in pain. "Your brother already wants to hitch us together. You should have known better than to ever enter my chamber alone in the first place. There is no excuse for entering it a second time unless you came here deliberately looking for trouble."

"If that is what it takes to make you stop avoiding me, then yes, I'm here to look for trouble."

"And what about the consequences? Are they not clear enough for you?"

"I shall accept them all."

"Even when it's marriage." His gaze bore into hers. "To me."

"You and my brother really are entirely too preoccupied with the topic."

"You are not preoccupied enough," he shot back.

"Why all this harping on the matter? It's not like Saville is going to the papers with the news that we kissed. Between us, as long as no word gets out, my reputation remains intact. Also, he will never know I came to your house if you don't admit to it again."

"Do you think all servants are tight lipped?"

"You don't trust your own servants?"

"It's that I don't trust human nature. We got lucky once. We might not get lucky again."

"I thought luck deserted you when you acquired your family curse." She strode over to the bed, a pinch of sympathy gathering in her breast at the pain he was clearly still feeling. "Does it hurt that much?"

"Yes."

"I'm sorry." At his grunt, Selena continued. "You created a list."

His gaze darkened as it met hers, confirming her suspicion that he would never have told her on his own. "Who told you about that?"

"My brother." She crossed her arms over her chest. "Why? Was not the whole point of it for me to find out?"

"No." He unfurled from his position and finally uncupped his hands from *that place* to wipe his eyes. "I don't know. I wasn't thinking all that much when I created it."

"But you were thinking of me."

Silence.

Selena wanted to punch him. "Were you also thinking of me while you were avoiding me this past week? Or were you just thinking about yourself and all the peace of mind my absence would bring you?"

A grumble. "Both."

"Really? Then why does it feel like you are not telling the whole truth?"

"I won't say it again," Warrick said with a deeper edge to his voice. "Leave. Now."

"Why should I leave?" A clear challenge meant to provoke.

"Because I'm not feeling like a gentleman at the moment, Selena. I'm feeling more beast than man."

"Oh? Should I be scared then?"

"Yes, because even I am terrified, damn it."

Oh? "I have never seen you terrified to face a challenge before."

"Do not test me, Selena. I'm hanging on by a thread even as we speak."

"Why not test you? Lord knows, I have been tested time and time again since that list was pasted into the betting book."

He shoved a hand through his hair. "You are going to make me bald at this rate."

"Always going on about your precious locks and so-called receding hairline. It's all in your head, you know." Receding hairline or not, the man was still handsome as sin. He'd be handsome even if he had no hair on his head at all.

"I have a mirror."

Selena scoffed. "Tell me something, Phineas. *Have* you found the peace you sought this past week? If not, just act the beast. What have you to lose by it?"

"You do not know what you are saying."

"You are done acting the gentleman, and I'm done acting the lady."

"You don't have to act the lady, you *are* a lady."

"Well, I don't want to be one anymore."

"Stop acting so stubborn. You will be ruined if you stay." That burning gaze dropped to her shirt, then he growled, "Did I not tell you never to wear those damn trousers again?"

Selena smirked. "Are you provoked? Good. My mission has been accomplished."

"*I* will ruin you."

"Is that what you meant by being more beast than gentleman?" Her heart sped up, and she inched a step closer. "You say ruin, I say explore."

"What has gotten into you?" he demanded.

"Perhaps I have turned into a beast as well." She paused. "Though I did call on you for a reason." She had intended to provoke him and then inform him about the note. But honestly, she could always tell him about the summons later.

"Out with it and then leave."

"But now I'm enjoying myself too much to leave."

"Selena, I've no patience for games today. Go before I do something we both regret."

Both regret? Selena was rather sure they had already sunk far into a bog of regrets. She wanted to free herself from it, which was why she'd suddenly changed her mind about telling him about the real reason she'd sought him out today.

A familiar rush of excitement washed over her.

Ah, yes, she'd often felt this thrill years ago whenever he'd spoken to her or even shared the same space with her. Only it was no longer the innocent kind of excitement that shot up her spine, but rather something much more tempting. Irresistible. An urge she no longer wanted to hold at bay.

"I may have come for one reason, but now I'm staying for a different reason."

"Selena." A low growl, one that brought a smile to her lips.

"Phineas, I am no longer a girl. I am a woman capable of making her own choices."

"I don't see you as a girl," he denied.

"Yes, of course. I am Saville's sister, a lady. If I carried any other title than that of innocent lady, you would not be shooing me away like a naughty child."

"I'm not shooing you away."

"You clearly are. I am nothing but a diamond that must be handled with care. A jewel that cannot be tarnished. Well I am rather sick of being a diamond. Why can't I be a stone or a rock? Even a pretty shell you pick up on the beach will be fine."

"Jewel, diamond, rock, stone. When you are in my bedchamber, I don't see you as any of those things. That is the bloody problem."

He paused, letting the full weight of those words—those splendid words—settle over her.

"But," he said, and she stilled, a breathless pause that filled with tightness. "I cannot ignore the possible consequences."

"Would it have been a problem if I were a widow?"

"A widow? Don't be absurd."

"No, answer me. If I, a widow, stood before you in your chamber tempting you to act the beast, would you hold back?"

He paused.

Hah! "I knew it."

"Fine." He scratched his chest. "I cannot argue against such logic. But the fact remains that you are not a widow."

Selena followed the movement of his hand, wanting to be the one to trail her fingers across his chest. "Pretend that I am."

"I beg your pardon?"

"What would you do right now if I were a widow? Or a courtesan? Or whomever *you* wish me to be."

He stared at her, his gaze intense. "Whomever *I* wish you to be?"

The lowered timbre of his voice sent a new wave of shivers down her spine. Selena swallowed and nodded. "What would you do?"

His lips arched in a smile she had never glimpsed from him before. He motioned with his finger for her to come closer. Selena inhaled deeply, taking one small step that brought her slippers up to the bed. "I would punish you."

Startled, she replied, "Punish me? Why? Didn't you say you are not the sort of man that *punishes*?"

"I'm feeling rather contrary at the moment." He pointed at his lower region. "For almost robbing me of the ability to sire children."

Selena blinked, half intrigued and half terrified, her smile slow in coming. "What punishment shall the beastly earl dish out then?"

His hand snaked out to snatch her wrist, and Selena found herself pulled onto the bed to lay next to him, shackled within his warm, strong arms. "Let me show you."

CONTROL HAD NEVER felt this good snapping. He had held onto it for far too long, and by Christ, her body was heaven against his.

Whatever you *want me to be.*

What those words did to him, she would never understand. Never had such a simple sentence jolted him to such an extreme that Warrick had to keep from pouncing on a woman. A lion who had caught sight of his gazelle.

Whatever he wanted her to be.

What *did* he want her to be?

He knew.

He just couldn't admit the words out loud. Nor could he bring himself to acknowledge the truth. Because the answer would leave him even more helpless, *powerless* than her entering his bedchamber alone after all they'd shared.

Yet she had given him permission to reveal, no, to act on his desire. And her smile . . . how had he only noticed this about her now? She was like rays of sunshine that pierced through the blackened sky. Then when she disappeared as clouds set in, all he could do, all that was left for him to do, was chase her. The light.

What would he do if he didn't have to hold back?

Everything.

His lips found hers in sweet desperation. If heaven had a taste, it would be Selena Savage. Unlike the first two kisses, he took his time with this one. No anger drove him to silence or to prove a point. This moment was all about savoring, and Warrick savored all the warmth his lips sought. The warmth that his dreams lacked.

He could never have imagined that the dream he'd been having before she brutally awoke him would come true.

His hand smoothed over her waist to press her close to him, as close as she could possibly get. "I hate these damn trousers. They drive me crazy." His hands tugged at her shirt, pulling it free from its tucked-in state.

"What are you doing?" she breathed against his lips.

Then his hands were on her skin. "What any beast would do

when a beautiful, headstrong woman enters its lair."

She let out a small gasp, then laughed. "Oh no, what's a woman to do?"

"Surrender." A predator-like glint gleamed in his eyes. "Just surrender."

"I guess I have no choice."

"Not if you stay here. You have one last chance to escape, Selena." His heart pounded in his chest like a swordsmith hammering at a piece of metal, waiting for her answer.

"You asked me if I wished to be ruined." She smiled at him, and his breath stalled.

Did that smile mean . . .? *Don't get ahead of yourself, little Phineas, that smile might mean a thousand things.*

"The answer is . . ." she paused, and he paused along with her. He didn't even blink, as if the fate of his future would be secured in her next breath. "The answer is yes."

God help him.

He should not feel as relieved as he did. Any last noble intentions vanished like a puff of smoke, making him question whether they'd even existed in the first place.

She'd said nothing about what would happen after, but he would not push. What mattered was this moment. And at this moment, she was in his bed. His lips curved slowly, his smile reaching his eyes.

"What are you waiting for?" she breathed.

He didn't know either. He lowered his head to scrape the swell of her breast through the material of her shirt with his teeth, drawing a small gasp from her. "I won't let you go anymore."

"You couldn't chase me away even if you brandished a candelabra."

"If you were the one chasing, I wouldn't run away." His eyes locked on hers. "Then you know what happens next?"

"You ruin me."

"No." He lowered his head to the arch of her neck and inhaled deeply. "I ravish you. But first, these damn clothes . . ."

Hands tugged at her shirt. "What are you even wearing? Or *not* wearing?"

"I was in a hurry, so this is my own brand of fashion."

That reminded him. "What made you rush over this early in the morning that you decided to fashion this style? Or was it purely to provoke me?" He suspected the latter. She would have remembered his warning. Minx.

She pressed a finger against his lips. "That's a conversation for later. But I must admit, I do enjoy wearing shirts and trousers much more than I do dresses."

"Seems to me like you had plans to ruin *me*, Selena."

"Perhaps I did." She pushed at him lightly. "Let me remove the shirt."

"Not very ladylike of you." He rubbed his cheek against hers, his gaze traveling to the buttons of her attire. Too many buttons.

"I'm not feeling like a lady at the moment, Phineas."

"Christ, I hate it when you say my name."

A soft, fair brow arched. "Hate? Truly?"

He smiled against her skin. "Too many shivers down my spine for my liking."

Teeth flashed, and Warrick could only watch in awe as she shrugged out of her coat and her shirt. She tossed the clothing aside, leaving only her corset and trousers. He cursed, his whole body tightening at the sight.

So beautiful.

His gaze flicked to the disregarded garments, his heart beating in his throat. "They fit you perfectly."

"I had them commissioned alongside the other items for our grand reveal of the betting book. Remember that?"

How could he forget. The shock had taken years off his life. Back then, it had overshadowed even his guilt about losing the list. The combination of that outfit along with the Turkish trouble . . .

"I'm going to cut these trousers up and toss them in the fire."

Her fingers moved to tug at the laces of her corset. As if sensing his anticipation, she paused, a slow smile forming on her face. "Aren't you going to remove your breeches?"

"You are doing such a smashing job of removing your clothes, I'm hoping you could remove mine as well."

She laughed. "That would take the joy out of watching you remove them."

He stared at her.

She reached out to trail a finger over his jaw. "I'm enjoying that look on your face more than I ought, Phineas."

Hell. Damnation. And everything in between.

"You are driving me mad, here," Warrick half growled, half groaned.

"I quite like that, too."

"Minx. What books have you been reading?" They should be outlawed. "Where did you learn to tease like this?"

"Have you forgotten? I don't read."

Of course. "Well then?"

The grin that lit her face stole his breath. "We women have a base instinct, too."

God save humanity. "A damn lethal one if you ask me." Warrick crawled over her, eyes burning into hers as he yanked those Turkish trousers down. "You are taking too long."

Soft laughter provoked goose flesh all over his skin. But that wasn't half of it. She did away with her corset, and the sight of her . . . he couldn't breathe. She was so damn alluring.

He cupped her breasts gently, testing their fullness in his palm before he captured their peak between his lips. She gasped beneath him, and the sound was like magic in his ears.

Ah, hell. "I want to take my time, do so many things to you."

Her eyes blazed. "Then do them."

"I can't." He lowered his head to hers, their noses touching. "I can't hold back."

"Then don't do that either. We are both beasts, remember."

Beasts . . .

I want to be so much more than a beast for you.

But this was not the moment. Not the time. This was all

about them, naked, skin against skin, together. She shimmied fully out of the trousers he'd already tugged down with impatience. And dear Christ, the gentleman inside him vanished.

Who was he to disobey?

His fingers circled the folds of her sex before pushing inside. He captured her gasp with his lips but let out a groan of his own, their breath entwining like their bodies. She clawed the tips of her fingers into his back and dragged them down.

Neither of them held back. Neither of them wanted to.

"Hell, Selena." His body was on fire.

"You still have your trousers on," she accused. "I removed mine, it's about time we remove yours."

"If my trousers go, it's over."

A skeptical look crossed her features. "What's over?"

"Me. You. This moment." He licked her neck. "I'll enter you. Claim you. Possess you."

"Is that the sum of lovemaking?" Her eyes sparkled with mischief. "You enter me? Claim me? Possess me?"

This damn woman. "Today, it is."

"Then enter, claim, and possess me, Phineas."

Warrick rose to his knees, his eyes refusing to release hers as he pushed his trousers down his waist. He wanted to own each look, each caress, each whimper that belonged to her. It might even become his life's purpose to collect them all.

Might?

No.

It had already been decided.

His purpose, his life—they belonged to her.

He fell back over her, shrugging his trousers from his legs. He lifted her chin with a single finger, male satisfaction filling every pore at the expression she gave his cock.

"Look at me, princess."

"Princess," she breathed as his hand cupped her core. "I'm not a princess."

"No, you are not."

You are everything.

Chapter Fourteen

T HE ACT OF intimacy had never been something Selena had given much thought, not even after she overheard the tales of debauchery of her brother and his friends. At first, she'd been detached from the role the women played in those stories because she was a lady and not a woman of easy virtue. They had no bearing on her.

Then, slowly, it became clear. In the minds of the men of the *ton*, romance was nothing but a pretense meant to appease. An illusion for the disillusioned hearts. A fairytale with no fairies and just tales.

Selena lost interest altogether in pursuing such a shallow offering.

But dear God, *this* was heaven.

She could only focus on fullness. And at the present, that *was* Warrick—inside her. His hands . . . *everywhere.*

She bit her lip at the sensations that sparked through her body with each of his thrusts. The pain of it had quickly turned to a slight sting, and now the feel of this man's body above hers, his lips trailing her skin, his possession, robbed her of any and all sense of the world around her.

She had come here to confront Warrick with the newest development of the secret club as well as find a way for them to move forward without cutting each other out of their lives. She hadn't anticipated such an outcome as this. But Selena approached new decisions with the same fearless manner in which she approached most things. This time was no different. She had decided to follow her heart wherever it led her.

She gasped as his teeth grazed the sensitive tip of her breast, absorbing all he bestowed, and he—he devoured all of her.

She splayed her hands over the span of his chest, soaking up the flex of his muscles beneath her fingers, his urgency to claim and conquer as strong as hers to claim and conquer him. And she very much wanted to conquer him—his attention, his focus.

And yes, his heart.

Selena jolted at the recognition, but amidst their bodies deeply connecting, for better or worse, she held onto him.

His hand fisted in her hair, and he dragged his mouth over hers, truly more beast than man, driving himself to the same heights she had moments before reached, the pain of his breach transforming once again into dazzling pleasure as he rocked her world on its end again and again.

A moan escaped her lips.

The man was insatiable.

So am I.

The pleasure she'd received at his hands, his mouth, his body was nothing short of wicked. And from deep within, an explosion erupted, the sparks rolling through her body, and escaped through her lips in the form of a cry. Her legs trembled as though they had lost all functionality. She barely noticed that Warrick had cupped her face between his large hands, dragging soft kisses from her temple to her cheek.

And in the aftermath of all the pleasure, his, hers, theirs, Selena's mind shut down. She curled up in Warrick's embrace, not allowing any thoughts of reality to penetrate the cocoon they had just woven. Over the years of knowing him, she'd grown accustomed to his scent, but in this moment, it took on a whole different fragrance.

She inhaled deeply.

She loved it.

She never wanted to leave these arms.

What am I even thinking?

"Selena," his low, gruff voice murmured.

Mmm.

"Princess."

"Not a princess," Selena murmured, not wishing to leave her daze.

A chuckle.

"Why are you laughing?" she complained dreamily. "Hold me. Don't say anything about marriage or consequences."

Strong, powerful arms gathered her up tighter into his embrace. "Who said I was going to say anything?"

She eyed him askance, and he nuzzled her shoulder. "It's written all over your face."

"You are not looking at my face."

"That's because I can hear it in your tone."

"I hadn't said anything," he protested, but there was laughter in his voice.

"Your body shifted in a way that told me you were preparing to bring up the topic."

He placed a soft kiss on her temple. "I won't bring up the matter of marriage or badger you on consequences. I'll wait until you demand marriage from me or badger me on the consequences."

She pulled away a bit to lift her chin at him. "Wait for me to demand marriage?"

"You ruined me after all. Should you not take responsibility in the future? 'Tis your duty."

"Duty, my arse," Selena teased in a deep, mock voice.

"A true gentleman you are."

"Settle in then, you might be waiting forever. I am quite the rake," she declared in her most rakish tone.

Another kiss. "Then I will have to come up with a plan to reform you, even if it takes forever."

Selena settled back into his arms. This was a side to Warrick that she had never experienced before. An uncomfortable knot formed in her belly. She didn't know how to deal with *this* Warrick. This Warrick had too much power. She could feel hers slipping through her fingers. "Let's not promise each other anything for now."

A short, albeit relaxed, silence fell between them before he said, "I shall not pressure you to do anything you don't want to."

She nudged him. "But you want to, don't you?"

"You know me too well." A kiss. "I'd lock you in this very chamber and never let you go if I had a say in the matter."

"You won't ever do that."

"You seem so sure."

She lifted her gaze to meet the smile in his eyes. "I thought you were not a possessive man. Or have I stumbled upon a grave secret?"

He chuckled. "It's not a trait I value or embrace, but that doesn't mean I don't feel it."

"Well, if you are going to act the possessive man, just lock yourself in here with me." Selena shut her eyes. It would be so much easier to be locked up. Then she wouldn't have to grapple with difficult decisions that life as an heiress with the world at her fingertips presented. "I'm sleepy."

A finger trailed her brow. "Let's rest for a few hours."

"We won't be disturbed?"

"No one enters my chamber without permission except you and your brother."

That brought a smile to her lips. "That's good. We don't have to worry about him."

His arms tightened in response.

Selena waited until Warrick's breathing evened out before she opened her eyes. Sleepy didn't mean she could sleep. Rather, the beat of her heart had yet to settle. He'd use up his forever to reform her? They had been teasing words, but they had struck at the heart of her. The offer of marriage . . . it was still there for her to seize. The only question remained, would she seize it?

Her gaze flitted over his face.

So handsome.

She wanted his heart, which meant . . . she had already given him hers. Of course, she'd already known she had *fallen* into lust with him, or she would never have made love to him. But the instant he'd shouted her name in pure ecstasy, Selena had known her infatuation had already bloomed into something more.

What did this mean for her?

If she stayed with him, if she married him, would her greatest attribute then become Warrick? Would her identity merely shift from sister to wife? Would she find herself or lose herself even more? And yet she couldn't help but recall the loneliness she'd felt with Theodosia at the alehouse when her brother had arrived instead of Phineas. And this morning, claiming him while he claimed her, she'd dropped all and any pretenses to deeper explore this attraction between them.

The scent of him curled around her, tempting her, teasing her, stealing all the wits she required to think. She didn't want to leave. Not like this.

But she didn't want to stay either. Not like this.

She could forget herself in moments such as these. She could surrender herself without question. And she wasn't ready for that. She needed time. They truly didn't do anything the conventional way. First they explored each other, now she had to explore the link between her head and her heart.

She slowly retreated from his embrace.

Living in her brother's shadow was one thing. She had no choice. They were family. But she could never live in Warrick's shadow.

Forgive me.

WARRICK SAT AT the edge of the bed and glared at the empty

space where *she* should still have been sleeping. He had awakened alone in bed, the warmth of her body absent, leaving only an unwelcome cold, bare spot in his bed. He couldn't recall ever falling asleep with a woman in his arms, and even if he had, it hadn't been in his house, in his chamber, in his bed. And he damn well enjoyed the feeling.

A sigh broke free.

He shouldn't have avoided her in the first place. Perhaps then his mind would not be wondering whether he had just been used. Whether she regretted their lovemaking. Whether he had been too beastly?

Given that it was Selena Savage, Warrick could not discard any one of these possibilities, and the thought left a bitter taste in his mouth. A deuced uncomfortable feeling, that.

No.

He refused to believe he'd been used. Or that she regretted his touch. Or that she regretted what they'd done. Or that he had been too beastly. No, she'd had ample opportunity to dash from his chamber beforehand, and she had enjoyed his touches. That hadn't been his imagination. Also, the clock that struck in the distance told him it was past noon already. She couldn't stay in his bed forever, could she?

His gaze drifted to the book on the floor—the book that had almost claimed his family jewels—and a wrinkled piece of paper sticking out of it.

Warrick's brows drew together.

He collected the paper, his eyes widening as the contents came into view. His entire body lost its warmth as he read the note to meet at an address he knew, just knew in his gut, was in an unsavory part of London.

Why hadn't she told him? Had she forgotten? Why sneak away like a thief in the night?

"Confound it."

This had to have been the reason she came in the first place.

She had sought him over this mysterious meeting request,

but the direction of her visit had taken a turn neither of them had expected. And he distinctly recalled she said they would discuss the purpose of her visit later.

Why then had later become never?

He turned over the note. No name. Just an address, date, time, and—he clenched his jaw—a sword entwined with roses.

Warrick tossed the note aside and snatched up his breeches. He needed to catch that minx. But first, he needed to have his men look into this location. Why the devil didn't she tell him? Did she realize she could lose her life? Did danger not mean anything to her?

Warrick strode from the room and descended the stairs. "Cameron," he called. "I'll be heading"—his words cut off at the sight of three men crowding his hall—"out soon."

Deerhurst raised a brow. "Dressed like that?"

Warrick scowled. "What's wrong with how I'm dressed?"

"You're not wearing a shirt." Deerhurst pointed at his chest. "Your skin is showing."

He glanced down. Ah, bloody hell. He looked back to his friends and shrugged. "What's wrong with showing a bit of skin?"

Avondale frowned. "Are you drunk?"

"Yes, I'm as pissed as parrot," Warrick snapped. "Of course I'm not bloody drunk."

"Your hair is a mess," Avondale pressed on. "Your hair is never a mess."

What the hell was this? "My hair took its own direction today. Should I ask it why it refuses to cooperate?"

Deerhurst eyed him up and down and then back up again. "You seem different."

Warrick glared the men. "If it's about my hair, I've been trying this new style, you can ask Mortimer behind my back. He has also commented on it. So, be off with you."

"Calm down, old chap. We aren't making fun of your hairline."

"Who was talking about my hairline?" If a brow could scold,

his would be throwing punches.

Silence.

"No need to get so defensive," Avondale spoke first after a moment, concern lacing his voice. "We are just worried about you."

"You are obstructing my path. Of course I'm in a sour mood." And why was Saville standing there detached and silent as a ghost? If he couldn't bear to look at him or even say a single word, why come?

But by Christ—*thank you for small mercies.*

Selena had already slipped away, and so did some of his annoyance that he'd woken up without her.

Deerhurst arched a brow. "How can we be obstructing your path? Were you really going to leave your house shirtless?"

Warrick dragged a hand through his hair. He hated nagging. "Why are you here?"

"An intervention," Avondale announced.

His hands returned to his head but this time to rub his temples. "Begone. All of you. I'm not in the mood for this."

Neither one of them moved. Even Silent Saville's boots remained rooted in place. Damn it. It seemed he wouldn't be able to escape this business.

"We are not leaving until you hear us out," Deerhurst said.

"If this is about the duel, don't bother."

"It's about everything," Avondale said. "You. Lady Selena. The duel. This rift." Avondale stepped forward. "Things can't go on like this."

Warrick sighed, resigning himself to his fate. "Let's hear it then."

"Can we retire to a more private setting?" Deerhurst asked, glancing between him and Cameron.

These blackguards. Couldn't they just say whatever they'd come to say and then leave? The moment they sat their arses on a cushy pillow, he'd be hard pressed to get rid of them at all today. He motioned to the door at the left. To Cameron, he directed,

"Don't ring for tea."

Cameron inclined his head. The man seemed a bit restless, as though he wanted to say something to Warrick but couldn't. His brows furrowed. He'd known Cameron for years, and though he was content in his position as a footman, Warrick trusted him with all his most delicate assignments and relied on the man's judgement. But before he could ask, his attention got diverted by Deerhurst.

"Not even brandy?" Deerhurst said. "We might need a drink."

Oh, no. "You can get a drink at the club after you've said your piece."

The men glanced at each other but nodded.

"Why do I get the sense that you'd like to be rid of us as soon as possible?" Avondale muttered. "I must say, it's a first."

Warrick arched a brow. "You're only sensing that now?"

He motioned them to the receiving room. "What would you have me do about me, Selena, the duel, and the rift anyway? Out with it so that you can clear off."

"My lord," Cameron stepped up to him and said softly, "can I have a word?"

"Marriage." Avondale's announcement echoed off the walls.

Warrick stopped dead in his tracks. *Not this again.* "You all know my stance on this."

"You kissed her, man," Deerhurst spoke up. "You need to take responsibility."

"Have *you* proposed to every chit you've kissed?"

"That's not the same," Deerhurst argued. "Lady Selena is Saville's sister. You should have known better than to cross that line. Think about how Saville must feel."

His jaw very much knew how Saville felt.

But this wasn't about Saville.

This wasn't even about *him.*

"Well, you can leave," he looked at Saville, "because I did suggest marriage to her, and she said no. You were there, remember?" Three collective frowns responded in answer. "I won't coerce any woman into marrying me. Not even if she is your sister."

"I'm sure she will see reason once Phaedra talks with her," Deerhurst offered.

Warrick held his ground. "It won't matter."

"Why the devil not?" Avondale snapped, his infuriating calm finally cracking. "Don't let this stubbornness turn you into a fool."

They hadn't even spoken to Selena and yet *they* called him stubborn. *Good luck, old chaps.*

He shrugged. "I'm holding out for love."

Deerhurst let out an oath, and Warrick directed a steely gaze at him and Avondale. "Since you both have managed to find love matches, you dare rob me of the chance?"

"That's not to say—"

"Stop," Warrick cut Avondale off. "You can't speak of other people's future feelings, so don't even attempt it. I'll say this one last time, I won't marry a woman I don't love and most especially not one who doesn't love me. The end. If you can't accept that, then I suggest you challenge me to another duel."

I'll deal with Selena my way.

Silence fell between the friends. Lengthy. Heavy. The only sound was a door shutting in the distance followed by gentle laughter and the soft patter of footsteps.

Wait.

He knew that laugh.

His back went cold with terror at the same time a soft, familiar voice called out, "Phineas? Is that you I hear?"

Dead.

He was dead.

"What the hell is this?" Saville's lips finally sprang into action with a bellow. "Selena! Why are you here? And what the devil are you wearing?"

Warrick inhaled a deep breath before he glanced over his shoulder to see Selena exiting the dining room. His eyes widened on the robe—his robe—draping her body. Too big, it swallowed her up whole, the hem dragging on the floor.

What . . . "Why are you still here? I thought you left." *Why haven't you left yet? And why the blazes did I just ask that?*

"You damn blackguard!" Saville roared. "Selena, get over here!"

Warrick stepped into his line of sight, cutting off their view of Selena. "Run," he growled over his shoulder.

Saville shot forward. "I'm going to kill you, you blackguard!"

"Run?" Selena exclaimed. "Are you mad? Run where?"

Damn it. Anywhere!

Warrick sidestepped Saville, grateful when Deerhurst and Avondale cursed, both leaping forward to grab Saville by the arms, holding him back.

"Field Savage," Selena called out her brother's full name, "don't lose your manners!"

"What bloody manners? I find you in his house and you dare say such a thing! Are you trying to anger me to death?" Saville stopped struggling. "Why are you here? What the hell have you been doing in this house?"

"It's not what it looks like," Warrick said, trying hard to keep the curses from flying from his lips, even though he knew that no explanation could appease the wrath contorting the lines of Saville's face. Damn it, he was being punished, wasn't he? This was the curse.

She was his curse.

"Yes, this can easily be explained," Selena said. "I seduced your best friend. What are you going to do about it?"

Warrick's jaw dropped as his head whipped to her. Admitting to a kiss was one thing, but this . . . There was no coming back from an admission like that. Not a path that he could see.

Unless . . .

Unless he married her.

Unless she married him.

Unless they both loved each other.

But all his thoughts with drowned out by a deafening roar.

Chapter Fifteen

N O GOOD DEED goes unpunished.

The lists of her regrets today kept growing and growing. She should not have given into the temptation of the scent covering Warrick's robe and worn it. She should not have wandered about the house and struck up conversations with servants to tease out information about their employer instead of thinking about the consequences of acting as though this were her house, and these her servants. She should not have admitted to seducing Warrick, angering her brother to the point of being dragged back home and locked in her chamber.

Locked.

As in he had turned the key and *locked* her inside.

Insufferable man!

Did he honestly believe a locked door could keep her inside their house? Had he forgotten she'd had learned to climb through windows and up and down trees as a child? She also had a meeting she could not miss. Yet another thing she regretted—this meeting.

Also coming alone.

Selena sighed. The chaos of this morning must have addled her brain. Amidst all the shouting, as she'd had been hauled off by her brother, she had not missed the unfathomable look in Warrick's gaze. There was no emotion, as though he had suppressed every last drop. Yet his gaze had remained so intense that the hairs on the back of her neck had only settled back down in the familiar setting of her bedchamber.

Why can't I say yes?

Yes to marriage, yes to him.

He was a good match, and she was quite fond of him. More than fond. He brought out in her a passion no other could claim to accomplish. And yet she could not utter the words that would clear the mess they were now mired in. Not even after acting the lady in his house!

She'd almost given in.

Almost.

Him standing strong, not allowing his closest friends rob them of her choice . . . it was so appealing that she'd almost acquiesced. But she would rather die than allow anyone to browbeat her into marriage.

Her gaze surveyed the ramshackle building falling to pieces brick by brick. Late afternoon, night had not yet claimed the day, but an overcast sky brought with it a light drizzle and moody feeling.

Well, it's now or never, Selena.

She cast one last look at the hired coach, the driver having promised to wait for her, before she entered the building.

The temperature dropped a degree.

She just needed to remain calm, quiet, and patient. Nothing bad was going to happen to her. Her death would assuredly give rise to inquiries, would it not?

She hadn't quite known where the person would meet her, but she didn't have to wait long. The pitter patter of footsteps alerted Selena to another person, and a woman's voice issued from the shadows.

"You came."

"You thought I wouldn't?" Selena asked with a guarded tone she reserved for those who were not enemies but not yet friends. They must have been watching her, and even if they weren't, the scene at the alehouse should have brought her to their attention, if nothing else, but what sort of attention that was, she could not yet say.

"I wasn't sure, to be frank." A figure appeared from the darkness. Cloaked in red. "I didn't think you would come alone."

"I'm here." But she didn't want to tarry. "And I'm not alone." A bluff if there ever was one. "Why did you ask to meet?"

"We have something you want, and you have something we want."

Now that was interesting, and it surprised Selena. "What could I possibly have that you want?"

"The betting book you stole from White's."

Her entire body froze and, for a second, even her brain. They wanted that old, cursed misery of a book? "Why ever would you want the book?"

"That is our business."

Fair enough. She didn't care anyway. "And what would I receive in turn for the book?" Selena already suspected the answer.

"An invitation into our club."

Finally. The long-awaited invitation.

How unfortunate that she felt no relief, no giddiness whatsoever, after receiving the one thing she'd wanted for so long.

"Do not tell me you don't want our invitation anymore?" the voice asked when she did not reply.

Anymore. The arrogance! Not misplaced though . . .

But why now? "Won't the book be my business too if I enter the club?" Selena asked instead of answering the woman's question.

"You are a sharp one." The woman chuckled. "Yes, it will, but that is business for when you join. And the betting book is the price of admission."

How curious. "Do all members pay a price of admission?"

"Of course. No club is without its membership fees. Ours is merely a once-off fee of money, object, or favor."

Money, object, or favor?

Theodosia would be dying of laughter by now, pointing a finger—*I told you so.*

"If the betting book is the price of admission, why ask for it only now? We've had it for weeks."

"Yes, but we didn't know who stole the book. Then a few of you released copies of its pages. After that, we had to observe you and decide who best to approach."

"And I'm the only one who showed blatant interest in joining your club."

"You have been quite obvious about it, yes."

"Why meet me in such a horrifying place?" Selena crossed her arms. "Could we not have met elsewhere?"

"My apologies for the unpleasantness of the location, but you have people following you, so we had to be careful."

Was she talking about Warrick? Selena didn't think that was the only reason she chose this as their meeting place.

"What if I don't have the book?"

"It would be best not to lie us, Lady Selena."

"How would you know if I am lying?" Well these people didn't know everything then. She honestly didn't have the book anymore.

"I assure you, we have our ways. You have two days to decide."

Her brows furrowed. "Only two?"

"Yes, and before you question our timeline, all members received two days to make their decision to join or not."

"Very well, but what happens if I don't hand over the book?"

The woman laughed, causing Selena to frown. Where had she heard this laughter before? It sounded somewhat familiar. "Then the next time we meet, it shall not be in a warehouse."

Shivers broke out all over her skin. She would not consider herself the best judge of character, but she was no simpleton. That one sentence was filled with unspoken meaning, and lined with a sly undertone an infant would recognize.

She should have alerted Warrick. But she hadn't. She'd thought a bit of space would help clear her mind, especially after the debacle with her brother earlier today. Yet another regret to dwell on.

"What is that supposed to mean?" Selena's gaze flicked to the shadows beyond the woman. Earlier she'd had her reservations, now uneasiness clamped down on her chest. What did they want with the betting book? Did *us* mean the club? Why not say *club* then? What if they were actually a cult rather than your run of the mill secret female club? And *how* did they know—or think they know—she had the book?

"Oh, nothing much," the woman said. "Merely that we have shown you a courtesy by allowing to hand the book over with your two hands and as a result, join us. We could use a lady such as yourself on our side."

"Then tell me this, what is your club about?"

"Liberation."

"Of whom?"

"Can you not guess?"

She stared that the woman's faceless form, her mind conflicted. Men? Society? The possibilities were too endless for a mere guess, but she didn't want to prolong this conversation further. "I shall consider your proposal."

"There is, of course, another condition."

Of course, there was.

Why was nothing ever simple with secret clubs? "What is it?" Selena asked. And why wait until now to reveal it?

"Cut all ties with the Earl of Warrick."

Selena blinked. Did she hear that wrong? "*Excuse* me?"

"Cut all ties with the Earl of Warrick. That is the last condition."

"Why on earth do you want me to do that?" What was it about this man? Everyone either wanted her to accept all ties or cut all ties. How tiring.

And . . . Selena narrowed her eyes on the figure. How did

they know there were ties that could be cut?

"You are not willing? It's a simple enough request."

Not true. There was nothing, not one single dratted thing, that was simple about it! Unless you call giving the man you fancy your innocence "simple." And besides, she did not want to cut ties with him. "That might be a bit difficult. He is my brother's best friend." *And mine.*

"That is neither here nor there. He's been following you around like a dog who has misplaced his owner. I want it to stop."

Unease spread through Selena. A dog who misplaced its owner? Then who would the owner be? "I daresay whether he follows me about or not has nothing to do with the club."

"Not the club, no. Me."

Selena went cold. "If you wish for me to cut ties with the earl, you must at least tell me why."

"Warrick is my lover."

His name on this person's lips, even if just the title, along with *lover*, caused Selena's breath to catch. Instant denial welled up within her. "That's impossible."

Because I am his lover.

"I assure you, Lady Selena, I very much am." The woman suddenly laughed. "I see you are quite shocked. Do not tell me you've designs on the earl."

"I have not."

Liar.

"That is good. I fear your heart would be broken if you did. In any event, those are the conditions. Hand over the betting book. Cut ties with Warrick." Selena flinched. "You have two days to decide. I will send you a new meeting location soon."

"Are you the founder of this club?"

A short burst of laughter. "Goodness, no. I am merely the spokesperson *she* chose."

Selena clenched her jaw. "Will *she* be at the next meeting?"

The cloaked woman paused.

"That is *my* condition." Selena lifted her chin, staring straight at woman. "If I am to cut ties with a family friend and hand over the book, I expect to hand the book over to the person in charge."

"As you wish. I am certain she won't have a problem accepting the book personally from your hands. She's been wanting to get her own hands on it for a while."

"Why did she not come tonight then?"

"Do you have the book here?"

Selena said nothing to that.

Another grating chuckle. "Until next time, then, Lady Selena."

Selena stood in the abandoned warehouse, staring at the spot where the woman had disappeared, lost in thought.

Warrick had a lover.

And it wasn't her.

She was going to throttle him. But only after she decided whether or not to join the club.

WARRICK CRUSHED THE note in his hand as he surveyed his surroundings. Whitechapel. One of the worst parts of London. Not a place any lady should wander about alone. His jaw ached just thinking how he had once again been left behind.

Selena Savage, just you *wait.*

He didn't have a good feeling about this as he strode up to the warehouse where the meeting was to be. He was late. Bloody drunken riots on one of the streets. Furthermore, it was dark, wet, and smelled like rotting carcasses.

He should have shackled them both to his bed when he'd had the chance. That way, they could have ignored reality for a bit longer. Instead, he was here. Cold. Miserable. Mood as foul as the smell in the air. He caught a glimpse of sandy hair dashing to a carriage ahead.

Oh, no, you don't.

Warrick quickened his pace, almost to a jog. He didn't go for stealth, his footsteps echoing through on the cobbles of the street. She glanced over her shoulder.

"Warrick?" Her face went slack at his approach. Good. "What . . . what are you doing here?"

"That is a question best left for you to answer." He snatched her wrist and tossed the driver three coins. "She'll be riding with me."

The man tipped his head and flicked the reins.

"I was not going to fight against you." She tugged at her wrist. "And you are here, so you must have guessed why *I* am here."

He lifted the note in his hand while leading her back to his carriage.

"So that's what happened," she murmured. "I thought I lost it."

Warrick held fast to his calm. "You sought me out to tell me about this, but you didn't. Why?" This bothered him the most. Why seek him out and then change her mind? Had he done something wrong? Even if she'd simply forgotten, she could have sent word to him later. But catching her in the act confirmed she hadn't meant to include him anymore.

"After what happened this morning, I thought it best not to involve you. I also didn't know whether I would be able to slip away without getting caught."

"Is that really your reason?" He ushered her into the carriage, brushed the rain from his hair, and followed her in.

She didn't answer.

Fine, then. He wouldn't push. "Just tell me if I did something wrong or not—if that is why you didn't tell me."

"Of course not," she said softly. "You did nothing wrong."

That was something, he supposed. A small release from the reservoir of other things that plagued him. Like, "Why, after you left my bed this morning, did you prance about my house without a care?"

Her cheeks flushed. "Yes, well, I have been regretting that particular deed of mine."

Warrick studied her. "If you were going to be so reckless, you could have stayed in bed with me."

"I couldn't stay there forever. I had to leave sometime." She exhaled a deep breath. "Then I had this mad urge, and you know the rest."

He would never forget that "rest" for the rest of his life. Still, "Why didn't you wake me?"

"Would you have wakened me?" she countered.

Warrick clamped his jaw shut. No. Not in a thousand years. "You see."

Fine, it was in the past, anyway. He rapped on the roof and the carriage shot forward. There were other more pressing matters. "Who did you meet here?"

She arched a brow. "Have you not guessed?"

"Do not be snippy, Selena. This is serious. Do you know how dangerous this part of London is for a woman? Alone? You didn't even bring a footman! You hailed a damn hackney. What if something had happened to you tonight? How do you think I would feel? How would your brother feel?" He removed his gloves and dragged a hand through his hair. "This is the exact reason why Saville put a *watchdog* on you. He was afraid of you running amok with no regard for your safety."

"I am not running amok," she protested, her brows furrowing.

"Then what are you doing?" Warrick challenged. "Do you even know? Not that I can blame you even if you don't. I hardly know what the hell I'm doing."

A hand settled on his knee. "I understand, all right?" Her eyes met his. "I made a mistake, I won't deny that." She patted his leg before retracting her arm and settling back. "I met a woman here. She was cloaked. They extended an invitation to the club."

His heart started pounding in his chest. "Does this look like a place any club with good intentions would extend an invitation?"

She shrugged. "Perhaps it was a test."

"Test, my arse. Tell me you are not going to join them."

"I'm not sure. They gave me time to decide."

He waved the note in her face. She could not be this naïve. "This is not an invitation, Selena. This is not a test."

"Then what is it, Phineas? Perhaps this is just their own unique method."

"How the hell should I know? If the club has this sort of an initiation, or whatever the hell it is, it's better not to join." Mortimer said the club was up to no good. That the people, women or not, were dangerous. This location, in his mind, confirmed the duke's suspicion. However, if he told Selena that, she might join just for the thrill of it. So what the hell to do?

"What initiation does White's have?" she asked.

"What do you mean initiation? The club has membership fees."

"Well, perhaps this is the price for joining this particular club."

"Are you certain it's worth paying?" He didn't think so. "From the looks of it, not only is the price steep, but it might also collect a good portion of your soul."

Her lips quirked. "A portion of my soul?"

"What?" he muttered. "It might very well be the case. And if not yours, then mine. You running about London as though no danger will ever touch you claims a bit of me every time."

She averted her gaze, and after a moment, a small sigh pushed past her lips. "You followed after me, didn't you?"

"But you didn't know that I would."

Her lips parted, then shut again.

Warrick shut his eyes. "What the hell happened? I thought we had an understanding."

"What understanding? You avoided me for six days, didn't you?"

His eyes opened to meet hers. "Then did I misunderstand you coming into my chamber alone? Kissing me? *Accepting* me as a lover?"

Her eyes suddenly narrowed on him, something indecipherable flashing in the depth of those dark irises. "Are we lovers? Or did we just make love in a moment of impulse?"

He couldn't have heard that correctly. "A moment of impulse? Are you telling me you only used me to satiate your desires?"

"Did we not use each other? I was not the only one with impulses."

"Damn it, I didn't use you, Selena." Why would she even think that?

He matched her probing stare, but to his surprise, she looked away first. That single action was like a punch to the gut. Saville's blows could not even come close. He could practically feel her dismissive air filling the carriage.

"This is not the time to debate this matter," she finally said, still not meeting his eye.

Warrick refused to look away from her for even one second. They had come such a long way since the days he merely followed her around, breached so many boundaries with each other, and taken the first step toward being together in a more permanent way. But this club . . . he was afraid she would choose to join it if he warned her against it, terrified she would if he didn't. Deep beneath this predicament, however, lay the true source of his fear—that no matter what choice he made, she would never choose him. That she'd always choose something else.

Another small sigh broke through the rattle of wheels and clapping hooves of the horses. It clung to the space between them. Her head turned back to him, her gaze filled with helplessness.

"This is all your fault, you know."

Warrick stilled. The blood drained from his body moments before it rushed back up. "I beg your pardon?"

"This is all your fault." That look of helplessness turned

sharp. *"Everything* is all your fault."

Warrick's mind just . . . froze. It was beyond the scope of his abilities to decipher what the hell was happening. What exactly was his fault?

She shook her head. "And I don't know whether to thank you or boot you from the carriage."

"Selena, it would be better if you explain to me what exactly I am to blame for."

"Did this not all start with you and the rest of your gang?"

Warrick stared. "Are you referring to the list?"

"Well, that is the start of it all, is it not?"

Yes, but, "I thought you had moved past that." How long has it been? Hell, she'd seemed quite over it this morning. Had something happened between then and now that she wasn't telling him?

"How can I, when I'm constantly reminded of how I am but a tip of a finger in this world of wagging claws?" A helpless note remained.

Warrick wanted to drag a hand through his hair, pinch the bridge of his nose, rub his temples, and slam his fist against a wall. He didn't have enough hands for all his urges. So, he settled for clenching them.

"Forgive me for pointing this out," Warrick said, "but you are not making a whit of sense. How are you a fingertip?" If she was a fingertip, what the hell was he? "You didn't raid your brother's liquor cabinet, did you?"

"How male of you to assume that if I'm not making sense, I must have been drinking."

Well, what else was he to assume? How else was he to get her to speak to him, to share what's truly bothering her? "If you wish to blame me forever, I can take it." His shoulders were broad. "But I sense there is more than just the list behind this, and I can't do anything if you don't tell me what it is."

Again, she looked away.

"Selena."

She kept her gaze averted.

"What aren't we telling each other?" He pushed the desperation that surfaced back down, but some still spilled out. "I can be whatever you want me to be, too. *Who*, is the only question. Who do want me to be? Who do you want me to be to *you*?"

Her eyes lifted to his. "Why should we define and claim inconsequential terms?"

Warrick stared at her. She knew how to make his heart palpitate in all sorts of undesirable beats. "Are you talking about us as lovers?"

"I am speaking in general."

Warrick shut his eyes. "Damn this miserable curse. It must be flaring up again."

Calamity would befall him if he didn't marry before the age of thirty. What was this if not a form of calamity? What was this if not form of a curse?

A bitter truth dawned on him: He was dancing with disaster, and at any moment, the music could stop. And when that happened, he would either be standing with her by his side, or utterly alone.

Chapter Sixteen

S ELENA'S HEART CHASED the beats of the furious clatter of Warrick's coach as it rattled through the streets of London. Her wrist still tingled where he had led her away in an almost death grip. She rubbed the spot gently, absentmindedly.

He'd been late, so he hadn't heard. He didn't know.

Cut ties with Warrick.

How many times had she almost blurted the truth to him from the moment they entered carriage? But she had held back. A part of her wished he'd arrived sooner to overhear her conversation with that woman. Another part of her dreaded the very thing.

She snuck a look at the man's grim face. Guilt jabbed at her heart. She hadn't lied to him, she told herself. Everything she told him was the truth. Not the entire truth, but still part of the truth.

Selena, you fool.

She shouldn't have made it sound as if they had used each other. That was the only part that couldn't be further from the truth. But she had floundered. She hadn't known how to act toward him in the wake of hearing that woman's conditions. That *one* condition.

Everything she wanted was within her grasp, but the price was hefty. And if she paid it . . . it might just be the cost of a chunk of her soul. He hadn't been wrong there. He hadn't been wrong with many things.

"Are you cold?" His question came so suddenly she jolted.

"I beg your pardon?" She hadn't even noticed the cold.

"You're shivering." He shrugged out of his jacket and draped it over her shoulders. Heat spread across her cheeks. The action was so simple, so intimate, it made her heartbeat jump. But then his scent enveloped her, mocking her with the memory of all she desired but hesitated to claim.

"I'm sorry." He deserved this much. "I made things harder for you, didn't I?" She felt those dark eyes on her, but she couldn't meet them. She would not be able to hold back if she did. She would blurt everything out. "I should never have stayed."

"Why did you?"

"I'm not sure myself. I suppose I was curious—too curious for my own good." Curious about all things Phineas North. Curious if her heart would keep skipping beats for him. It still did. She wasn't sure it had ever stopped.

"I suppose I can't blame you," he murmured offhandedly. "If I were you, I'd be loath to leave a handsome man, too."

She snorted, a bit of the tension draining her body at his attempt at dry humor. "There is no such thing."

"When it comes to you, Selena Savage, there is no such thing as no such thing." A short pause. "We don't have to define terms if you don't want to, but what are we going to do about this situation we find ourselves in?"

Her eyes met his, and the burning in their depths intensified, refusing to leave her in peace.

Peace.

Lord, she finally understood why Warrick desired his peace of mind. Selena wanted nothing more than to fall back onto her bed, curl up surrounded by all of her pillows, and shut out the world.

However, that woman had robbed of any peace even if she were to do exactly that. "I realized something tonight," Selena said slowly, collecting her thoughts. "You are the reason I haven't been invited into the club."

"Me? How so? Is that what the person you met said? Is this what you meant when you said everything was my fault?" A brow shot upward. "You give me too much credit, Selena."

She shook her head. Revealing the woman's claim that they were lovers would open the conversation to the conditions of entering the club. She couldn't reveal this. Not yet.

Two days . . .

Just two days.

She would claim every minute of those two days and clear her head and consider her options.

"The credit is deserved," she replied simply. "You and your long legs, big head, and brawny shoulders are the reason I have not received an invite."

"It's astonishing how you can turn what ought to be a compliment into an insult."

The corner of her lips twitched. "But it's true." She leaned forward. "You speak of curses. Is there even such a thing? If there is, then you are as much my curse as I seem to be yours."

"Because I've been protecting you from fortune hunters?"

"Following me."

A stormy furrow gathered between his brows. "Protecting you."

"Why are protecting me in the first place?" She shot back, regretting the impulse as soon as the words left her mouth.

"Bloody hell, Selena. You know why. How long are you going to crucify me for that mistake? Yes, it's my scrawl on the list. Yes, I lost the list. I'm the reason the list made the betting book. But you should know better than anyone how easy it is to misplace a scrap of paper."

Selena let out a heavy breath. He wasn't wrong. She couldn't blame him forever. At some point, she had to let it go.

Cut ties with Warrick.

This man . . .

Who am I? Who are you? Who are . . . we?

Until she could answer those questions, she could not claim

him, his heart, or anything else for herself.

She gave a curt nod, mostly to herself, but also in acknowledgment of him. "You are right, of course. It's time to let the past go. You made a mistake. All of you. You shouldn't be cast into the fire for it. Lord knows, mistakes are part of being a human." She'd made too many recently to count on all her fingers.

Fingers. Fingertips.

He slanted her a skeptical look. "You aren't just saying this to appease me, are you?"

Selena shook her head, her gaze dropping to her hands. "Anyone can lose a scrap of paper." Look at her. Hadn't she lost one, too? The very same one that led him to the warehouse.

Oh, lord.

She couldn't breathe.

If she had the world at her fingertips, why did it feel as though her world was slipping through them?

I can't do this right now.

She used one of her fingers to part the curtain covering the window. They'd already entered Mayfair.

"Please stop the carriage," Selena blurted.

"What? Why?"

She could hear the frown in his voice. The confusion. A tight vise gripped her throat. What was happening to her? She couldn't breathe.

"Please," Selena exclaimed. "Stop the carriage! I need it to stop." *Need to get out.*

He rapped on ceiling, signaling for the driver to draw the carriage to a halt.

"What's wrong?" She heard a rustle. "You look pale."

"I need to leave." The moment the carriage stopped she pushed open the door and leaped out, inhaling a deep breath of air.

"Where are you going?" Warrick demanded, climbing out after her. "We haven't arrived at your home yet. It's dark, Selena. Dangerous. Get back in."

"I'll be fine. Don't follow me." The coolness of the air relieved some of her anxiety. "You wish to get rid of your curse? Just get rid of me. There. Done. Curseless."

"What are you talking about? My curse is a family curse about marriage."

"Is that why you are here?" *Stop, Selena. Don't say anymore.* But the words still pushed past her lips. The fear. "You are looking for me to break the curse? Not Selena the curse, but Selena the curse breaker."

"What's wrong? Obviously, something happened that you're not telling me. I've never seen you as a curse breaker or whatever. I've only ever seen you as Selena."

What *was* wrong? Selena herself couldn't say. No, she could, she just didn't want to say it. So, she found something else to latch onto. Her only goal, her only aim at present, was to get to her bed.

"This is what you believe?" he continued. "You think I'm using you to break the curse?"

She pinched the bridge of her nose. "If we wed, your curse is broken."

"That's hogwash and you know it. Did you not enter my chamber on you own?"

"It doesn't matter anymore." Or it did. She couldn't find the right words. Her temples started to throb.

A loud curse. "It doesn't matter? What do I mean to you? Am I merely a pillow on your bed? Was I a method to a madness I do not grasp? I don't understand what is happening right now. I might even be the mad one."

No, he wasn't. This was her. "Let's stop here, Phineas."

"What do you mean?"

She still couldn't look at him. If she did, she might falter. Just two days . . . "Let's take some time to think about what who we are to each other."

"I already know who you are to me," he said softly. "I don't need time."

Oh, God. She could feel herself wavering. "Let's just take some time," she repeated, unable to find more words.

"I love you, Selena."

Her breath caught.

He . . . he . . . She shut her eyes, her entire body going numb at those three words. "How . . .?"

"How do I love you? Simple. You bring me torment."

She pressed the back of her palms against her eyes. "Torment is not love. Torment is torment."

"A man can only be tormented by a woman he is madly in love with," he denied. "And I love you."

Selena couldn't listen anymore. Her brain refused to digest his confession, could hardly form a sentence that made sense. "Let's speak about this later, all right?"

"*Selena*."

"Please." She lifted a hand to stop him saying anything more. She couldn't hear it. She didn't have the heart to. She didn't have the *mind* to. "Goodbye, Phineas."

SOMETHING WAS WRONG. Very wrong. So wrong that the chill from their encounter hadn't yet left his body. What had happened between the time she'd left his house and the time he'd found her in the warehouse? Whatever it was, it was something that she didn't trust to tell him about.

A string of foul words flew from his lips.

He'd told the woman that he loved her, and she said they could discuss it *later*?

Why had he ever thought he could unravel the shroud of distrust that shackled Selena? He couldn't. Instead, he'd been the one to unravel, just as he'd originally feared. He was still bloody unraveling. The threads . . . he could feel them fraying as he lost his sanity, his heart, his very soul. What about her? He'd felt a palpable change in her that hadn't been present earlier that day. Hadn't even been present as she'd been dragged off by Saville.

Ah, Saville.

Even his closest friendship was on the brink of ruin.

Would this damn curse claim everything dear to him?

No, he refused to give that blasted word any more power. Curse? What curse? If Warrick were a cursed man, it was a curse of his own making. He had been so focused on everything that had gone wrong for him that he had been half blind to all that might go right. Had he even been open to anything but curses? The moment the first thing had gone wrong after he turned thirty, the idea of the curse settled into his mind, and he hadn't been able to push it back out.

Everything turned into a curse.

And some of the wrongs had clearly been his doing. Ridding himself of this so-called curse would not be accomplished by marrying, and marrying would not rid him of his problems. He needed to begin righting wrongs.

Selena wanted space, so he would give her space even if it killed him. He'd start making amends with Saville instead.

With an apology.

He *had* crossed the line. Though he would not be badgered into marriage, he could have handled certain things differently.

The rain had stopped about the same time Selena had left him at the side of the road, but no one could escape the frosty nip this night brought. Despite the chill, he knew where his friend would be after a day like today, and he'd come straight here after following Selena from a safe distance to make sure she arrived home safely. Warrick jumped from the carriage the moment it drew to a halt strode over to his friend who sat on the bank staring off at the Thames River.

Saville didn't glance over his shoulder at his approach, just growled, "What the hell are you doing here?"

"Can't I enjoy the riverside view?"

A snort. "How did you know I'd be here?"

"Did you forget we've been friends for years? I know the spots you go when you are near angered to death."

"I didn't forget anything. You are the one who forgot."

"You are right." He wouldn't deny his wrong in this.

"What the hell do you want? I'm not in the mood to chat."

Warrick settled in beside him. "I'm here to apologize."

Saville took a swig straight from the bottle of brandy he held in his hand. "Then marry my sister."

"I will."

Dark, skeptical eyes settled on him. "I've never heard a man change his tune so quick. Weren't you dead set on standing your ground earlier?"

Warrick picked up a pebble and flicked it into the river, watching the dark ripples grow bigger and bigger. "I'm not scheming. I'm telling the truth even while I'm still standing firm."

"But you will marry my sister?" Saville asked, looking over to him.

"In a heartbeat."

Saville's eyes narrowed. "When?"

This was the part his friend wouldn't like. "The moment she demands it of me."

"Bloody hell." Another swallow.

Warrick held out his hand. "Give me some of that."

"Get your own bottle."

"I didn't bring one."

Saville grabbed a second bottle Warrick hadn't noticed resting beside him. "Here." He tossed him the bottle, and Warrick caught it with both hands.

Warrick's brow pulled upward. "You brought two bottles?"

"Well, I was planning to drown myself in drink tonight. Do you have a problem with that?"

"No." Indeed, Warrick had no different idea. "I'll join you."

"I suppose my misery could use company."

Warrick uncorked the bottle and took a long swig. He welcomed the burn of fire trailing to his belly, and some of the chill vanished. Saville hadn't chased him away. Had brought two bottles. No man could drink two all by himself. He must have hoped for company. But he wasn't going to expose his hunch.

He took another swallow, watching Saville mimic his earlier action and tossed a pebble into the river. "I didn't plan for any of this to happen. You must know this."

"You didn't stop it either."

"No, I didn't." Another swallow.

"Your sister . . ." What to even bloody say? "I am hers. Everything else is—"

"Once again, you are ignoring the fact that I am her brother." Dark eyes moved to him. "Everything else is what?"

Warrick gave him a flat look. "Irrelevant."

Saville grunted. He traced the rim of his bottle with a finger, the action almost pensive. "Do you love her? Do you love my sister?"

Warrick couldn't help his brows from furrowing at the memory Saville's actions evoked. He sighed deeply. "I care for her deeply, yes." She had his heart, his everything.

"Then why wait until she demands marriage from you?"

"Your sister is not ready to decide what she wants." Whatever, *whomever*, that may or may not be. "Give her a moment to collect her thoughts."

"You mean unlock her bedroom door?"

As if a locked door could hold her.

"You really are clueless at times, my friend."

"You're one to speak.

Quite right. Warrick raised his bottle and clinked it against Saville's. "To clueless friends."

"Hear, hear," Saville said before tossing back liquid in this throat. "Ah, I love the sting." He looked to Warrick. "Anyone pinch your arse lately?"

"Don't bring up that bloody experience." Another swallow burned down his throat. "What about you? You seemed quite taken with Lady Theodosia. Have *you* perhaps fallen in love with the chit?"

"What the devil are you talking about? That woman drives me mad."

"That doesn't mean you don't care for her." Just look at him. He had fallen head over heels for his own tormentor. "And you *are* still following her around."

Saville blew out a breath. "No, I'm not. Not since her birthday."

That surprised Warrick. "Why not?"

His friend lifted his shoulders in a heavy shrug. "We set out to protect the heiress from the scum of London crawling out of the crevices."

Warrick nodded. "The consequences of the list."

"Yes, well, there are no longer fortune hunters sniffing around her skirts. She doesn't need my help."

"The lady is a force to be reckoned with," Warrick agreed.

"How the hell do I know what love feels like, anyway?" Saville muttered. "At the very least it should feel good. It's love, after all."

"I'm not sure if *good* is the word I'd use to describe the sentiment."

"Then what word would you use?"

"Not a word," Warrick said, contemplating his next sentence. "Rather, I'd describe giving my heart to someone feeling like I did the first time I raced my phaeton against you across Hyde Park at full speed. Only, I am not holding the reins. She is. It's both thrilling and terrifying at the same time."

"Bloody hell, are you drunk already?" Saville glanced at the contents of his bottle before looking back at the Thames. "It should still feel good. Poets are always going on about it."

"You haven't read a single page of poetry have you?"

"Why the hell would I do that?"

"Never mind," Warrick said. Hopeless. Why wouldn't these Savages read? "And who are you calling drunk? I can go all night."

"Then whoever is overcome first has to carry the other to the carriage."

"Are you a bloody child?"

Saville shot him a glare. "Why yes, I am a child. I am infantile, remember? Besides, are you afraid you won't be able to carry this child?"

He shouldn't have said anything. *Just ignore it.* "Then you are planning on being overcome first?"

Saville snorted. "Of course. I've got half a bottle on you already. Unless you plan to pour half down your throat now."

"No, I—"

A woman's laughter interrupted him, followed by, "Well, well, well, whatever do we have here?"

Warrick shot a glance over his shoulder, his brow furrowing at the appearance of four cloaked figures. Three wore black cloaks. One wore a sickening shade of red. It reminded him of blood. By their stature, they were all women. A sense of foreboding filled the space between the beats of his heart pounding in his chest. The secret club?

"Who the hell are you?" Saville growled.

"Oh," the woman in red said, "we shall get to it soon enough, but first you shall have to come with us."

Were they being *kidnapped*?

"We are not going anywhere with you." Saville stretched out a leg lazily. "Run along. You weren't invited to the party."

Four pistols appeared from beneath the cloaks and pointed straight at them. "As you can see, we are not giving you a choice."

"Well, why didn't you just start with that?" Saville asked, stumbling to his feet. He swayed. "We don't want any trouble."

Dear God.

"Warrick, dear," the woman said. "You, too."

Warrick, dear? Why did her voice sound so familiar?

"Warrick, dear?" Saville arched a brow at him, his eyes shooting daggers. "Love is truly grand."

"Don't start. I have no clue who this woman is." Warrick

studied the figures. "But I suspect you are from the secret club that has recently surfaced in London."

Soft laughter filled the air. "Why, you are correct. I must say, I never thought Lady Selena would tell you about us. I daresay that's where you heard about us, is that correct?"

Warrick paused. This had to be the woman Selena had met at the warehouse.

"My sister?" He looked at Warrick then back to the women. "What does my sister have to do with you?"

"Oh dear, the Earl of Saville doesn't know anything," the woman murmured. "How interesting. But to answer your question, my lord, your sister has *everything* to do with us. She is, after all, in possession of something we want."

"What the devil could Selena have that you want?" Warrick demanded. Did this have something to do with how she acted after he retrieved her from their meeting?

More laughter rang out. "She told you about us, but she didn't tell you about this? What an interesting girl. It seems she might be leaning toward meeting our conditions to join us after all."

"My sister will do no such thing," Saville bit out.

Her hooded head turned to Saville. "That is not up to you, my lord."

"What, no Saville *dear*, for me?" he mocked.

"Of course not, that endearment is meant only for my lover."

Warrick froze.

Her what?

Him?

The sting of steely eyes settled on him once more. "Don't look at me like that. I only have one lover and that's—"

"*That's?*" Saville's entire body puffed up. "That's who?"

Warrick clamped his mouth shut. No need to poke the bear again. He turned to the women. "Why kidnap us?" She'd mention conditions. He didn't have a good feeling about that at all. "What do you want?"

"Insurance, Warrick, dear. Insurance." She motioned with her pistol to a carriage waiting in the street beyond. "On you go."

On you go?

Just like that?

What the hell was happening right now?

Chapter Seventeen

TIMING WAS EVERYTHING.

Or so Shakespeare had claimed. Selena had always found it to be a matter of fate. Was it fate that finally gave her the one thing she'd been searching for weeks only to douse her joy with that one single condition? Was it fate that made that one single condition confess love to her that very same night?

A day had passed without as much as a word from either Warrick or her brother. It was like the two of them had vanished from her world. Perhaps they were both giving her space. Which could be expected of Warrick, but her brother . . .? Then again, it also wasn't unlike him to douse his anger at White's, or wherever young men went to douse their anger.

Their absence, however, was not what Selena was worried about.

A whole day had passed, and she still had no idea what she would do about the conditions or the confession. Since the very minute she'd first heard of the secret women's club, she wanted to find this it in the hope of carving an identity for herself that moved beyond heiress, the sister of the Earl of Saville, and lady. She hadn't known what she would find, but there had been a renewed sense of purpose in her heart even in the searching.

Now . . . the timing of everything seemed a bit off.

For one, she didn't have the book anymore. Theodosia had it.

She knew if she were to ask for it back, her friend would hand it over in a heartbeat, but it was not her book to give to the club. All the heiresses had a say.

Selena paused to consider her progress. "Something seems to be missing," she murmured to herself.

"Did you say something, my lady?"

Selena glanced at the maid below her and shook her head. "No, I was merely talking to my brother."

"The earl . . ."

Selena smiled. In one hand she held a palette filled with colors, and in the other a paintbrush. She pointed her brush at the portrait of Saville that decorated a large portion of the wall in the blue drawing room. "I like this version of my brother better. He is silent and does not retort back with whiplash comments. Quite pleasing to hold a conversation with him in this form. I should have done so much sooner."

"My lady, be careful on the stool."

"Oh, do not worry. I won't fall. But tell me, how does my brother look with this mustache?" She thought it rather fine.

"Very good, my lady."

She tapped her chin with the wooden end of her brush. "I think I shall give him a pair of devil's horns as well."

The maid retreated with a small bow. "Then I shall take my leave."

"Oh, Lucy," Selena called out. "Do retrieve all my brother's waistcoats from his closet and bring them here."

"My lady?"

"Along with a pair of scissors."

A hesitant pause. "As you wish, my lady."

Selena grinned at the painting before her. "It's so delightful to vent, do you not think so, brother?" She dipped her brush in a spot of red and proceeded to paint a small horn on his head. "What do you think about the conditions the club set? Shall I accept or not?"

Hand over the book.

Cut ties with Warrick.

One was manageable. All she had to do was calling a meeting of heiress and ask their permission. If they refused, the matter would be out of her hands. But the other condition . . . that was not so manageable. That was near impossible. Because he had confessed to her. He said he loved her.

Loved. *Her.*

Her infatuated heart couldn't be more overjoyed. However, the mere memory of that woman in the warehouse still left a sour taste in Selena's mouth. She had claimed they were lovers, dousing her joy every time she recalled it.

"I suppose I can't allow one woman to ruin this moment for me. Warrick's lover? What utter nonsense." She added more color onto her horns. "What do you think, brother? If she were Warrick's lover then she wouldn't be so desperate for me to cut ties with him, would she?" Selena paused. "It's an obvious test."

If she failed, they would retract their invitation. And it did also feel so *personal.*

And why did they even want the betting book? It was filled with nothing but a record of ridiculous pastimes of the masculine realm. In other words, they wanted a book filled with wagers of bored men.

Unless they wanted to use those wagers to blackmail certain people?

"Not so farfetched an idea . . ." She finished the other horn and leaned back slightly to observe her handiwork. "A much better representation."

Two maids returned with waistcoats in their arms, followed by Theodosia, who stopped dead in her tracks.

"What on earth are you doing?" her friend asked. "No, forget about that, what are you *wearing*?"

"Oh, this?" Selena glanced down at Warrick's robe. "Do you like it? It's my newest fashion craze."

"I shall pass," Theodosia said. "I prefer the Turkish trousers."

Selena stepped down from the stool, setting the palette and

brush aside on a table. "You are just in time." She waved a hand over the waistcoats the maids placed on the divan before excusing themselves. "We are snipping these up." A little revenge for daring to lock her in her chamber, regardless of the futility of it. She couldn't move on without getting him back.

"Your brother's, I presume."

Selena nodded.

"As much as I wish to join you in your rampage, I don't have much time to spare. I came to tell you that I shall be leaving London on the morrow."

Selena blinked away her surprise. "I never thought you'd take my advice."

Theodosia picked at one of the waistcoats. "It's good advice. I'm also taking the betting book. I can't have that thing in the house when my brothers return, and I want to escape their scolding altogether."

Ask for the book. "Is your mother joining you?"

Theodosia shook her head. "Which I'm forever grateful for. If I have to sit through one more cursed blind match up I might commit murder."

"She's just concerned for you."

"I know. I believe she is worried about my brothers' reactions to everything that's transpired so far this season, so she is allowing me to retire to our country estate."

"Well, that is good." *Now is your chance. Ask for the book.* "What time will you be leaving?"

"I'm not sure. Noon, perhaps. Why? Care to join me?"

Wouldn't that take care of everything and nothing at the same time! "I wish I could, but that would mean my brother would be following me."

"Please remain at home then." Theodosia grinned at the painting. "I'm surprised he didn't burst into the room to stop you."

"He has been avoiding me for the past day."

Theodosia nodded thoughtfully and took a seat against the

pile of clothing, glancing at the waistcoats with interest.

"Tempted?" Selena asked.

"A little bit."

Selena handed her the pair of scissors. "Try it. I promise you will find it rewarding."

Theodosia paused, but only for the briefest of seconds, before accepting the scissors, inspecting the various selections of waistcoats. A purple one caught her eye. "I think he wore this one when he hounded me in the cardroom that time."

Ah, yes. Selena recalled that night. It was the night Warrick had stood up for her to her brother. Her heart did a little somersault. "Well then, it's the perfect one to slice into pieces."

Theodosia nodded, and a moment later the sound of snipping filled the drawing room. A smile blossomed on her face. "You are right. It is rather rewarding."

"I told you so."

Theodosia continued to snip. "Have you heard anything about your club yet?"

Selena stared at the mountain of cloth before her. She should open her mouth and ask for the book. She should tell her friend about the demands of the club. She *burned* to confess everything about Warrick, what they had done, how she felt.

But she couldn't.

Theodosia wouldn't leave London then, and her brothers might catch up to her. No, she couldn't put this weight on her friend's shoulders.

"They are as elusive as ever." She supposed that still remained true. They were also more questionable. More than ever.

"Well, if you cannot find them, you can always start your own. Nothing is stopping you."

"Oh, and would you join my club?" Selena asked with a smile. The idea did hold some appeal.

"I might consider it if it's you. We can all gather and discuss how to deal with the men of our families."

"That would make for an interesting topic." Her suggestion?

Snip up their favorite clothes and turn them into devils.

Theodosia's eyes flicked to the painting of her brother again. "I must admit, my fingers are itching to apply some coal to his eyes and rouge to his cheeks."

"That . . ." Selena inspected the painting again. "That is a marvelous idea!" She pointed to the paintbrush. "Feel free to indulge your itchy fingers."

I can always ask for the book tomorrow before she leaves.

Yes, she still had time.

She would use every second.

WARRICK HAD BEEN furious many times in his life, but this was the first time he'd been livid to the point where his heart wanted to explode from his chest. *Kidnapped.* What infuriating madness was this? Who dared to kidnap two earls? To tie them up in a suspicions room and leave them to rot?

Whoever it was would surely pay for this.

This night had turned into a true, real-life nightmare. Just when one thing seemed to go right, another veered horribly wrong. He wanted to find Selena, but by the looks of it, they weren't escaping soon. He only prayed she was not in any danger.

"How tight are your bindings?" Warrick strained his arms against the rope that bound his hands behind his back. Nothing. He tried his legs, which were fastened to the chair. Nothing there either. He glanced down at the rope that circled his chest and secured him to the chair. These women weren't taking any chances.

Saville groaned, his voice straining. "Too tight to free myself." Saville glanced over. "They know how to bind a man."

Warrick grunted. "We should have gone for one of their pistols."

Saville shook his head. "I already got shot once. It still hurts like the devil."

Warrick hadn't forgotten about Saville's injury. "Don't push yourself too hard. I'll try loosening mine." They had to escape. The sooner the better. If not, then perhaps they could come to some sort of understanding with these women.

"Why did they cover our eyes anyway?" Saville asked as his gaze swept the room. "Any dolt could tell we're in a brothel."

Yes, and a cheap one at that. He surveyed the room. There wasn't much else besides a bed, a washstand, and the two chairs they were secured to. Red, time-worn wallpaper covered the chamber and had begun to peel, and a cold breeze escaped through a ghastly set of matching curtains. Other than that, the laughter of women, distant grunts, and the cloying scent of perfume mixed with that of old furniture gave their location away.

A tavern. A warehouse. A brothel. This group of women really had masked themselves well.

The door opened and the red-cloaked woman entered, followed by a big bulky man with a scar on his face. Warrick snorted, sneering, "I see you dressed to match the mood of the room."

She didn't rise to his taunt. "And I see you've settled in nicely. We would have taken you to the warehouse, but we decided to bring you here, where at least your limbs won't freeze from the cold. What do you think? Are you comfortable?"

Damn it. He knew that voice. *Think, man.*

"How gracious of you, madam," Saville mocked. "I shall be sure to show you the same sentiment when I'm freed."

The woman let out a faux sigh. "We never intended to involve you, Earl. Unfortunately, you were at the wrong place at the wrong time."

"So it's me you want?" Warrick asked. "Why? What insurance can I provide?"

"I'd also like to know the answer to that, since I am Selena's brother."

"Yes, but you are at odds with your sister. I daresay she

would let you rot here before she helped you."

"You haven't answered my question yet. What is that that you wish to gain from Selena?" Warrick demanded.

"I suppose it won't hurt to tell you." The women leaned closer. "We want the betting book."

Sure enough.

This damn book had come back to haunt him. If only it could be the ghostlike type of haunting instead of the kidnapping sort of haunting by a bunch of madwomen. Why could it not have been a bloody ghost haunting?

"You want the betting book?" Saville asked. "Why?"

"Let us just say there are wagers in that book that are of importance to us."

"How can our club's wagers be useful to you?" Warrick asked. This couldn't have anything to do with the heiresses. Something else was at play here.

"That is no business of yours."

"Well, you've set your sights on the wrong heiress," Saville said. "Selena doesn't have the book."

"My sources tell me otherwise. And even if she does not have the book, she has one day left to retrieve it."

That caught Warrick's attention. "You plan to keep us here until you get the book?"

"Of course. As I said before, you are our insurance that she hands over the book."

Warrick narrowed his eyes on the red hood obscuring a mystery face. "You don't plan to include in her your club, do you? Or else you wouldn't have gone as far as kidnapping to force her hand."

"What need would we have of her? She is of no use to us beyond the book." The woman shrugged. "Perhaps in a few years."

"Damn crazy bat!" Saville growled. "Why don't you show your face?"

"Yes," Warrick agreed. "I would like to see this face of my

lover."

"I'm hurt that you cannot recognize my voice." The woman pulled back the cloak and smiled at him.

Shock spread through Warrick.

Saville laughed. "Lady Ridgeland?" He looked at Warrick. *"She* is your lover?" *Your taste leaves something to be desired*, Saville's tone implied.

"She is not," Warrick bit out. She had only ever been a nuisance. "She never has been."

"Glad to hear it," Saville muttered under his breath, but not out of the earshot of anyone present.

Lady Ridgeland's smile froze. "Well, you might be glad to hear it, but Lady Selena was quite ready to believe in our connection—and quite shocked."

Warrick froze. "What the devil did you say to her?"

"Oh, just what you suspect, I'm sure."

"You mean you lied to her about us." Was that the true reason why Selena had acted so out of sorts when they last saw each other? But why hadn't she demanded answers from him? Given her character, she ought to have verbally boxed his ears.

"It's a lie for now."

Warrick sneered. "It's a lie forever."

"Needless to say, I felt spurned that day you rejected me at the Ashworth ball."

Warrick's mind raced. Had Selena believed this woman's words?

"Lady Selena has quite the decision to make, Warrick, dear," Lady Ridgeland continued. "She's been told that if she wants to join the club, she has to hand over the book and cut ties with you."

Warrick's temples ached. Had he known last night would take such a turn, he wouldn't have drunk brandy straight from the bottle. He could still feel the aftereffects of the alcohol, and his head had yet to fully clear.

"Why reveal your identity now?" Saville asked. "Is your little club not secret? What are you playing at?"

"Oh, I am but one member, and the power of denial is still strong in this world."

"Not when it comes to secrets," Warrick said. "All you need is a rumor."

"Yes, that's utter nonsense," Saville agreed. "And if you are but one member, it means you are not in charge. We would like to speak to whoever you are taking your orders from, please."

"I'm afraid that is not possible. I am tasked with procuring the book. How I do it is up to my own ingenuity, but no other members will be further involved."

"And would your founder be happy that you revealed yourself to us?"

"She is too busy to worry about such irrelevant matters."

"To worry about your games, you mean. Is that why you lied to Selena and demanded she cut ties with me?" Warrick demanded.

This troubled him more than he liked to admit. He cared little about the betting book, though he'd rather not have it fall into the hands of Lady Ridgeland. However, Selena might hand over the book for a chance to join.

But cutting him out of her life . . .

He didn't know where he stood with her. She had resisted marriage to him even while barging into his chamber. Her actions did not always align with her words. Hadn't she herself jested about fickleness? Then there was his failed confession. And most unnervingly, there was also the week *he* had cut ties with *her*. Though his intentions had been good, it hadn't been perceived that way. She could, he realized—she could very well cut ties with him. She could very well give him up to try to join a club she had declared she wanted to find above all else. The comprehension burned in his gut.

"My sister won't cut ties with Warrick."

Warrick glanced at Saville in surprise at this defense.

"Can you claim that with absolute certainty?" Lady Ridgeland asked with a smile that shot cold shivers down Warrick's spine.

"Yes," Saville said. "She loves him."

Warrick's eyes widened. "Saville," he said in a warning tone. *What are you doing? Don't goad the madwoman.* In the same breath, his heart did things it didn't normally do. Could Saville truly know such a thing about his sister?

"What?" Saville blinked at him innocently. "The two of you are more lovers than you are with this creature before us." He turned his attention back to Lady Ridgeland. "They kissed. We almost dueled over it."

Her eyes narrowed. "Your attempt to provoke me won't work."

"I even found her in his house, wearing his robe. Damn near stopped my heart."

"Saville," Warrick ground out. Did he realize he was aiding in his sister's ruin?

Lady Ridgeland huffed. "I suppose that shall make watching her choose us over him all the more rewarding."

Warrick scowled at her.

"Don't worry. I don't truly want you as my lover, Warrick, dear. I'm merely enjoying your anguish."

"Why the hell would you do such a thing?"

"Punishment, my dear." She sauntered over to him and traced a gloved finger over his jaw. "You see, when you reject a woman and make her feel like a dirty piece of cloth, there are consequences."

"That was never my intention," Warrick bit out, hating her hands on him.

"And yet that was how I felt."

He averted his gaze and grit his teeth. "How you feel is not my responsibility."

"I beg to differ," she said cheerily.

Warrick bit down on his teeth. There was no arguing with a woman who refused to own up to her actions.

Unbidden, thoughts of his curse surfaced. If he had wed before thirty, would he be dealing with such a crazed creature? But then, if he *had* married before thirty because of a curse, it wouldn't have been Selena.

And he very much wanted to marry her.

Chapter Eighteen

S ELENA LAY ON the sofa in the library, her gaze remained locked onto the arms ticking in her pocket watch—three seconds past noon. Theodosia must be departing by now.

No betting book.

No ties cut.

Although, it would appear that the ties had been cut—again—from Warrick's side. She hadn't heard anything of him in two days. Oddly, her brother hadn't shown his detestable face either. Had they dueled again and shot each other to death?

No, she would have gotten word by now.

Her gaze flicked to the crumpled note on the floor, the one that contained the date and time to meet that cloak woman with the grating voice. It had arrived this morning. She ought to have been elated at the invite. Giddiness should have invaded all her pores. Violins should have struck up a sweet tune in her head.

Why did she need to join a club to find herself anyway?

It's a super-secret club of women.

Yes, but it wasn't *that* secret anymore. It hadn't been a true secret the moment she herself had discovered them. Now her friends knew. And Warrick. The secret element didn't hold as much of an appeal anymore. Plus, they'd only invited her because they wanted something. Once again, she was overlooked as a person, seen only for her connections and what she could provide.

And *that* woman was one of them.

Who did she want to be anyway other than Saville's sister, heiress, lady? Wife? Spinster? Pariah?

Lady adventurer would be nice. Lady rebel had an interesting ring to it as well.

Selena sighed.

Lady Lazing Lazily was her title of today.

Her gaze fell on a cabinet opposite her. A bottle of golden liquor shone like a beacon through the glass pane. Was brandy not Warrick's preferred method for receiving peace? Selena could do with a touch of that—peace of mind.

Or the reawakening of her inner composure.

She rose and padded over to retrieve the bottle. Saville enjoyed his drink, just like Warrick. She wondered when he ever drank in the library. Her brother was much like her—he didn't read. With one exception: the papers.

He loved the gossip rags more than the busybodies of the *ton*. Come to think of it, Saville *was* one of the busybodies of the *ton*.

She uncorked the bottle and took a swallow without bothering with a glass, wandering back to the sofa, patting her chest as a trail burned from her mouth to her gut, holding back the urge to cough.

Lord, it was strong.

Did all brandy claim a person's breath like this? This was not peace.

But she took several sips more just to be sure and felt her mind begin to change on the subject.

This is not peace—this is life.

This was the sort of burn that could trail across all you believed to be true and turn the world to chaos and ash. But once that burning settled, the universe danced at your fingertips.

Selena let out a small laugh. Theodosia would give her the evil eye if that thought ever became known. She wiggled her fingers, sliding into a reclining position, swallowing another, smaller sip. Beer did, however, taste better. No contest.

A knock at the threshold bounced off the spines of the books in the library and echoed in her ears. "My lady?"

Selena strained her neck to peer over the sofa and settled down again. "What is it, Miles? Has my brother finally shown his face? Show him to his waistcoats."

"No, my lady. The Duke of Mortimer has requested an audience with you."

Selena bolted up right, bottle clutched to her breast. "The Duke of Mortimer?"

"Yes, my lady."

Interesting.

"Are you sure it's not someone impersonating the duke?"

"I am sure, my lady."

What business would the duke have with her?

The book.

Right, of course. She fell back down onto the pillows stacked at her back. The only reason anyone approached her—that cursed book.

She waved a hand in the air. "Show him in. Don't bring tea."

"Very well, my lady."

The solid click of footsteps approached, paused, and then continued until it stopped before the couch.

"Lady Selena."

Selena glanced over to the man but did not bother to rise. "Duke. Take a seat."

He stared at her a moment before lowering himself down into a chair. His gaze shifted to the bottle then back to her. "You seem to be going through a patch of difficulty, my lady."

"A patch." She reluctantly rose from slouching to a little less slouching. The man was a duke after all. He deserved *some* form of courtesy. "What brings a duke to our humble home?"

"Your brother."

A twist. "Saville is out and about."

"Warrick?"

More of a twist? "Should you not call on *his* residence if you desire an audience with the earl?"

He leaned forward so that his elbows rested on his knees. "Lady Selena, I'll be frank. Have you been searching for a club with a crest of roses and a sword?"

So, he knew, too. Why did she not find that surprising? She would not bother to deny it. At this point, nothing could astonish her anymore. Confuse her, yes, but not stun her. "You are quite impressive, Duke. You even know this much."

"I saw you at The Rose."

It took a moment for his words to sink through all the sips of brandy and connect to the alehouse she'd visited. "You were there?" Then it dawned on her. "The mysterious man in the corner with a cap on his head."

One single nod to confirm.

"I thought there was something familiar about you. Why were you there? Were you following me, too?"

"No." He sat back and crossed one leg over the other. "I've been investigating that club for some time."

"Aren't you also searching for the betting book?" The last words slurred a bit, which caught Selena off guard. Was she a bit foxed?

"Is the book in your possession?" Mortimer asked.

"No." Selena shuffled into a more upright seating position. "Not anymore."

He stared at her.

"What is with that gaze, Duke?"

"You are the first heiress to provide me that much information."

She nodded slowly. "I am an heiress."

His eyes crinkled at the corners, a faint hint of a smile. "You are."

Her head fell back onto the rest of the sofa. "I want to be more."

"Then be more," the duke said. "Why can you not be? You

seem to be more already."

Selena shifted her gaze to Mortimer. "Very well, Duke. Let us both be frank. This club is rather elusive." She took another small sip. "They want the book as well."

He sat up straight. "They reached out to you?"

"Don't look so surprised. Am I the only person in London who cannot fathom why I, and any other of the heiresses, did not receive an invitation to this secret club as soon as our scandal broke? They have been using it, after all. Why not include us?"

"You are still more pure than they are, Lady Selena. This is not an organization you can compare against White's as a social organization. This is one that operates in the shadows. You yourself said you find it strange, given all the chaos perpetrated at your hands, why you've not been invited."

"They must have their reasons."

"Then, did you even wonder at the sort of women that are members of this club?"

"Ladies. Free spirits. Women of the future." *That* woman.

"Ladies, yes. But dangerous ones. With illegal business dealings."

Truly? "Well now you want to make me join them more."

"Forgive me for pointing this out," he cocked his head, studying her, "but you do not look like you mean to join them."

She blinked. "I don't?"

"Your posture speaks of dejection. You did not bother to put on shoes. And this robe . . ." His observations turned speculative. "Is it your brother's?"

Selena's head snapped down.

Dear God. Was she still wearing Warrick's robe? She sniffed at the neckline. His scent had already disappeared.

"This is my *house* clothing."

The duke did not comment on it further. Instead, he went on, "Lady Selena, these women operate in the shadows for a reason. I cannot explain it clearly since part of the puzzle still eludes me and I'm inclined to avoid premature assumptions, but no good will come from giving them the book."

"Very well, very well." She pointed at the crumpled note. "An hour has passed since I was to meet them."

The duke's brows knit together, and he picked up the scrap. "This is helpful."

"Go on ahead." Selena plopped back down. "Tell them you are my answer to their demands."

"I am aware that this is none of my business, Lady Selena, but I've learned, in a world full of wretched beings—people with dubious intentions whose actions howl louder than your own thoughts—all you can do is trust your gut."

She sighed. "What is there to trust? My gut drove me to find and join this group."

"But you did not."

"Only because their second half of my membership fee was a bit too steep."

"Allow yourself to acknowledge your worth a little more, my lady. And then dance to the tune that moves you—and that tune alone. You don't need to change to prove anything if you do not wish to. After all, what is that but another version of allowing the opinions of others to dictate how you view yourself and what you do? You can simply stay as you are."

"As I am? Are you sure? I've been called the princess of trouble, you know?"

"Amongst other things," he agreed. "A person never carries just one title. If you are the princess of trouble, perhaps you should find your prince of trouble."

Selena scowled at the man. "Is that your indirect way of suggesting I get married?"

A chuckle. "I never mentioned marriage."

Such a sly man. If not marriage, then did he mean a scandalous relationship? Surely not. But . . .

She already had one.

She narrowed her eyes on the duke. Did he know about her and Warrick? It wouldn't come as a shock.

A footman knocked on the door. "My lady, excuse me for intruding."

"What is it now, Miles?"

"A note arrived for your ladyship. The person who delivered it said it was a matter of grave importance."

She motioned the footman over and accepted the note, breaking the seal and removing a card with a single sentence scrawled at the center.

Bring the betting book in exchange for your Earl of Warrick.

She flipped the card over. On the back, a time, location, and that annoying crest mocked her.

"Is something amiss?"

"Duke, I'm not sure if my eyes are deceiving me. Would you please read this note aloud?" She handed him the scrap of paper.

"Bring the betting book," the duke paused, "in exchange for your earl." His eyes lifted to meet hers. "Warrick."

"So I'm not mistaken." She shot upright. "I cannot believe they would go this far!"

"I will deal with this."

Selena leaped from the sofa, placing the liquor on the side table. "I will come, too."

He rose as well. "Lady—"

"I shall come whether you take me with you or not." Her chin rose. "And if you leave be behind, who is to say I won't accidentally thwart your strategy if I act alone?"

Silence. His gaze swept over her robe and then the half-full bottle.

She straightened her back. "Besides, I've dealt before with the woman who sent this note. You haven't. Trust me, Duke, you need me."

"Very well, but the moment danger presents itself, you leave."

Of course not! "What danger could possibly present itself?"

"According to my findings, I believe this organization is the most dangerous smuggling group in all of England."

They were . . . what?

⟫⟫⟫✖⟪⟪⟪

"MY ARSE HURTS."

Warrick shifted in the chair. How many hours had it been? It was impossible to keep count since at some point they had both nodded off.

He tested the tightness of his bindings. They weren't as tight this time. After Lady Ridgeland left them, the man with the scar on his face had stayed behind, so he could only stealthily attempt to loosen the rope that bound wrists. But even that hope was thwarted. They weren't total lunatics. Their captors had allowed them to do the necessary, but that meant each time the bindings were replaced they were rebound just as tightly as before.

Though the man wasn't in the room at the moment.

"Mine too." Saville rolled his neck. "We have been severely mistreated."

"Your sister . . ." Warrick trailed off. He didn't know how to express how he was feeling.

Saville understood. "We wouldn't still be here if she'd agreed to their conditions."

But did that mean she didn't? Wouldn't? Where they were in relation to the exact deadline remained uncertain, and he still worried he would be cast aside. Hah. Like a dirty cloth.

Warrick paused, noticing a familiar cravat on the floor. He gazed down at his gaping shirt. "Why the hell is my shirt open?"

"That crazy bat came in the middle of the night and removed your cravat, murmuring that you would be more comfortable without it. At least that is my vague recollection. You were deep in the land of nod." Saville lowered his chin to his chest. "I'm insulted. Why not remove my cravat too?"

Damn Lady Ridgeland. Who did she think he was?

"Am I being punished or am I cursed?" he muttered. "It's hard to tell at this point."

"Both, old chap. Both."

Warrick shot a glare at Saville, who taunted him back with a smirk.

"But it's not all that bad," Saville said, his eyes glinting. "What's wrong with a bit of skin?"

Warrick flinched at the reminder of their little intervention. "Well said."

Saville chuckled.

Warrick motioned to a stool in the corner. "How long as he been gone?"

"Not sure. He was gone when I woke up."

Warrick strained and wriggled against his bindings. They weren't as tight this time. "We need to get out of place."

"Would it be too much to ask for sustenance? My head is killing me. The behemoth could at least stuff some food in our faces after we relieve ourselves. They let us do that but not eat? Or drink? I could kill for a sip of *anything* right about now."

"It's worse because we had brandy." Warrick said. But with his mind clearer and his belly aching, his determination to leave this godforsaken place nearly exploded from his body in a surge of impatience. Even if he had to lose an arm, he would leave here today. "It's unlike them to leave us alone."

"Perhaps they are preparing food for us. They cannot let us starve."

"We'd be lucky if we were tossed a scrap of meat," Warrick muttered. He wriggled his wrists again. Since no one was keeping watch over them, if ever a chance was presented to escape, this was it. "I'm breaking free of this rope."

"I'd love to help, but my arm has gone numb. Sorry, old chap, you are on your own."

Warrick cast his friend a worried look. "How are you feeling?"

"Other than discomfort, pain, and a newfound level of annoyance, I'm doing well."

"That's a relief." A small mercy that his injury from the duel hadn't been more serious. But it did mean that escaping would be up to him. He focused his mind on one singular goal: breaking fee. Beads of sweat formed on Warrick's brow, and he strained against the damn rope. Every creak of the chair, every tug on the bond, urged him to strain a bit more.

"Christ, man, you're going to pop a vein if you keep doing that."

Warrick ignored him.

"We must look on the bright side, old chap. We shall be released soon."

"If we are, that would mean your sister has joined their ranks." And met their demands.

"I shall rake her over the coals after we leave this place," Saville said simply, then muttered, "they better not set up a meeting in a damn brothel."

"Unlikely. It will probably be the abandoned warehouse in Whitechapel."

"Whitechapel?"

"That's where Selena met Lady Ridgeland last time."

"I beg your pardon?" Saville's demanded. His voice turned to steel. "When the devil was this?"

"The day after you caught her at my house."

"*That* day?" Saville let out a rather foul curse. "I locked her in her chamber, for saints' sake."

"Did you honestly believe that would work?" Warrick bit out as he strained a bit harder. "Your *sister*?"

"I had some hopes," Saville muttered. "Futile hopes."

"At least you are aware."

"I shouldn't be surprised, given all the secrets that you've been keeping from me."

"This is your sister's secret, not mine."

"Well since you are sharing them, what other secrets have you been keeping for my sister? Since when has she been itching to join this club?"

Warrick relaxed his muscles, letting out a deep breath. He flexed his fingers. "I'm not sure."

"But you still found out about this little plan of hers."

Warrick sighed. Of all his friends, he'd have to be stuck with Saville. The head of nagging in their group. Where was the silent ghost from his foyer the other day? It seemed he had found rest and crossed over. "She told me the day of the Turkish trousers parade."

"Why the hell didn't you tell me Selena was searching for a damn dangerous club the moment after you found out?"

"Have you forgotten?" Warrick challenged back. "I am the one you assigned to protect her." He wanted to say more, vent his frustration, but he refrained. No good would come from tossing blame back and forth.

"Are you saying I should never have trusted you with my family?"

"I'm saying you should have protected your family yourself." Warrick glanced at Saville. "But look on the bright side, *old chap*—it's not too late to mend your wrongs."

"I get it," Saville ground out. "I am being punished alongside you." A short silence ensued before he sighed, before begrudgingly admitting, "You are right. I shouldn't have lobbed my responsibility onto you."

"Apology accepted." So long as they could go back to the way things were before the rift, Warrick didn't even need an apology from Saville. Any resentment he might have felt had long since disappeared. Only gratefulness remained.

"It shouldn't be this silent, should it?" Saville suddenly commented.

Warrick frowned. "I don't know."

"Are all brothels this quiet in the morning?"

As if summoned by the question, the door creaked open and the one woman Warrick never wanted to lay eyes on again waltzed into the room. *Her* again. She was followed by two women carrying trays in their hands.

"What happened to my shirt?" Warrick demanded even before Lady Ridgeland could part her lips to speak.

She smiled. "I thought you might be more comfortable. And if I am honest, I've fantasized about doing that for weeks. Even if it's just a hint of skin, it's a sight worth looking at."

"Now I'm really insulted," Saville muttered. "Is my chest not a sight worth looking at?"

Warrick shot her a glare. "Bedlam has a room for you, madam."

She laughed. "In any event, your Lady Selena has made her choice. She did not show up for our meeting."

Selena did not show?

Selena didn't show.

The tension that had gripped his body slowly trickled out in a breath of relief. Did that mean she refused to cut ties with him? Perhaps she didn't believe this vixen was his lover.

"I see you are quite pleased. Of course, this is not ideal," Lady Ridgeland sauntered over to him and raked a finger over his chest. Distaste filled him. "Luckily for us, we have the two of you. So we sent her a missive to inform her that we have her beloved earl."

He stilled.

Saville gave a very loud snort. "And if my sister misses *that* assignation, it means . . ." He grinned. "Well, who is to say what it means? What would happen then?"

Warrick blinked at his friend. His silent mockery had been just as loud as that exaggerated snort. His lips twitched.

"*Then* we would send news that we have her *brother* as well. That might do the trick, I believe. It would be rather shocking if she did not respond to her sibling being caught in our web as well."

Loathsome woman.

"My sister won't show because she won't believe you have Warrick, and neither will she believe you have me."

"Are you certain? You've been gone for two days."

"Selena is smart." Warrick squared his shoulders and lifted his chin, sending her a slight yet confident smile. "She won't fall for your tricks. If she doesn't show, it means she will not be blackmailed by you. She must have changed her mind about joining your mysterious little club. I wonder how the club will feel about your failure."

Lady Ridgeland's smile took on that syrupy—sickening—edge as she stepped up to grab his shirt with both her hands and yank, ripping it right down to his navel.

"What the hell are you doing?" Warrick roared.

She leaned in even closer. "I'm not in the best mood, Warrick dear. But looking at your body along with your face lined in anger will make me feel better in no time at all."

"You better hope," Warrick ground out between clenched teeth, "by the time I am free from these binds, you are not within my sight."

I'll drag you to Bedlam myself.

Chapter Nineteen

"**P**ERHAPS HE IS cursed after all."

The duke glanced at her. "I beg your pardon?"

Selena shook her head, indicating she'd spoken to herself, and peered from the top of her horse at the warehouse she recognized all too well. She had decided to change into her Turkish trousers, which made riding a horse astride more comfortable than riding sidesaddle.

She scowled at the building.

How unoriginal. Just like their crest.

A twinge of worry—small and prickling—nudged at her when she considered the possibility of Warrick having been kidnapped because of her.

By his supposed lover.

Her annoyance flared again, obliterating any concern that had bubbled to the surface. How could he get caught? He had some brain to go with all his brawn! How did this happen to an *earl* of all people? Titles truly didn't mean all that much, did they? The meaning attached was the meaning one gave.

"I still don't understand why we did not show up for the meeting. They have Warrick." More to point, *that woman* had Warrick. Not that it bothered her. She didn't believe they were actually lovers. He loved *her*. He could only be *her* lover.

And she didn't want anyone other than that brawny man. She

had decided.

Selena threw her head back with a groan. She was lying to herself. It did bother her.

It bothered her a lot.

If fact, it bothered her more than anything else had ever bothered her before. Two days of suppressed bother was threatening to erupt!

"Patience, Lady Selena," Mortimer answered. "Also, word to the wise, you shouldn't drink straight from the bottle. Brandy tastes better in a glass."

"I'll keep that in mind." She pointed to the building. "And they have already arrived. How can you be patient? Just how patient do you want me to be?"

"You are tipsy, so remain calm. Just a little bit more patience."

"Duke."

"Yes?" Amusement.

"I'm not anything of the sort. And also, I don't know if you have learned this in all your years of life, but I shall tell you now, for the sake of your happy future, never tell a woman to remain calm. It has the opposite effect."

"I see. Then, by all means, lose your composure as you deem fit."

"Are you mocking me?"

"I wouldn't dream of it."

Selena snorted. Silence fell between them, and she didn't think he would say anything more, but he suddenly noted, "Your earl isn't here."

Selena turned to him. "Warrick's not here?"

"The women in cloaks arrived, which means they weren't here from the start."

"Warrick is not here," she repeated flatly.

He lifted a brow, then shook his head. "You understand, do you not?"

Understand? No, she didn't understand anything more! How

had her ability to deduce the obvious hit such an all-time low? *Could she be tipsy?* She shook her head twice, collecting all her thoughts, her mind racing over the possibilities of what him not being here might mean. "Then we are waiting for them to leave," she guessed. "You want us to follow them back to their true lair."

"Correct."

"If they are so dangerous, shouldn't we inform the law?"

"I am the law."

She opened her lips, then shut them again. The loftiness of this man took arrogance to a whole other level.

Very well, Duke. You are the law. But it seemed the duke's sleuthing abilities were as dismal as hers. Otherwise, "How have you not been able to find this club before?"

"They've never come out of the shadows so boldly before. And I'm mostly interested in the founder. The Madam they call her. Now," sharp eyes locked with hers, "all thanks to you, to you heiresses, I am closer to unmasking her."

"You should thank Warrick and his gang, too, I suppose, but I shall accept the thanks. I am happy to oblige, though I am curious. You have been searching for the betting book."

"I have."

"Yet you have not asked me for it. Why not?"

"Would you hand it over to me?"

The horse shifted beneath her. "Knowing what I know now, perhaps."

He nodded. "I've decided for the time being, the book is better off with the heiresses."

Oh? "Why on earth would you decide that?"

"Call it a hunch." His lips quirked upward, only a bit, but a welcome change from his usually cold face. "When I require the book, I shall come retrieve it."

"I love your arrogance."

"I don't call faith in my abilities arrogance, my lady."

"Is asking for something considered an ability?"

"For a man, of course."

Selena shook her head, looking off into the distance. This part of town was quiet, but not without peddlers roaming about. Curious glances were sent their way, but everyone gave them a wide berth. Selena glanced at the duke from the corner of her eye.

He told her to stay calm, but with each second slipping by them, her impatience taunted her and made her question all the decisions she had made of late. All the ones she hadn't made. All the ones she'd avoided.

This was what happened when you left important matters up to fate and timing. Had she missed her time?

"They're leaving," the duke said in a low voice.

Selena perked up, burrowing deeper into the hood of her cloak. "After only after ten minutes? Is that not a bit premature? What if I am just late?"

"Four went in; only three walked out. They must have left someone behind on the chance you'll still appear."

Selena nodded, and when the cloaked figures entered a carriage and set off, she and the duke nodded at each other and nudged their horses to follow in their wake. A red cloaked figure had been amongst them. They followed the carriage to the fringes of Covent Garden where it finally drew to a halt, and Selena watched as the three women excited the carriage and entered an establishment across the street.

The Rose.

"Of course it's named The Rose," she muttered. The unoriginality continued.

"A brothel." Mortimer's curled his lips. "This is their lair?"

"An alehouse, an abandoned warehouse, and now a brothel. The women of this club sure do make their rounds."

"I presume the brothel is used as a front, just like the tavern."

"Still, ladies who use a brothel as a lair?" Selena was supremely disappointed in this club. "Where is their class?"

"This isn't about class. It's about money." He glanced at her. "You should remain outside."

"Not a chance, Duke." Warrick was in there. She wasn't about to wait outside and leave his rescue up to fate.

"This is no place for a lady."

"Now is not the time to develop scruples." She dismounted her horse. "You already brought me along. In any event, I've never been in a brothel before. I am quite curious." Would it be tasteful or seedy? Debauched or opulent? Would her earl be in one of the rooms? Would there be women? She hadn't forgotten about all the tales she overheard throughout the years.

But that wasn't what was important here. She'd followed the duke's instruction and been patient about waiting outside the warehouse and following the women here. But Warrick and her brother had been missing for two days. Two days that she'd been none the wiser about their fate! She had been patient long enough.

"Fine, but please take care of your safety."

"Oh, you do not have to worry about me, Duke."

She could hold her own.

WARRICK HADN'T LOST an arm.

Neither had he escaped this godforsaken place. But that didn't stop him from continuing to try. His wrists burned, but just a little more loosening and he would be able to free his hands. They had been stuck in this room for hours on end. His arms hurt. His legs hurt. And his arse had finally lost all feeling. And damn it, worry clamped his gut tightly.

"She must have a plan . . ." Not knowing Selena's plan, her whereabouts, her doings, however, drove him damn near insane. This was the first time in weeks he hadn't received any report on her. The first time he had felt truly separated from her. Even when she'd rejected him over and over, he hadn't felt as distant as he did sitting here tied to a chair.

"Who?" Saville asked. "My sister?"

"Yes. There must be a reason she didn't go to that meeting."

"She will show up for me," Saville said, a hint of pride lacing his voice.

"You sound supremely optimistic, yet I'm not so sure. Selena is no simpleminded woman. She also doesn't think like your average lady." She didn't accept things for what they were. She loved to challenge. She loved to defy.

"She will probably convene all the heiresses to deal with this club and cause another scandal," Saville remarked.

Maybe. "But this is no simple club, either."

Saville cracked a mocking smile. "You only realized this now?"

"No, I've thought so for a while," Warrick admitted. "Ever since I found Selena in a tavern on the docks. One they presumably own."

"*Tavern?*" Saville shot a glare his way. "My sister? When the hell was this?"

"Does it matter at this point?" It was all in the past.

"I am throttling you both when we settle this madness. A tavern? What the devil was she thinking?" Dark eyes narrowed on him. "Was Lady Theodosia there, too?"

"Wouldn't you know if she had been?"

"Not necessarily. The chit commissioned a girl with similar features to lead me around the nose for an entire day. Who knows how many times she made a fool of me."

"And you fell for that?" He wondered if *he* had fallen for that, too. No. He didn't believe he would ever mistake Selena for anyone else.

"They looked alike," Saville defended.

"Very well, they looked alike."

Saville's stomach gave a loud growl. He let out a deep sigh. "Hungry."

"Why didn't you eat the sandwiches they brought earlier?" Warrick sent a sidelong glance his friend's way.

"Why didn't you?" Saville shot back. "Have a stranger feed me? No thank you."

Yes, Lady Ridgeland had gone out of her way to make a mockery of them, demanding they open their mouths and say "ah." Feed them? Who did she imagine they were? He'd rather starve to death than take a morsel of food from her hand.

The door opened and soft laughter followed.

As expected, the moment you talk of the devil it appears.

"Do you have a damn ear to the door, madam?" Saville echoed his sentiments.

She sauntered over to him with a smile. "You must be starving, dear. Are you sure you don't want a bite to eat?"

"Lost my appetite the moment you revealed your face."

Her smile slipped. "What a rude thing to say to a lady."

"A lady?" Saville snorted. "A title that does not suit the likes of you, madam."

"Perhaps I shall send you to another room, earl. Your voice is quite unpleasant to the ears."

Warrick shot a warning glance at his friend. *Keep your mouth shut.* He did not want to be alone with this unhinged woman in a chamber. In a brothel, no less.

Saville averted his gaze with a scowl.

Warrick drew a deep breath. "You never struck me as a fool, Lady Ridgeland. But this—are you sure you are ready for the consequences?"

"Of course, dear." He flinched at Lady Ridgeland's purring tone.

"Stop calling me that."

"But I do so enjoy your death stares whenever I do. It makes me want to punish you even more than a pinch on the arse here, a candelabra there."

His veins turned to ice. "You were behind those incidents?"

"You rejected me so many times; I had to find a way to vent my frustration."

Heat rushed to his chest as shock sparked through his body,

but only momentarily. In its wake, relief remained. He'd been *punished*. By *her*. A living, breathing woman. Not random acts brought on by any curse. He didn't have to speculate anymore. However, that still didn't excuse her damn actions. "You are a bloody nuisance to society, madam."

"Oh, don't be like that, it was nothing serious."

"Why target me, then?" Warrick demanded. "There are many men who would be happy to give you what you ask. Why did you latch onto me?"

"Because unlike those men, you didn't fall for my abundant charms, and I do so enjoy a challenge." She trailed a finger over his exposed skin. "And you do have a body that is to my taste."

If Warrick had any hair left at all after this, he would bloody rejoice. "Do not touch me." He felt damn violated.

"Are you a lightskirt, madam?" Saville asked from the side.

Her head snapped to the right. "What did you just call me?"

Saville shrugged. "I didn't call you anything. I merely asked if you are a doxy. I mean, it's not that farfetched a question. You brought us to a brothel, and now you are fondling a man against his will."

"Men have done far worse to women over the ages."

"Not all men, and that doesn't excuse your behavior. You do realize when we will leave this place, there will be consequences for your deeds."

"You underestimate us, my lord." Her hand paused. "It shall be your word against all the people who will vouch for my whereabouts. You are merely two men who went on a two-day run of debauchery."

The chafing of his wrists and ankles would prove otherwise, Warrick thought darkly, but said, "So you have thought of everything then."

She smiled at him. "You shall find I am a very thorough woman."

And you will find, madam, that I am a very unforgiving man.

"Shall I place a kiss on this body of yours? Show you what

you have been missing?"

"Don't you dare," Warrick growled, just as a knock sounded on the door. He'd never been so relieved by such a timely interruption.

"Enter." Lady Ridgeland straightened, but her paws didn't leave his body, only shifted to his shoulder. He would need a bath—two, no, three baths—to wash away her touch.

A woman entered.

"I thought Turkish trousers were the latest craze," Saville muttered. "Seems to be cloaks with big, awful hoods."

"What is it?" Lady Ridgeland asked. "Do you have news of that wretched girl?"

"That wretched girl," the woman pulled back the cloak from her face, "brings news of herself in person."

The breath left Warrick's lungs.

"Selena?" Saville found his voice before Warrick could utter even one. She was such a beautiful sight. "How did you find us? No, what the hell are you doing in a brothel?"

Her eyes swept over the both of them, falling on his exposed chest and then flicking to the hand of Lady Ridgeland resting on his shoulder before locking with his eyes.

Confound it.

What was with this timing?

Her gaze turned to Saville. "I could ask the same of you, brother. Is this a kidnapping or a new rage in roleplay?"

"What the devil do you know of roleplay?" Saville asked, yet it came out as more of a mutter than a demand.

"I'm impressed, Lady Selena," Lady Ridgeland said. "You didn't respond to our missives so that you might follow us back here."

"Oh, I cannot claim all the credit. I had help. A voice of patience. A voice of calm. A voice of a man even more determined to find you than I was."

An unfamiliar feeling spread within Warrick's chest.

A man. *What man?*

Lady Ridgeland titled her head to this side in thought. "There are many men who court my favor."

"Then why go to such lengths? You know kidnapping is a crime. One you shall pay for dearly."

"We shall see about that."

What damn man?

Chapter Twenty

S ELENA REMOVED A pistol from waistband and pointed it at the woman before her, who she finally recognized as Lady Ridgeland. Wife to the Earl of Ridgeland and a distinctly unpleasant woman. "Let us see your hands. Any sudden movements, and I shoot."

Lady Ridgeland slowly lifted her hands away from her body, Warrick's body, palms up. "Careful now, you wouldn't wish to act on an impulse you might regret later."

"I assure you, I won't."

Honestly!

Selena had mistakenly thought nothing could surprise her anymore, yet the picture before her had her blinking—inwardly— not once, not twice, not even thrice. If any tipsiness remained, she had completely sobered up at the sight of Warrick, tied to a chair, muscles on display beneath a gaping shirt! Just what had happened here?

All in good time, Selena.

Now was not the time for her curiosity to bloom. Now was the time to stand firm, point a pistol, and wait while the duke made short work of any lingering threats in the establishment. His title alone had been enough to scare nearly everyone witless when they'd entered.

"Selena! You brought a bloody pistol?"

Selena cast a quick glance to her brother. "Of course. How else do you rescue someone?" Her gaze swept over the room. "I must admit, I am quite surprised at the cheap interior. I thought the rooms would be flusher and a bit bawdier." She turned to Lady Ridgeland. "You must be the cloaked woman from the warehouse."

"I am," Lady Ridgeland said. "I see you don't have my book. Is it with this man you spoke of? I'm rather curious as to this man searching for me."

"I'm rather curious too," Warrick muttered.

A figure filled the doorway. "Then allow me to appease your curiosity." He arched a brow at Selena's pistol, and then at Lady Ridgeland, his eyes taking on a steel edge.

"Ah, Duke, you are just in time," Selena said. She patted the duke on the shoulder, eyeing Warrick. "Mortimer offered to help me find the club, and he did."

"Mortimer." Warrick's gaze shifted between the duke and Selena, and for one miniscule second, she rejoiced in the emotion she saw flash across his face. Her gaze flicked briefly to his bare chest before meeting his gaze. Drat her heart. Always skipping beats when their eyes collided.

What on earth was this feeling?

She loved him, she loathed him. She wanted to punch him and hug him. He was both her longest infatuation and her most ardent opponent. Selena was conflicted in so many ways and about so many things. But one thing she was certain about, one thing she had no doubt about.

She wanted Warrick.

In her life.

Her heart.

Her bed.

She would *never* cut ties with him.

She blinked. Now was not the time to be thinking about such things!

The duke stepped forward. "I'll take the pistol," he said, and expertly transferred the weapon to his hand.

Selena blinked again, stepping aside. *That's what you get when you're distracted by a man.*

"It's over, Lady Ridgeland," Mortimer announced.

Lady Ridgeland. "Today, perhaps. It's such a shame, as I've been having so much fun." She tapped Warrick's shoulder. "With this one in particular."

Warrick scowled. "It's not what it looks like."

"Oh?" Selena asked, arching a brow. "What does it not look like? Because from where I am standing, you are bound to a chair and bare chested with a woman pawing you." She glanced at her brother. "And with an audience on top of that. Quite the compromising position you find yourself in."

"Not willingly."

Selena bit down on the inside of her lip. Seeing him with her own eyes, though he was a bit disheveled, some of her good spirits returned. And now that the duke was here, he could remove *that* woman.

"That is enough." Lady Ridgeland said to the duke, "You have no power here, Your Grace. Elias will return any moment now. I suggest you leave before he does." Those eyes settled on Selena. "And I suggest you retrieve that book for me."

"If you are referring to the man with the scar," Mortimer said, "he is already in my custody."

Selena glanced over her shoulder. "He is? When? I thought you said you weren't going to call for Runners."

"Not Runners. My men. They've been following us from the start."

The man left nothing to chance. "Why did I even ask?" Selena muttered. She turned to Lady Ridgeland. "I have a question. What was the goal of the trousers?" She wiggled a leg. "What did you gain from that parade, if you can even call it that?"

Lady Ridgeland let out a huff. "Who are you to ask me questions about things that aren't any of your business?"

A few days ago, Selena would have faltered at the question.

She'd started this journey questioning her selfhood. But now, this very moment, she had no hesitation whatsoever.

"Who am I?" She strode up to Lady Ridgeland. "I am Selena Savage. And I have every right to question your business."

"You are nothing but—"

A swift, crisp crack echoed through the room. Lady Ridgeland head jerked to the side; her hand clasped her cheek in shock. Selena's palm burned. But it was a satisfying burn.

The screech came an instant later, "How dare you?"

"You touched my earl. Also kidnapped him. And you lied to me about being his lover." Selena looked at Mortimer. "She's all yours."

Mortimer motioned with his hand and two men strode in.

"The trousers and parade were a distraction," the duke answered her question as his men secured Lady Ridgeland in two firm grips. "Everyone's attention was focused on the misbehaving women of the *ton*, allowing movement of smuggled goods from the underbelly of London to the upper classes."

"You have no proof." Lady Ridgeland struggled against the two men. "Do not touch me."

"How would you know, madam?" Mortimer asked. Cool words. Utterly chilling.

If ever a woman with a death wish lived, Lady Ridgeland would be that woman today, for she simply glared at Selena and demanded, "Where is the book?"

Ignore a duke? Hah! At your own detriment.

Selena scoffed. "Why do you want it so badly?"

"Their organization has long been employing the betting book to smuggle in the form of wagers." The duke's cold tone dropped to a new degree of chilliness. "The women use their husbands."

"This is worse than I thought," Warrick muttered.

"A damn atrocity," Saville agreed. "Let's see if I don't pick this organization apart until there is nothing left of it!"

"That is why I am here," Mortimer said.

"The wagers in that book have always belonged to us." Lady Ridgeland sneered. "We've been controlling the outcomes for decades now. It's a rather profitable business. One you and your friends ruined when stealing the book and distributing copies all over London."

"So, *this* is why you didn't want to let me into your little club? Revenge?"

"On the contrary. The reason you never received an invitation is because you do not qualify."

"Because I don't have a husband that you can control, correct?" Selena crossed her arms. "Well, even if I did have a husband, and even if I did have a scandal or two to hold over his head, I would never hand it over to you. So, you are right, I suppose I'll never qualify. But then, who wants to live like you?"

"You mean who would want power and money when they are the driving forces of the world? Honestly, girl. Besides, our husbands are also winning in this situation. The money benefits their pockets as well. That is why they never go against us. That is why you can't do this to me, Duke."

Lord save her.

Had Selena stepped into an alternate world where nothing made sense? She cast a glance to Warrick. He made sense. He made everything worthwhile.

"I can do whatever I please," Mortimer said.

"Not against us," came her sneer. "Our network is too big."

"Just like your mouth," Selena said. "Even if the Duke of Law doesn't have much evidence, you've given him more than enough leads today. And he has your betting book."

The woman's eyes widened. "You gave the book to the duke? I don't believe it!"

"Why not? I arrived with him today." She raised a brow at him. "Although, you are a member of White's. You had access to the book all along."

"That their organization used the book only became known to me a few weeks before it was stolen. I'd been studying who was placing wagers and when they were placed." His gaze raked the two bound men. "Then a list appeared, and the book *dis*appeared."

"And to think that I searched for what I thought was a club because I was searching for meaning."

"What a lousy thing to search for," the lady jabbed.

"Yes, well, as lousy as it may sound, I didn't know how else or onto what else to latch myself. How wrong I was. And shame on you," Selena stabbed back. "Luckily, it has recently occurred to me that I've always been in possession meaning." She'd just been slow in rediscovering hers. *I am already all I need to be.*

"Take her away," the duke ordered. "And bring me Lord Ridgeland."

"You can't do this to me," Lady Ridgeland screeched, struggling against the two men. "You can't do this to me!"

"You kidnapped two gentlemen of the realm," Mortimer said, dusting off the sleeves of his jacket. "If nothing else, that is a serious offense."

"What a satisfying sight," Saville said with a grin.

"I found these men like this! You have no evidence that I kidnapped them!"

"I have the notes that were sent to Lady Selena. I'll have the testimonies of the staff in the brothel within the hour, but most importantly, Lady Ridgeland, I have ears."

"Yes," Selena piped up. "And the duke's ears are all he needs. The duke is the law." She looked to the duke. "You go, I shall take care of my brother and Warrick."

Mortimer nodded, inclined his head at them, and strode from the room.

Selena turned to the men still tied to the chairs. "Well, this is a sight I'd love to capture in a portrait."

"Are you going to untie us or not? My arse is numb. I cannot believe you did not notice I was missing for two days! What if I had been harmed?" Saville complained.

She crossed her arms over her chest. "Weeds don't perish so

easily."

Her brother's face went blank. "Did you just call me a weed?"

"I borrowed a phrase from Theodosia."

His eyes narrowed. "Did *she* call me a weed?"

"You shall have to take it up with her."

Saville craned his neck to look toward the open door. "Is Theodosia here as well?"

"No, of course not. I would never involve her in matters she has no interest in."

"Good," Saville said. "Now can you please unbind us? I can't feel any part of my body anymore." He paused. "What the devil, are you wearing those Turkish trousers again?"

Selena shrugged and her cloak parted further to reveal a pair of Turkish trousers, covered by the prominent robe she still wore. He hadn't noticed them back at Warrick's house, but he noticed them now? "You should be more worried about your clothing than mine."

He jolted. "Why? Don't tell me you cut up my waistcoats again!"

She shrugged. "Theodosia and I had a spot of fun."

"Selena."

One word, that was all it took to set her heart aflutter. They hadn't seen each other in two days, and she could hardly drag her gaze from him.

Her brother's voice faded into the background.

WARRICK STARED AT Selena, unable to tear his gaze away. Anyone who saw her now would think she was a scandalous mess. She was. A glorious, scandalous, mess. And she'd arrived with Mortimer, tall, handsome, and in possession of an amazing head of hair.

He couldn't help but feel a tiny twinge of jealousy.

Just a tiny twinge.

What had Mortimer asked him back at the tavern? Something about whether Warrick would warn him off if he were to approach Selena about the book. He hadn't, since he didn't mind that, but *this* situation—running about town together dressed in those damn trousers again, entering a brothel together—stabbed at his gut.

Just a little bit . . .

And what was "the duke of law" all about?

"Why are you here with Mortimer?" Warrick asked as though they were the only ones in the chamber.

"He arrived on my doorstep, and with impeccable timing, I might add. We received the note that demanded the book in exchange for you." Her gaze trailed over him.

"Impeccable timing, indeed."

She strode over to him. "Envious?"

"God, yes." A touch. "Interacting as though you've been friends for ages. A pat on the shoulder. A private joke. Smart smiles."

She laughed. "But I am here for you."

The pinch in his chest was replaced by warmth.

"Helloooo," Saville drawled. "We are still tied to chairs!"

Warrick ignored him. "Did you really hand over the betting book to him?"

"I already passed it along to Theodosia at her birthday party," she admitted. "He can claim it at any time to aid his investigations."

"Theodosia has the book now?" Saville perked up.

"Yes," Selena said. "Why are you here with my brother? Did not the two of you have a falling out?"

"Can we discuss this later?" Saville wriggled against his binding. "Untie us."

Warrick glanced at Saville. "We probably shouldn't untie your brother for time being."

Saville's head whipped to him. "Why the hell not?"

Warrick's eyes locked with Selena's. "He wants to throttle us both."

Selena reached over to test Saville's bindings. "How unfortunate that these ropes are bound so tightly. How ever can I, a simple lady, untie them?"

"Selena," Saville said sternly. "Untie us."

She laughed, and Warrick shut his eyes for a moment. A beautiful contrast to the last time they saw each other. He'd never been so thirsty for the sight of her as he had been today. When she had slapped that madwoman across the face, the pride that had swelled in him had rivalled any he'd ever experienced for himself.

"I shall untie you in a moment. I have some matters to settle." She trailed a finger over Warrick's jaw. "Lady Ridgeland seems . . . preoccupied by you."

"That is no business of mine. I have done nothing to encourage her madness."

A soft, quizzical brow rose.

"*Nothing.*"

"Very well, I believe you."

"I have your trust just like that? You don't doubt me?" God, that felt good.

She pursed her lips before replying thoughtfully. "Nothing is ever without any doubt, but I doubted her more than I doubted you."

"How touching," Saville said. "Now untie me."

"Shall I have charges brought against her?" Warrick asked. He didn't know what plans Mortimer had, but he wanted to see that woman rot in prison or rot in Bedlam. Either would do.

"Don't worry, the duke will handle her."

Warrick's gaze narrowed. "You trust him that much?"

"I have faith in his abilities, and I trust that people kneel to his title." She sent a meaningful glance at the door. "Even when the reverence is slow in coming."

"I have a title, too."

She grinned at him. "Yes, you do." She leaned closer to whisper in his ear. "I might kneel for you."

Warrick groaned. Inside, his heart hammered.

"I can hear you," Saville said, his voice dry as dust. He glared at the two of them. "Untie me. Now. So that I can escape this torture."

"I don't mind if you hear us." She pinched Warrick's chin between her fingers and gave him her full attention. "You said I must take responsibility."

Warrick's whole body erupted in goose flesh. "I did." His voice came out hoarse.

She lowered and fiddled the ropes, slowly undoing that woman's handiwork. The moment his legs were free and she stood up again, he stretched his legs out to capture hers, pulling her to him. With a gasp, she tumbled onto his lap. He grinned. "Reach around me to untie my hands, as well."

"What the hell I am seeing?" Saville muttered.

She laughed. "Why, I am merely untying Warrick."

"You better not untie me at all. God, I've chills all over my body."

Warrick ignored the man, his eyes only on Selena. "You said something about taking responsibility."

She nodded. "Yes, I am taking responsibility for you and, since we now find us in such a compromising position, I demand that we marry."

"What changed your mind?" Warrick asked. Every limb was screaming from being tied for so long, and yet all he wanted to do was pounce on Selena and claim every last breath she had.

"*I did.*" She laughed with a short shake of her head. "Who am I? I am Selena Savage. I'm a woman that follows her heart. It simply occurred to me that I can never be stuck in my brother's shadow as his sister or your shadow as your wife. I am just too brilliant for shadows." She leaned close to him, their lips almost touching. "So, you must marry me. And I will need your answer soon."

"And if I refuse?"

"I'll demand your reason."

"I'm holding out for love." Warrick's voice went gruff. "I'll only marry for love."

"You are in luck. I'll only marry for love, too." She grinned at him, her hands all over his chest. "Riches, titles, the world is mine to claim, Phineas. Will you join me?"

Did she even need to ask? "Hell, yes."

"Thank God," Saville said from the side. "Now can you please untie me so that I can cast up my accounts elsewhere in peace?"

Selena glared at her brother. "You are ruining this moment for me."

"You shouldn't be having this moment here, with us being tied, in a brothel!"

Warrick freed her from his legs so that she could unfasten his hands. The moment they were loose, he slowly rose from the chair, his bones cracking as he stretched out his arms and legs. He didn't waste any time. In one smooth motion, he hoisted her into his arms and strode to the door. "Your brother is right. A brothel is no place for a lady."

"What about me?" Saville called out after them from his chair. "A brothel is no place for a gentleman, either!"

"I'm sorry, old chap, bear it a bit longer."

"You cannot be serious!"

"I will send one of the women of the establishment to you soon," Warrick tossed over his shoulder.

"You blackguard! Who is to say what might happen to me?"

Warrick stepped from the room and quickened his pace to leave that bellowing voice behind.

"He is going to be furious with you," Selena said with a small laugh.

"He'll get over it. I'd rather not have an audience to provide commentary for what comes next."

"Oh? What comes next?"

"Me and you. Alone. Kissing. Loving."

Forever his.

Chapter Twenty-One

S ELENA WRIGGLED AGAINST her earl in her bed.

Her Warrick.

Her betrothed.

Her man.

She liked that last title best. Simple. To the point.

Her man.

Selena was learning that happiness was not always what a person gained in life, but rather found in the voyage one took to achieve those rewards. And yet, who was to say when that voyage ended? Her own journey was still very much in motion. She was still en route breeching boundaries, overstepping norms, and hurtling through points of no return.

She also plucked a few rewards along the way. One of which was in her bed.

Selena kissed his shoulder.

A delightful grunt. "We are crossing the line again," Warrick breathed against her skin as he trailed kisses along her neck before kissing the inside of the palm that had slapped Lady Ridgeland. "Your brother will be here soon."

"I love crossing the line with you." Crossing lines was what they did best. Soon enough, they'd be wed and there would be few lines left, so Selena wanted to enjoy every single one.

"Are you saying we've crossed so many lines, crossing one

more won't hurt?"

"Exactly that." She nipped at his lips. "Don't you love crossing them with me?"

"Too much."

"You know," she said teasingly, "you started it first."

"That's debatable, princess."

She laughed. "Then, let's debate some more." She traced a suggestive finger down his arm.

"I have a better idea," he breathed, his tongue slowly trailing her lower lip. "Let's elope. Because I can't stand the thought of living apart from you."

She arched her neck back to glance at him. "You don't have to live apart from me. You can move into my chamber until we marry."

"I want you in *my* chamber. *My* bed. A place where Saville doesn't prowl."

She laughed. "He doesn't prowl there?"

"Good point."

She snuggled closer. "Isn't eloping a bit too much?"

"No." He trailed his thumb over her lower lip. "We can have fun traveling."

"You mean you will have me all to yourself." She wasn't opposed. She could do with a bit of a reprieve from the strain and pace of these past days.

The kisses continued to trail. "I can seduce you in a carriage. In a field outside." He lowered his voice. "Everywhere."

"Is that what you mean by having fun?" She lifted onto her elbows to stare him down. "We shouldn't have *too* much fun before we marry or else there will be no more fun to be had, will there?"

"I disagree. There will always be fun to be had when I'm with you."

"Insatiable."

He tugged at her trousers. "In my heart we are already man in wife."

She laughed. "Well, I shall still require paperwork to make it legal. After all, knaves are best put on a leash." She nuzzled her nose against his neck.

"Leash?" He grinned, lifting his head. "Selena Savage, I didn't know you were into that sort of play. I'll oblige you."

"I'm not, you beast."

"But now you have put the picture in my mind. How ever shall you remove it?" His hand moved along her leg. "And didn't I tell you never to wear these trousers again and what do you do? Wear them and go off with a duke."

"On your rescue expedition."

"I don't care. Take them off."

Before she could tease him further, a voice bellowed through the house.

"Selena! Selena Savage! You are dead!"

Warrick stilled, and Selena sat up straight. She glanced at him. "That is not the roar of a man we left tied to a chair at a brothel."

"No?" He arched a brow, backing up against the pillows on her bed. "Then what roar is that?"

"It's the roar of a man who entered the drawing room first in search of us after he filled his belly."

"Dare I ask?"

She bit her lip and shrugged. "Well, the drawing room contains the remnants of his waistcoats. Also, a portrait of the current earl that has recently undergone renovation."

"Ah."

Selena tried not to grin too delightfully. "Theo joined in on both activities. I wonder if knowing that will calm his anger at me?"

The thud of footsteps drew close.

Strong arms circled around her. "We are about to find out."

The door slammed open, and Saville appeared in the doorway like the grim reaper, ready and eager to reap.

"Aha! When I heard your *fiancé* was still in the house but the two of you were nowhere to be found, I just knew you were up to things no unmarried man and woman should be doing!" His glare turned acid. "I see you are not even scattering apart at my presence."

Selena rolled her eyes.

"I'll say this again, old friend," Warrick murmured, his arms securing her more firmly against him, "but your temper will be the death of you one day."

"No matter," Saville waved a hand. "I'll let it slide today."

Selena blinked. That was it? "Let it slide?" Her tone held a wealth of suspicion.

He shrugged. "In my mind, you are already married."

Hah! That just confirmed Selena's belief about the male brain—it could convince itself of anything. Her gaze shifted between her brother and Warrick. Her earl. Her future husband. Her man. And she? Wife, sister, and whoever the hell she chose to be.

She understood now.

Who was she?

She suddenly laughed.

She was Selena Savage.

Saville sent her a worried look even as the arms around her flexed. "Why are you laughing like that?"

And Selena Savage loved riling up her brother. "Oh, I just imaged you searching for us in the drawing room first."

He jabbed a finger at her. "You can say that when you destroyed my face? Do you know how many hours I stood for that painting? How many days?"

"That was not *just* my handiwork. Theo loaned her expertise."

He froze. "What did you just say?"

Selena grinned, sending out a small apology to her friend. "Theo is responsible for the rouge on your cheeks and coloring your eyes black."

His brows furrowed, unfurrowed, then furrowed again. "She turned me into the devil?"

Selene wriggled her fingers. "She had a hand in it. Just a tiny hand. A brushstroke, really."

Warrick gave a soft snort beside her.

"That little minx," Saville complained. "I shall have to pay her a visit and demand retribution."

"Oh, that won't be possible."

"Why not?"

"She is in Brighton," she informed him brightly.

"She left London?" he exploded. "Why the hell did she leave London?"

To escape you. "That is a question better directed at her."

Steely eyes narrowed to slits. "You are right."

"I am?" She was? Saville rarely agreed with her. Well! Just when she thought she could never be shocked or surprised again!

"It *is* a question I should direct at her. Directly."

Had her brother finally lost his mind? She could practically see it racing.

He gave a nod. "And demand compensation for my destroyed property while I'm at it."

"Are you sure that is wise?" Selena asked slowly.

His next words confirmed that he had indeed, lost every last ounce of sanity.

"I'm leaving London. Warrick will have to see to your needs."

She wanted to laugh, but she didn't know at which part—him leaving to chase her friend or his remark about *his* friend—so she just blurted, "He has been seeing to my needs, dear brother."

"You damn brat! Where are your manners? You cannot speak of such things. I've been casting my eyes elsewhere, but you admit to your affair so bluntly, I'm caught off guard every time."

There was the brother she knew. Selena threw her leg over Warrick. "It's just as well you are leaving London." She suddenly grinned. "I have it on good authority that the King brothers are on their way to town. They might want your head."

"Well, then." He waved at them with a look of disgust. "I'll be off then. Behave in the meantime. Get married or something."

Selena blinked, then laughed at his back as he marched out. "I do believe he is in trouble."

"So do I." Warrick rolled her over, pressing her into the bed. "But care more about the trouble in my arms." He kissed the corner of her lips. "Now where were we?"

She pushed at him. "You have such a male brain."

"Then appease it, princess."

"I still want to apply ointment on the spots your skin chaffed," she protested. "That harridan . . ."

"Later. First, we need to remove these trousers."

"Why?" That dark tone didn't bode well for her trousers.

"They are dying tonight."

Her eyes widened. "You want to cut up my trousers?"

"They cut me up every time I look at them."

"But, I've grown quite attached to them." She flashed her teeth. "I love them undoing you too much for you to cut them up."

"Saucy wench. They are still being cut up."

"Later." She'd commission more. "First, let's see what damage that rope did."

He flipped her again and this time she was on top. Selena stared down at him, hands resting on his chest. She liked this.

"All right." His gaze bore into her, but this time all those unreadable emotions revealed themselves. "First, touch me."

Lord. "Where?"

"Everywhere." His face took on a meaningful edge. "I need to replace that creature's touch with yours."

That, Selena was happy to do, and do it forever. She dragged all ten fingers down his chest. He groaned. "You know," she leaned over to whisper, "I love how your body feels beneath mine."

"Ah, Christ."

Christ, indeed.

The next day

WARRICK STARED AT the luggage lining the wall of his parlor. Selena. She had insisted on sending her belongings to his residence while keeping an iron hand on the process. He shook his head, following the line of trunks to the drawing room where she discussed a list of her instructions to her maids.

He leaned against the door with his shoulder.

God, what an endearing sight.

Thank you.

Thank you for her.

He had lived a privileged life. A few trials here and there. But Selena . . . she wasn't one of those trials. She'd always been part of his life. Since he and Saville became friends as boys. But she stormed into his heart like a tempest, sweeping away everything in her path and fully claiming her space.

He was a man who learned from his mistakes.

But he hoped he would never learn everything when it came to Selena Savage. *I look forward to being corrected.*

"Warrick? What are you staring at?"

He blinked away his musings, smiling when Selena walked up to him. She was here. In his home. She was his in every sense.

Well, almost. "Not much," he murmured. His gaze swept over her trunks again. If this was a dream, Warrick never wanted to be disturbed from his sleep. "I can't believe your brother left London, and he left me with you. Alone."

"Not that hard, considering all that happened, and we are leaving today as well."

Yes, they were eloping.

She had agreed last night, and of course Warrick, as a gentleman, had to seal the agreement with a night of devotion. Too much devotion. Especially for someone who had been tied to a chair for two days. His body could barely move today.

"You look tired." Selena led him to a sofa and pushed him down. "The carriage is being readied. You can rest once we are on the road, or we can delay another day."

"No delays."

"So hasty." She poured them each a cup of tea.

He tracked her movements, smiling when she handed him his cup. "Thank you."

"A pleasure." She took a sip of tea, and promptly sprayed it all over the table.

"Not a pleasure after all?" Warrick teased. That had been his own reaction when he first took a sip of this particular tea, reminding him why he preferred the strong brew of coffee.

"This is terrible!" She frowned and sniffed the tea. "Has the tea gone bad? Dear Lord."

He shrugged. "It's the tea you sent me as a gift."

Her eyes widened. "Surely not."

Warrick nodded and took a sip. He'd grown accustomed to the taste. "The very same."

"And you drink this?"

"The stuff is atrocious, I agree." His eyes delved into hers. "But you gifted the tea, so I drink the tea." And she mentioned it helped with hair growth. A man had to try all the remedies he could get, didn't he?

She set down her cup. "Why on earth would you torture your tastebuds so?"

"You get used to the taste." He nudged her foot with his. "Do you understand how much I love you now? This is the only tea I drink."

"Shall I purchase you more?"

"Please don't."

She snorted. "So much for this love. However, even if you don't drink this stuff, even if you turn bald, I will still love you. Don't drink stuff you don't like."

Warrick's heart warmed. And he said he'd *try* all remedies, not commit to them for the rest of his life. In that regard, he only needed one. He only needed her. "Turn bald? Don't even utter such blasphemy."

Her brows suddenly puckered. "By the by, I seem to recall you prefer older women."

It was his turn to choke. "Where the hell did you hear that?"

"I overheard you talking to my brother once."

He set down the tea, turning to her. "When?"

"Years ago."

"Lord, woman, I have said a lot of things over the years and didn't mean half of them. Do not take it to heart. Even if I did at the time, now I only prefer you."

"Are you sure? Best tell me now before we leave for Gretna Green."

"Are you threatening to leave me? Don't. I will lock you in my chamber."

Selena laughed. "No bedchamber can hold me."

"That's true." A begrudging admittance. She did have a way of slipping from a person's grasp. But not his. Not anymore. "Any *more* questions before we depart?"

She tapped her chin thoughtfully. A gesture he'd come to find endearing.

"No questions," she said after some time. "Only a statement."

Dear Lord. "Why am I getting shivers down my spine?"

She punched him in the arm lightly. "Do not jest. From now on I shall be your protector, too. See, this time I rescued you. I am strong, too."

"You seem to be under a mistaken impression, love." Warrick smiled at her. This woman planted all sorts of miraculous seeds in his heart. "I didn't protect you because you were weak. I protected you because you are important. Much more than even I first imagined, but instinctively I knew."

She sidled closer to him. "When did you get such a slick tongue?"

He pulled her into his embrace, lowering his head to her neck and inhaled. "Shall we test how slick it can get?"

"Knave!"

Warrick laughed.

What an intriguing ever after this was going to be.

The End

About the Author

Tanya Wilde is an Award-Winning author that developed a passion for reading when she had nothing better to do than lurk in the library during her lunch breaks. Her blazing love affair with pen and paper soon followed after she devoured all their historical romance books! In 2020, she won the Romance Writers Organization of South Africa (ROSA) Imbali Award for Excellence in Romance Writing for Not Quite a Rogue.

When she's not meddling in the lives of her characters or pondering names for her imaginary big, white greyhound, she's off on adventures with her partner in crime.

Wilde lives in a small town at the foot of the Outeniqua Mountains, South Africa.

Website – www.authortanyawilde.com
Instagram – instagram.com/tanyawilde
Facebook – facebook.com/groups/843373666456177
BookBub – bookbub.com/authors/tanya-wilde